School Reunion

DI Strong and DS
attacks which s ... ool
that DS Knigh ... who is
doing it, and w ... , the past
begins to unravel ... s.

Other books in the ... ong series

The Anniversary

In the first book of the DI Strong crime thriller series, Andy Austin's family are killed in a road accident. With a sense of injustice, he becomes obsessed on seeking revenge. He befriends DI Strong and uses him to help carry out his plan. As the police get closer to catching him, it becomes clear that there are a few people with guilty secrets.

The Deal

Detective Inspector Strong hatches a plan to use Andy Austin, a wanted murderer, to help him deliver justice to serious criminals he just can't convict. As Strong gets more and more confident with his scheme, he begins to make mistakes and leave himself exposed to a greater risk of being caught and ruining his career. This is the second great book in the DI Strong crime thriller series, following on from The Anniversary.

Other DI Strong series books (cont.):

Loose Ends

This is the third book in the DI Strong Crime Thriller series, following on from The Anniversary and The Deal. DI Strong has been bending the law to get the justice he can't achieve through conventional police methods. But is Strong taking too many chances and arousing suspicion? Too many people are becoming involved, too many loose ends, which Strong knows he will have to do something about.

Two Wrongs

Two Wrongs is the fourth book in the DI Strong Crime Thriller series. Detective Constable Knight is keen to progress her police career but is struggling to shut down the current criminal turf war. Strong looks to help, unaware that DI Campbell and DC Harris have their suspicions on his methods of working and they are watching him closely.

Other books by Ian Anderson - The Jack Burns series:

Jack's Lottery Plan

This is the funny and moving story of Jack Burns. One day he finds out that a friend has secretly won the lottery and he embarks on a clandestine plan to get a share. But his plan goes hopelessly wrong impacting Jack and his friends in ways he would never have imagined.

Jack's Big Surprise

Jack Burns is planning a surprise proposal for his girlfriend Hannah. But as is usually the way with Jack, things don't go to plan. Instead, he finds himself hopelessly involved in a series of hilariously funny and unfortunate incidents. This is the sequel to Jack's Lottery Plan and finds Jack just as chaotic as always.

For more information, please visit my website at:
www.iananndersonhome.wixsite.com/iananndersonauthor

Or find me on Facebook at:
www.facebook.com/IanAndersonAuthor

School Reunion

By

Ian Anderson

100% of the profit from the sale of this book will go to the Motor Neurone Disease Association.

Author website:
www.ianandersonhome.wixsite.com/ianandersonauthor

Facebook:
www.facebook.com/IanAndersonAuthor

December 2022

Chapter 1

What had he said again? It was just banter? Banter? Really? Was that all he thought it was? He'd pleaded with James, but he didn't deserve any mercy. No, he deserved to suffer, like James had. James stretched out his full six feet two inch frame and ran his hands through his blonde hair, smoothing it back across the top of his head.

Stephen Jones had made James Gray's life hell. Two years of it. Daily. Until James had got a transfer to another school and joined their gym club. He'd soon lost weight then and muscled up, and no-one at his new school ever thought of him as the fat guy, or pig face.

When James had gone to visit Stephen Jones, he hadn't even been able to recall James's real name at first. That was the reality of it. No doubt he only remembered him as "fatty" or "piggy" or any of the other names he, and the others, had called him over the two years he'd spent at Danesborough High School. Two years of pure misery. James had come home from school every night and thrown himself onto his bed and lay there crying.

He'd pleaded with his mum to do something about it, and she'd tried her best, but there didn't seem to be much she could do. She'd gone to the Headmistress, and she'd promised to sort it out. But it didn't stop. It just became more underhand. Little comments, things said when no teachers were around. In some ways it was worse. Every remark cut like a knife. His dad told him he needed to man-up, but James didn't know how to do that. He'd thought about ending it all many times. He'd looked up different ways of doing it. Slashing his wrists, drinking bleach, taking a load of pills? They all had their pros and cons. He'd gone to the train station once and stood on the platform where the fast trains went through. Swooshing past, throwing up a blast of air. The ones that didn't stop. They just hurtled onwards. Unless someone jumped in front of them.

Jimmy Bragg was driving the morning train to Cardiff that day. It was the fast train, total journey time was just under two hours. The day was slightly overcast, with a thin layer of white cloud, but Jimmy had good clear visibility through the front window of his cab. The trees and bushes were rushing by on either side of the tracks, before the scenery turned into houses and gardens as the train approached the next station. Jimmy slowed the train slightly, although it wasn't a stopping station, it was an automatic reflex for Jimmy. It was something he did ever since that day two years before. The day when a young man had decided that Jimmy would end his life. His name was Patrick Campbell, Jimmy had found out later when he was being interviewed by the police. Jimmy hadn't even seen him. The train was passing through a station, and Jimmy felt the bump and heard a noise. But it was the bump mostly. He felt it, and he immediately knew that he had hit something. He hoped it was a thing and not a human being. But of course it was. Twenty five year old Patrick Campbell. Now, when Jimmy approached stations, he slowed down slightly and became very attentive to the platforms as they came into view. It was something they'd taught him on the rehabilitation course he'd had to go through after the Patrick Campbell suicide.

Jimmy saw the boy standing at the edge of the platform, on his own. He wasn't moving and he wasn't looking at the approaching train, He was just staring straight ahead. A shiver ran down Jimmy's spine. It just didn't look right. It reminded him of Patrick Campbell, although he hadn't seen him. Just something. He gave the train horn two loud blasts as it entered the station and it seemed to wake the boy up from his trance. He suddenly looked up at the train and Jimmy saw his face clearly. It was deathly white. The boy stepped back from the platform edge and Jimmy's train rushed through.

But all of the bullying had been fifteen years ago and maybe James should have got over it by now. Moved on. And he had in some ways. He had a good job, a career. After leaving school, he'd worked hard and qualified as an anaesthetist and he now worked at The Royal College Hospital which was five miles from where he lived. Over a few years, he'd saved up and managed to buy a small two bedroomed flat. It wasn't much, but it was all his, and he enjoyed having his own place. He still saw his parents most weekends. His mum liked to cook him a Sunday lunch and they'd sit around the kitchen table and eat it, like they always had. James got on well with his mum, his dad not so much. They didn't seem to have much in common, nothing to talk about, and so when his mum was in another room the two men would tend to sit in silence, James thought it all harked back to the problems he had at school, his dad not really understanding it, and they had just become used to not talking much to each other.

There had been periods when he'd almost forgotten his schooldays, but it was always there in the background of his mind, not completely erased.

Then it had all come back to the fore when he'd received the email about the Danesborough High School reunion. It had come from a woman called Jenny Broughton who he vaguely remembered from his time at the school. He thought she was in another of the classes in his year. How she had got his email address he didn't know but he guessed, with social media and everything else that was easily available on the internet, it wouldn't have been too difficult. Indeed, he'd done the same since to find out where some of his ex-schoolmates now lived. Jenny Broughton's email had then been followed up by a bright, sparkly invitation through the post. He remembered getting it and just staring at it for a while. Not really reading the words but just holding it in his hand and looking at it, remembering what it had been like at Danesborough High School. It hadn't been all bad, had it? There had been times when he'd had fun, had a laugh.

Even with those that bullied him most. But then when he thought they might be starting to like him, it would suddenly turn and they'd be on him again. Prodding him, pulling his hair, spitting on his blazer. Calling him a fat bastard. And laughing. That was the thing that hurt most, them all laughing at his pain.

But, as he looked at the invitation, he began to think maybe this was it. Maybe this was what he needed. Perhaps it would help to meet them all now, as adults, and clear out all the past from his head. Get rid of all the rubbish and really move on. The school reunion could be his chance to do that. He could see them all again, all of the bullies, but now he would see them in a different light, a new light. Everyone had grown up, they would all be different now. All adults, all sensible, no longer silly little schoolkids. The more he thought about it, the more he convinced himself it was the right thing to do.

When the day of the reunion came round, he had a few doubts about going, a few last minute nerves, but he reassured himself it was still the right thing to do. He'd discussed it with his mum the previous Sunday and after he'd explained why he wanted to go, she agreed with him that it was a good idea. Even his dad, for once, had joined in the conversation, and seemed to be supportive in his own way.

'They do a good pint in that hotel,' he'd said, 'but it's not cheap. You'd be better having a drink in The Bull's Head across the road before you go in, it's cheaper there.'

James had arrived early at the hotel and, not wanting to be one of the first arrivals, he'd parked his car and walked across the road to The Bull's Head, by chance taking his dad's advice. He was wearing his favourite black jacket, a white shirt and black trousers and shoes. He walked up to the bar and ordered himself a drink. He stood there, sipping his pint and looking around the bar, over the top of his glass. There were a few small groups of people, but no-one that he recognised, although he wasn't sure how many of his ex-schoolmates he would now know. Fifteen years had passed, and no doubt people would have changed physically. He certainly had. From being a small, overweight boy, he was now a tall, fit young man. He had been a regular at his local gym for many years now and the results showed. It would be interesting to see how many of them recognised him now!

The bar door opened and a group of four young men entered. They were all talking loudly and laughing, and everyone looked at them as they walked up to the bar. James thought he recognised them, three of them definitely, and a shiver ran down his spine. Stephen Jones, Nigel Harrison and Danny Blake. James remembered the three of them very well. He remembered what they'd done to him when he was their schoolmate. Schoolmate! Ha! That was the wrong term if ever there was one. No way had they been his mate! James continued to sip his pint, it appeared they hadn't noticed him, and he tuned in to their conversation.

'Who do you think will be there tonight?' Stephen Jones asked the group before taking a long drink from his pint of lager.

'I wonder if Carol Jenkins or Anne Watson will be there,' the fourth young man said. James half recognised him, but he couldn't put a name to his face.

'I think I saw Carol in the High Street a few weeks ago when I was visiting my mum.' The man continued. 'She looked all right. Maybe a bit fatter than she used to be, but not too bad for her age.'

'Well, lets face it mate, we've all put on a bit of weight,' Nigel Harrison replied, reaching over and patting his friend's stomach as they all laughed.

'What about old pigface? Do you think he'll be there?' Nigel asked.

'I doubt it. He'd be worried we'd bump into him in the Gents and flush his head down the toilet again,' Stephen replied laughing.

'Oh, God yeah, I'd forgotten about that,' Nigel replied, laughing along with his friend.

James had turned slightly away from the group, but he could still hear everything they were saying, and it was bringing back memories. Bad memories. He could recall that day very clearly still. It had been at morning break, James had gone to the toilet before classes started up again and while he was in there, three other boys had come in. They were laughing and pushing each other around, but they stopped when they saw James standing at the urinal.

'Well look who's here,' Stephen Jones said. 'It's old pigface. What are you doing in here?' he asked, with a serious looking face. 'This isn't for farm animals, this is for humans, oink, oink.'

The three boys laughed, and they walked towards James, one of them prodding him in the back as he hurriedly pulled up his trouser zip.

'This little piggy needs a wash I think,' Stephen said, and he grabbed both of James's arms and turned him around, pushing him towards one of the open cubicles.

He forced James inside and, with the help of the other two boys they pushed him down onto his knees and pushed his head down into the pan. Then one of them flushed it and the cold water ran over James's hair, down his face and neck and onto his shirt. He tried to call out, but he knew it was useless. No-one would come and help him, they never did. After what seemed like a long time, but was probably only a few seconds, they let him go and the three boys ran out of the toilet, laughing loudly amongst themselves.

James got to his feet and tore off some toilet roll, dabbing it against his face and neck to try and dry himself off as best he could. He walked out of the cubicle and stood in front of the washbasins, looking at himself in the mirror. What a sight! He was a real mess. His hair was wet and sticking out in all directions and his shirt collar was dark with damp patches all over. He smoothed down his hair and, looking in the mirror, he started to cry.

And now, fifteen years later, those three boys were back. Stephen Jones, Nigel Harrison and Danny Blake. And it seemed like they hadn't changed.

James watched out of the corner of his eye as the four young men finished their drinks and decided to make their way over to the hotel where the Danesborough High School reunion was taking place. As they left the pub, James turned back around to watch them go. He wanted to go after them and punch them in the face, one by one, but he knew he wouldn't. Instead, he waited for a few minutes and finished his drink before leaving the pub himself and walking back to where he'd left his car in the hotel car park. It had started raining and he got in his car and sat there for a few minutes, thinking. Thinking about what he'd just heard. Remembering all the things that had happened to him during his two years at Danesborough High School. Thinking about what he'd gone through and what he'd done since. Realising that he'd done nothing about it, all these years. The people that had bullied him, that had made his life hell, had got away with it and even now were still laughing about it. They thought it was one big joke. They thought he, James Gray, was just one big joke. It was then, sitting in his car in that hotel car park, the rain pouring down, that he decided he needed to do something about it. They needed to pay for what they'd done to him. He started his car, switched on his windscreen wipers, and drove out of the car park heading back home.

Chapter 2

Over the next few weeks, James Gray did his research and found out as much as he could about his ex-schoolmates. Where they lived, where they worked. What their social lives were. Everything he could find out on-line, which was quite a lot, and he carefully documented it all as he went. A couple of them had moved abroad, South Africa and America, but the majority of them were still living locally.

On one of the girl's social media sites, he'd come across a school photo of his old class at Danesborough High School. Miss Hardy's class. It showed all of his classmates, except for him. He wasn't in the photograph. He remembered he'd been off sick that day. In fact he'd been off sick quite a lot, mainly due to the stress he was having to go through during his time at Danesborough High. He printed off several copies of the class photo and used it as a reference for the main people he wanted to target.

Stephen Jones was the natural first priority for James. He had been the worst. The cruelest of them all. He was the one who had constantly called him names and the one who had always taken it that bit too far. Like the toilet incident.

It had been easy to find out where Stephen lived and worked, it was all available in a combination of his, and his partners, Facebook and Instagram pages. Stephen lived with a woman called Maria Khan and they had a young child. He worked in an office in the centre of town, doing some kind of IT work. James had found out as much as he could and then he'd driven to Stephen's house a couple of times and parked his car down the street, just watching. It seemed that Maria regularly took the baby and visited her family, often on Tuesday and Thursday evenings. Having got that information, James decided that he would call round and give Stephen a surprise visit from an old schoolfriend on one of those days.

Having decided he was going to go and see him, James still wasn't sure exactly what he was going to do when he got there. He wanted Stephen to understand what he'd done to him, how he'd suffered, how it had impacted his life, all of that. But then what? He didn't know. Did he want an apology? Was that enough? Or did he want more? But what? He didn't know. And he still didn't know when he was standing at Stephen's door waiting for him to answer it.

Stephen hadn't recognised him at first. To be fair to him, James had changed quite a lot, physically. He was no longer the short, chubby schoolboy Stephen had once known, he was now a fully grown, well-conditioned man. Even when James had introduced himself it had taken Stephen a few minutes to register it, who he was. Of course he'd never used James's real name, only those other names. Those names that had ruined James's life.

Stephen invited James in.

'It's just me tonight, my partner and the baby have gone to visit her mum, they're usually gone for a few hours,' Stephen explained, not aware that James already knew that. 'Take a seat, emm, James,' he said. 'Do people call you James or is it Jim or Jamie or something? James seems a bit formal.'

'No, James is fine,' James replied smiling.

The two men sat there, chatting about things. This and that, nothing really. It was all very awkward with regular moments of silence as the conversation stalled.

'Can I get you a drink…James?' Stephen asked, still finding it difficult to call him by that name, it felt strange. He was also unsure as to why James was actually here, he hadn't said.

'No thanks,' James replied, weirdly finding the whole awkwardness thing somewhat satisfying.

After another stilted conversation about holidays, James glanced at his watch and decided it was time to move things on. He wanted it all over before Stephen's partner returned home with their baby. He still wasn't sure what he was going to do, or what he actually wanted out of this, but he was ready to start and see where it took him. He clenched his fists by his side, digging his nails into the palms of his hands.

'So do you remember our time together at Danesborough High?' James began. 'I was only there two years. It was the worst two years of my life.'

'Really?' Stephen replied, shifting position in his seat. 'I, emm, I quite enjoyed it there. Some of the teachers were crap mind you. You weren't there long were you?'

'No, two years. Two years of Hell. Do you remember what you used to call me?' James asked, moving forward in his seat and looking directly at Stephen, whose cheeks were beginning to redden.

'Emm, no, emm, there was a bit of name calling, a bit of banter wasn't there? I think most people had nicknames, didn't they?' Stephen replied hesitantly.

'Do you remember when you stole my uniform from the changing rooms when we were doing P.E.?' James asked. 'Maybe you remember holding my hand down and stubbing out a cigarette on the back of it. Or maybe spitting in my hair, you must remember that surely, the amount of times you did it?'

James was strangely enjoying himself. It felt good to get all of this stuff out. To say it out loud to the person who did it and watch his reaction. He could see that Stephen was feeling very uncomfortable. He couldn't sit still and couldn't look directly at James. He kept glancing towards the door as if he was wishing someone would come in, but James knew his partner wasn't likely to be home for another hour yet.

'What about flushing my head down the toilet, surely you must remember that one?' James carried on, smiling at Stephen as he spoke.

'They…it wasn't just me….it was just kids….you know, doing what kids did. We were….it was just fun…We all did it. We didn't mean anything. It was just, just, …we were just having a laugh,' Stephen replied, finishing with what he hoped was a friendly smile.

It was the smile that got James. The thing that tipped him over. He hadn't even apologised. He'd no idea of the hurt he'd caused him. Suddenly he knew what he had to do, after all these years. He rose from his seat and before Stephen could move, James had him in a bear hug. He marched him out the room and down the hallway, guessing where the room he was looking for might be.

'What…, what are you doing?' Stephen said, struggling to free himself from James's hold but it was too tight. 'Let me go please, please don't hurt me. It was only banter….honestly.'

James had reached a white door at the end of Stephen's hallway and he stretched his foot forward, around his captive, and kicked the door open. It was the bathroom, just as he'd hoped. He walked Stephen inside and forced him down onto his knees in front of the toilet.

'What….what are you doing? You can't. Please…we're grown men now. Not schoolkids. Please, let me…'

Stephen's voice was muffled as his head was forced down into the toilet. He tried to struggle but only succeeded in banging his face and head against the sides of the toilet bowl. He could feel a strong hand on the back of his neck, forcing him further down until his face met the water. Then there was a roaring sound, as loud as an aircraft. and he felt a rush of water pouring over his head. He closed his eyes and began to pray.

James was enjoying this. He knew this was what he needed to do. He should have done it years earlier. The flush had completed but this was too good an opportunity to miss and so he pulled the lever for a second time. He stood there watching, smiling as the water poured over Stephen Jones's head again. When it finished, he let go of his hold on Stephen's neck and his victim slid backwards and slumped down onto the tiled bathroom floor.

Satisfied that he'd done all that he wanted to do, James walked away from the bathroom and back into Stephen's living room. From inside his jacket pocket he took out one of his copies of Miss Hardy's class photo and with a red pen he drew a circle around the head of the young Stephen Jones and then put a cross over his face. He left it on the coffee table, a little memento for Stephen Jones, James thought, as he walked out of the house.

Chapter 3

'Can I have a word with you Mo, in private?' Councillor John Aitken said as he gently took DI Strong's elbow and led him towards a corner of the large function room.

Detective Inspector Strong was a senior police officer, Head of the Serious Crime Team, and, in that capacity, he often had to attend events, representing the Police Force. This particular event was being held to recognise people in the local community who had gone above the norm and done their bit to help others. They had all been nominated and whittled down previously by a judging panel, of which Strong and Councillor Aitken were both members, until they had reached a number of forty deserving people. Those forty were then invited along to the awards event which was held in the Council offices and consisted of a number of speeches, awards, and a sumptuous five course dinner. It was a yearly event and, as always, it had been a great success. The formal part of the evening was now over, and the award winners and other attendees were mingling amongst the tables, reviving old connections and making new ones.

DI Strong and Councillor John Aitken had first met around five years ago when John had first been elected on to the Borough council. Being local dignitaries, the two men were often invited to the same events and over the years they had got to know each other and often ended up chatting together over a brandy at the end of the evening. On this particular evening though, they hadn't quite reached the point of having a brandy, Strong had still been chatting with other guests when Aitken had approached him. Strong noticed that the Councillor had a serious look on his face as they walked towards the corner of the room. When they had reached a quiet spot, Aitken stopped and turned to face the Detective.

'I was wondering if I could ask you a favour Mo?' Aitken started. 'I'm not sure if you can help, but I thought I'd ask you anyway. Someone I know suggested you might be able to help.'

'Oh, who was that?' Strong enquired.

'Irene Hardy, she's retired now, but she used to be a teacher at Danesborough High, when I was on the board of the school governers there,' Aitken replied.

'Ah yes Irene. Lovely lady,' DI Strong responded, smiling. He couldn't remember an Irene Hardy, but guessed he must have met her at a public function at some point. He'd certainly attended many of those over the last twenty years and shaken hands with a lot of people.

'How can I help you, John?' Strong asked the councillor.

'Well, it's a situation where I…emm…we, seem to have hit a bit of a dead end and…emm… we're not sure what we can do,' Aitken replied.

'Okay, it sounds intriguing. Why don't you tell me more about it, and if I can help in any way, '

'Right, well, it's a long story but I'll summarise it as best I can,' Councillor Aitken began. 'It goes back to our schooldays. I was at an all-boys school for a few years, from the age of eleven until I was fourteen. I used to lodge there and came home most weekends. On the whole it was a good school, I enjoyed it and made quite a few good friends. I still keep in touch with them to this day. But unfortunately, it wasn't all good. There was a P.E. teacher there, Mr Sandown who liked to get close to us boys, if you know what I mean?' Aitken stopped talking to look at the detective. Strong nodded his head.

'At the time we never discussed it amongst ourselves,' Aitken continued. 'I think each one of us thought it was just a random thing he occasionally did to us individually. Like I thought it was just me, and it was only now and again, and so nothing really to make a fuss of. But I mentioned that some of us still meet up for a lunch or a beer every so often, and it was at one of these lunches a few months ago that the full story emerged. It transpired that Mr Sandown had been doing his thing with all of us. Some worse than others, I was relatively lucky, if you can call it that. But, in short, he had been sexually assaulting all of us boys, without anyone saying anything about it. We decided then, after a very emotional lunch, that Sandown should pay for what he'd done. He should be brought to justice, and most of us were prepared to stand up in court and testify against him, even though it meant exposing ourselves to the world, and bringing back some awful memories that we'd largely managed to hide.'

Aitken stopped talking to take a breath and he looked directly at DI Strong.

'I'm sorry to hear that, John. It sounds terrible. What can I do to help you? Do you need me to find this Sandown for you and bring him to justice?' Strong asked.

'Well yes, but no, not exactly,' Aitken replied. 'We have tracked him down, we know where he is, but he's no longer in the U.K., he's living in Switzerland now and he has citizenship there. And the problem is our lawyers are advising us that unless he returns voluntarily to the U.K., it is going to be very difficult to extradite him from there. I guess, I don't know, seeing you here tonight, I just wondered if there was anything you might be able to do. Do you have any police contacts in Switzerland that might be willing to help get him back here? I don't know, something like that maybe? What do you think?'

'Mmm…it's a tricky one. I can't think of any Swiss contacts off the top of my head, but I do know a couple of people in Germany. Maybe they could help. Let me have a think. Can you email me what you have on Sandown? His address, any personal details you have that will allow us to identify him, anything like that,' Strong replied.

'Sure, I'll send you what I've got in the morning,' Aitken replied. 'I appreciate anything you can do to help Mo. We'd all really like to see him brought to justice for what he did.'

'No problem,' Strong replied. 'Just one thing John, it'll be best that we just keep this conversation between ourselves. No-one else should know that you've spoken to me about it, do you understand?'

Councillor Aitken nodded his head and the two men turned back towards the room, ready to renew their conversations with the rest of the invited guests. Just as they reached the first group, DI Strong's phone started to ring. He took it from his jacket pocket and saw that the call was from DS Harris, one of his team.

'Yes,' he said, abruptly into the phone, turning his head away from the nearest group of people.

'Guv, we've got a body. Looks suspicious. Do you want to come and see?' DS Harris asked.

'Yes, of course,' Strong replied. 'Text me the location and I'll be there as soon as possible.'

Strong had spent long enough at tonight's community event and he was glad of an excuse to leave. Aside from that, he also still really enjoyed doing proper detective work, and the thought of investigating another dead body was one that greatly excited him. He'd shaken enough hands tonight and so he quietly slipped out of the room and made his way to the exit.

Chapter 4

'What do we know so far?' Detective Inspector Mo Strong asked the young police constable as they both looked down at the lifeless body lying on the bathroom floor at their feet. Strong had seen a lot of dead bodies in his time, too many, but that was just one of the things that came with the job. You couldn't expect to head up the Serious Crime team without getting involved in…well, serious crime. And sometimes that meant looking at dead people.

The police constable referred to his notebook, he didn't want to get anything wrong in front of the Detective Inspector. He was an important man. His big boss. He began to read, slowly and carefully.

'The victim has been identified as Mr Stephen Jones. He is, … sorry was, thirty years old and worked in town for an IT company as a Project Manager. He lived with a Maria Khan and they have one child. The victim's partner, Miss Khan, returned home from her mother's just after eight pm. She entered the house and couldn't find Mr Jones, who she expected to be at home. She tried calling his mobile and heard it ringing from somewhere in the house. Eventually she traced it to the bathroom and found Mr Jones lying on the floor, apparently unconscious. She tried to wake him up but he was unresponsive and so she called the emergency services. A paramedic arrived twenty minutes later and pronounced him dead at the scene.'

The police constable paused for a breath and to check if this was what DI Strong wanted from him. He had his theories as to what might have happened. but he didn't feel confident enough to air them in front of the big boss. The Detective nodded and signalled for him to carry on.

'The cause of death wasn't obvious, but the paramedic noted some bruising and cuts around the area of the back of the neck and also to his face and head, although he didn't think these were serious enough to have been the cause of Mr Jones's death.'

He paused again, wondering if he should add his thoughts at this point, but decided not to.

'The paramedic also noted that the man's whole head was quite wet,' the police constable carried on, 'with there being no obvious explanation for that.'

The young policeman stopped talking and looked up at DI Strong who was standing leaning against the bathroom doorframe, his head almost reaching the top. He was a tall man.

'That's all I have sir,' he said, hoping he'd given the DI what he wanted.

'Okay, thanks, good job Morton,' DI Strong replied. 'Can you join the others and see if any of the neighbours saw or heard anything before you go back to the station. We'll all catch up again after that, probably in the morning. But call me directly if you get anything important.'

DI Strong walked back down the hallway and went into Stephen Jones's living room. It just looked like a normal living room, in a normal house, except there was a dead body in the bathroom and there were several members of the police SOCO team working their way around the house, including in this room. These were the scene of crime officers (SOCO) whose job it was to gather forensic evidence from the victim and his surroundings. They had been called early to the scene and were dusting for fingerprints, examining the furniture, and taking photographs.

Strong looked around the scene in front of him and his attention was immediately drawn to an A4 sized photograph lying on the top of a small coffee table in the centre of the room. He slipped on a pair of blue disposable gloves and picked it up carefully by one corner to take a closer look. It appeared to be a print-out of a photo of a school class, possibly from a few years ago, judging by the look of the schoolchildren's clothing and hairstyles. One of the pupils had a red cross over his face and a red ring drawn around his head. Strong peered closely at the face, but he couldn't make it out behind the red pen markings. It was a boy, that was as much as he could say.

'Does anyone know what this is? Why it's lying here?' he asked generally to the room.

'No, it was there when we arrived,' one of the SOCO team replied. 'It's been checked Guv.'

DI Strong popped the photo carefully into a clear, plastic evidence bag, handing it over to another uniformed policeman who had entered the room behind him.

'Make sure this gets bagged as evidence,' Strong said. 'We need to find out what it is exactly, and who is in it, especially the face with the cross through it. See if the victim's partner knows anything about it will you? If she's able to.'

'Will do Guv,' the policeman replied, and he walked out of the room in search of Miss Khan.

Strong had a quick look around the rest of the house but found nothing else out of place. Everything looked normal. Miss Khan was sitting in the kitchen with another woman comforting her, and a policewoman making them both cups of tea. Strong decided there would be nothing to be gained by him barging in and asking her more questions now. She would have had enough of that, and Strong would be able to read all of the reports in the morning. He had a good team. Strong had one last look at the body of Stephen Jones on the bathroom floor, before turning away and leaving the dead man's house.

Chapter 5

Ordinarily, Detective Sergeant Laura Knight would have been the lead on this case, but she was away at the annual police conference in Birmingham. DI Strong had called her and given her the brief details of what he knew so far. It was only an unexplained death at this point, not a murder, he'd said. There was no evidence of any forced entry or struggle of any sorts, other than the slight injuries sustained to Stephen Jones's head and neck. But Strong confessed to her that his instincts were that there was more to this than first met the eye.

Strong told Knight that she should stay at the conference as planned and that he would run the operation until she got back the following week.

'It'll be good for you in the long run, good for your career to make contacts, connections, with some of the other delegates,' DI Strong had told her. 'There'll be a lot of senior policemen there from different regions and you should get amongst them and get your face known. I'll keep you in touch with what's going on here, so you can take over when you get back. It could be nothing anyway, you know how these things are.'

DS Knight understood the logic, it was *the* conference to attend if you wanted to get yourself known in the senior police community and potentially seek out future career opportunities. Normally DI Strong would have gone to it, but on this occasion, it clashed with the week that his daughter, Sophie, was moving back home from Leeds, having got herself a new job in London. DI Strong hadn't told DS Knight that was the real reason he had asked her to go in his place, but she didn't need to know that, and it was true that the conference would still be good for the Detective Sergeant's career aspirations.

Having taken the call from DI Strong, DS Knight was left feeling a bit disappointed. She didn't want to be stuck in a hotel at a police conference when there was an unexplained death to investigate back at home. That was the sort of excitement she'd joined the police for. It would be her first major investigation since she'd been promoted to the Detective Sergeant role, and she was keen to get stuck in and make a good job of it.

DI Strong's call had already whetted her appetite for the case. She wanted to find out if this man had been unlawfully killed and, if he had, find whoever had done it quickly and get him, or her, behind bars. Locked away. Him or her, that was a funny one. The police had to be careful nowadays not to label people, or to make assumptions. Even though the vast majority of assaults and murders were committed by men, they couldn't just jump to that conclusion when they hadn't yet identified a suspect. Knight was pretty good at getting all the politically correct terminology correct, but some of her older, male, colleagues weren't quite as sharp and would regularly make mistakes. However, putting political correctness to one side, DS Knight knew that if this had been a murder, then it was most likely that a man had carried it out. The stats don't lie.

The hotel where the police conference was being held was probably the most luxurious hotel DS Knight had ever stayed in. No, not probably. Definitely. Although to put it in some sort of context, she hadn't really stayed in many hotels before. And when she had, it was usually the cheapest one she could find. A travel lodge or equivalent. Just a bed for the night.

But this one was in a different class. No expense spared. Which was fine, as she wasn't paying for it. Immediately, from the grand, open, reception with the glass chandeliers and the long oak style reception desk, to the spotless corridors and lifts taking her up to her luxury room on the fifth floor, the hotel just demonstrated it's five star rating.

Knight had a double bedroom with a huge, king size bed. She could lie horizontally across it and her feet still didn't go over the edge. She knew that because she had tried it.

She'd managed to make it through the three day annual police conference, most of which had been pretty tedious, presentation after presentation from various police officers or related hangers-on. There had been a couple of interesting sessions though, she had to reluctantly admit, from experts in specific areas. The one on the latest forensic techniques had been fascinating, as had the one on using technology for facial recognition. Although that had worried her a bit too, thinking about the way that technology could be manipulated to produce false evidence. When questioned about that, the man from the technology company giving the presentation hadn't really come up with any sort of convincing answer.

Anyway, it was all over now and she'd soon be able to return to her day job. The job she loved. Being a detective and solving crimes. Penalising criminals and getting justice for their victims. All she had left to get through was the final evening of the conference, which was a gala, black tie dinner. More middle-aged policemen making boring speeches no doubt, but there was also a comedian booked to do the after-dinner speech who she vaguely knew from a comedy panel show on Channel Four. And of course the dinner and wine would be top quality, so at least there was that to look forward to.

DI Strong had told her that this was an important part of the whole three day event. It was her chance to mingle with some of the other senior police officers from different regions. Get to know them, let them know who you are too, Strong had said. Everyone else will be doing the same.

'It's a competition, a beauty parade, although that's probably not the right term to use nowadays and not many of them will be that beautiful anyway, present company excepted of course,' Strong had laughed. 'But you know what I mean. It's your chance to get your face known so that people will remember you when further career opportunities come up. You should make the most of it. get to know as many people as you can. You never know when they might come in useful.'

DS Knight had changed her mind a few times before deciding on which dress she should bring for the gala dinner. She didn't want to look too frumpy, she was only thirty, still quite young, but also she didn't want to look tarty either. She needed to hit the right balance, formal but still something that showed off her curves, showed that she was a confident young woman. Of course, in the end, she chose her little black dress.

There was a seating plan and DS Knight found herself at table number thirty three, sitting between a DI Jones from South Wales and a DI Collinson from the North East. It was a large round table and there were five other people with them, but after quick introductions, due to the overall noise of everyone talking in the room, they all gave up trying to shout across the table at each other and instead focused on chatting with their immediate neighbours.

The food was gorgeous, probably one of the best meals DS Knight had ever eaten. She wasn't much of a cook herself, although it was always something she wished she could do better and several times she had resolved to spend some time learning how to do that. But that was the crux of it, time. She just never seemed to have enough of it. Her job took up most of her day and when she was feeling hungry, she would usually make herself a quick meal, just because she knew she had to eat, before getting back to work. The only other thing she did regularly was sleep.

In between the starter and the main course, Knight learned all about DI Jones's family and how his eldest boy, Lloyd, she thought he said, was a promising young rugby player. A winger, was that a rugby position? She had thought that was to do with football. DI Jones spent most of his weekends watching his son play rugby and he explained to Knight how he hoped he might be taken on by one of the top teams in the next few years. Knight wasn't really listening, but she smiled and wished him the best of luck.

Between the main course and the pudding her head was turned to the right and DI Collinson told her about his lifelong passion for Newcastle United football club. How he had gone to see them since he was a young lad, his words, with his father and grandfather and how he'd had a season ticket for the last twenty, or was it thirty, years. Knight asked him if they had any good wingers, and she was surprised when he appeared to get excited by her question and started reeling off a number of names she didn't recognise, and instantly forgot. She told him she hoped they would have a good season this year. She hoped that was the right thing to say.

Neither of the two men seemed to have much interest in DS Knight, other than asking if she had a boyfriend or partner or any children. By the time the sweet course came, DS Knight couldn't see herself working in either South Wales or the North East of England.

After the meal was finished and the plates cleared away, most of the guests got up from their seats and moved around the tables, renewing old acquaintances, and making some new ones. DS Knight had gone to the bar and bumped into a police officer from the Merseyside region, a Detective Constable Keown. He insisted that she come back and join him at a table with some of his colleagues. Not knowing anyone, Knight couldn't think of an excuse not to go along with him and so she found herself sitting at a table with DC Keown and three other male police officers, all from the Merseyside region. There was a DI and two DS's. The DI was a Detective Inspector Murphy, and being their boss, he dominated the conversation. The drinks were flowing, and DS Knight was doing her best to keep up with the Merseyside group. At some point, Keown and the two Detective Sergeants must have gone off to their rooms, although Knight couldn't remember seeing them going, leaving just her and DI Murphy at the table. Murphy glanced at his watch.

'It's getting late, shall we have a nightcap, one for the road?' he asked and without waiting for an answer he signalled to a waiter and ordered two large brandies.

The waiter brought the drinks across to the table and DI Murphy raised his glass,

'Cheers!' he said, and he drank it down quickly, holding his glass up and looking at DS Knight with a smile on his face.

Knight realised he was expecting her to do the same and so she lifted her drink and gulped down the contents, holding up the empty glass towards DI Murphy. She wasn't going to be beaten by a DI from Merseyside, or anywhere else for that matter.

'Cheers!' she said back to him, smiling drunkenly.

'Come on then, it's getting late. I'll see you to your room,' Murphy said, and he took DS Knight's arm and guided her towards the lift.

Knight stumbled a bit as they walked, but she put that down to the heels she was wearing tonight. She was much more used to wearing flat shoes.

A few minutes later, they had exited the lift and were walking along the corridor on the fifth floor of the hotel.

'Which room is yours then?' DS Knight asked DI Murphy as they walked along the brightly lit corridor.

'Oh, I'm on the twelfth floor somewhere,' DI Murphy replied.

'Oh, well, good night then, it's been nice meeting you sir,' DS Knight said as they reached her room door. She tapped her entry card against the sensor and pushed the door open.

As she stepped inside, she sensed DI Murphy was still there, behind her, and she turned around.

'It's still early yet, let's see what's in your mini bar, shall we?' he said, smiling at her and, over his shoulder, DS Knight saw the door swing softly shut behind them.

Chapter 6

Doctor Cathy Elton was an experienced forensic pathologist. One of the best. She'd lost count of the number of dead bodies she'd seen over the last twenty years. Too many to think about. But from an early point in her career, she'd learned to think of them simply as her work canvas. What she did was an art form. There was a skill to it, and she had become a talented performer.

This latest body had been an easy one though. The young man had died of a cardiac arrest. A heart attack. That was obvious. And that was the message she was now delivering to Detective Inspector Strong, a man she had worked with on many an occasion, and who she had a great deal of respect for. Dr Elton had also spent a couple of evenings with him many years ago, setting the world to rights over a few bottles of good red wine, as their discussions on a particular case had carried on into the night and wandered into other topics. The first time they'd had dinner together, Dr Elton briefly wondered if there might be a chance something would develop from it. He was a good looking man and Dr Elton was single at the time. The trouble was though, DI Strong wasn't. And from their discussion over dinner, it had soon become clear that he was happily married and deeply in love with his wife, Catherine. Not long after that, Dr Elton had met Alan and he was a good man. You wouldn't describe him as being dynamic, but he was stable and solid. He always did the right thing. She'd agreed to marry him, and they'd had two beautiful children, Eloise and Nick, who were both now at university, both doing science degrees. She sometimes wondered what life might have been like with Detective Strong, but, ah well, que sera sera, Dr Elton thought as she stood facing the Detective now.

'So, Cathy, what you're telling me is that he died of a heart attack,' Strong said to the pathologist. 'So, are you in fact saying that we're not looking at a murder case here at all? There's no evidence that he drowned?'

'Ah, well, if only life were that simple, eh?' Dr Elton replied smirking knowingly. 'But I can tell you that he certainly didn't drown. There was no water in his lungs, not a drop, and yes, he definitely died from a cardiac arrest, as you can see from my report, but….'

'Ah, here it comes, there's always a but, isn't there?' Strong interrupted, smiling at his colleague, who he knew well enough to be able to inject a little humour into what was rarely a pleasant meeting due to the nature of Dr Elton's job.

'Well, not always, but in this case, yes there is,' Dr Elton replied, smiling back at the detective.

'The bruises and cuts to his neck, face and head, and the fact his head was wet with water, all needed some explanation, I think. Those, along with the position he was found in, on the bathroom floor would lead me to hypothesise that shortly before he died, he was perhaps forcibly held down with his head in the toilet, which was then flushed over him.'

'Mmm…' Strong murmured. 'How certain are you of that, and have you ever seen anything like that before?'

'I'd say ninety per cent certain, from the positioning of the cuts and bruising. He had bruising on the back of his neck which would be consistent with someone holding him forcibly in that area. And, to answer your second question, no I haven't seen that before,' Dr Elton replied. 'It's the sort of thing you hear schoolkids doing, isn't it? Flushing someone's head down the toilet.'

'Yes, yes, funny you should say that,' Strong replied.

'Why do you say that?' Dr Elton asked him.

'Well, it's just that we found a photo near the body and it looks like a school class photo,' Strong replied.

'Did it belong to the victim?' Dr Elton asked.

'Well we don't know at this point, but my guess is probably not. It looked like someone left it there to be found. Maybe as a kind of message,' the Detective replied.

'Ooh…that's a strange one,' Dr Elton replied. 'Please keep me posted on what you find out. I only get to see this part normally. The gruesome bit, you might say. I often don't find out what happens afterwards, and I'd be interested to know if there's more to this one.'

'It's not my fault you chose the wrong career,' DI Strong replied, laughing as he walked towards the door. 'You should have become a detective,' he added, still laughing as he pulled the door closed behind him.

Strong made his way back to the police station and called his team together in the large conference room on the second floor. The Detective Inspector was sat at the head of the long table, and around the remainder of the room there were twelve members of the Serious Crime team along with several other police officers, ranging from Police Constables through to Detective Sergeants. With Detective Sergeant Knight still being away at the Annual Police Conference and several of the women officers otherwise engaged, today's meeting consisted entirely of male police officers.

DI Strong welcomed them all and opened the meeting by summarising their initial findings.

'Stephen Jones, a thirty year old IT Project Manager was found dead at his home yesterday evening. His partner, Maria Khan, discovered him when she returned home from a visit to her parents. Stephen was lying on the bathroom floor and it was subsequently found he had died of a heart attack. However, there was also some unexplained bruising and cuts around Stephen's head, face and neck. It is possible he was attacked, his head pushed into the toilet, and the attack led to him having a heart attack and dying. At the moment we are treating this as an unexplained death until we find out any more evidence to indicate what might have actually happened.'

DI Strong then opened up the meeting to the room for further discussion on the case. The first person to speak was one of the Serious Crime team, Detective Constable Peters.

'Guv, the SOCO team took a closer look at the whole scene, covering all of the bathroom area. They found some of the victim's hair, skin and blood on the inside of the toilet pan itself, although these were all fairly minute as the toilet had been flushed. However, their conclusion was that this indicated that the victim's head had been forced into the toilet and that it banged against the sides of the toilet as it was held down, or he struggled in the process and banged it in doing so. The toilet was then flushed over the top of Mr Jones's head, which would have washed away some of the evidence. The SOCO team also found some markings on the hallway walls, leading towards the bathroom door, which they believe were also made by the victim, trying to resist being pushed into the bathroom.'

'Okay, thank you,' Strong replied. 'So, in summary, we are saying it looks like someone forced him into the bathroom and then put his head into the toilet itself, before pulling the flush over him. After that he had a heart attack and died.'

'Yes, I believe that's correct,' Peters replied. 'The SOCO guys said it would be impossible for him to have done this on his own. He wouldn't have been able to have his head so far down the toilet and flush it at the same time. He would not have been physically able to reach the lever.'

'Okay, okay.....' Strong murmured, nodding as he spoke. 'Anything from the door to door enquiries? Did any of the neighbours see anything?' he asked the room.

A few of the police officers shook their heads and another Detective spoke up, this time Detective Constable Morgan. He was new to the team and Strong hadn't got to know him yet although he had heard that he was a good, hard worker.

'Guv, DC Morgan,' he said, taking the opportunity to introduce himself to the wider team as well as reminding his boss who he was. 'We spoke to all the immediate neighbours and others further along the street. No-one saw or heard anything and unfortunately no-one has any CCTV cameras on their properties. It's quite a quiet residential area,' Morgan concluded in a soft, Welsh accent. 'We're now expanding the area to see if we can pick up anyone entering the street that evening, from further afield. Perhaps in a car.'

As he finished speaking, another of the team raised his hand slightly to indicate that he had something to say. Strong recognised him as one of the longer term members of the Serious Crime team, Detective Constable Harris. Strong nodded to him.

'Guv,' he began. 'As you know there was a photo found in Mr Jones's living room which appeared to be out of place. We asked Mr Jones's partner, Miss Khan, if she had seen the photo before and she said she hadn't. Nor could she recognise anyone in it. She was pretty sure it didn't belong to her partner Stephen Jones. As it looked like an old school photo, we also showed it to Mr Jones's parents and his mother immediately identified it as being from Danesborough High School around fifteen years ago when Stephen would have been around fourteen or fifteen years old. His mother was also able to give us the names of several of the other pupils in the class photo. She also confirmed that the child with the red ring drawn around his head and the cross through it was her son, Stephen Jones.'

'Okay, good work Harris,' Strong replied. He was pleased to see that DC Harris was continuing to put in the groundwork. The good, solid policing that always needed to be done, and the type of work that Harris had always been good at. Harris had recently been passed up on promotion to the role of Detective Sergeant, in favour of DS Knight, and DI Strong had worried that he might have taken that badly, but he seemed to be carrying on as normal.

'So, I think what we have here is a man who has been assaulted in his own home by an, as yet, unknown assailant,' DI Strong addressed the room. 'It is not clear whether the assailant meant to end Mr Jones's life, but, in reality, that is what has happened. The school photo seems to have some connection to the attack, it looks like it may have been left there by the assailant. We will have to investigate the meaning of that further. With the knowledge we have so far, I have decided that we will now treat this as a murder case. Carry on with the CCTV and door to door checks and I'll assemble the team back here again in the morning with an update on where we are.'

Chapter 7

'Okay, so who's next?' James Gray said, staring at the photograph of Miss Hardy's class on the table in front of him.

There were three rows of children, twenty nine in total, with two adults standing, one at each end of the back row. James wasn't in the photo, he'd been off sick that day, one of the many days he'd missed school during those two years he'd been at Danesborough High. Any excuse to stay at home. He'd often invent an illness or make himself physically vomit, trying to persuade his mum that he couldn't go to school. But she had her work to go to, and she could tell when he was putting it on, so she'd usually get him dressed and send him on his way.

Scanning the class photo, James definitely wanted to give Miss Hardy a visit, he needed to have a discussion with her. She was an adult and she had been in a position where she should have been able to help him. But she hadn't. Maybe even see what was happening. But she hadn't. She'd done nothing. Just like all the others.

But Miss Hardy would have to wait for now. The next person on James's visiting list was

Nigel Harrison. Nigel had been Stephen Jones's best friend at school and had usually been there when they were doing something to James. He had been one of the gang that had flushed James's head down the toilet, and he'd also been there when they'd burned his hand and forearm with a cigarette. Nigel had been the one with the cigarette, while the others held James's arm flat on the table. James remembered him doing it as if it was yesterday. He particularly remembered Nigel's face, he was smiling, like he was really enjoying what he was doing. It was like a game to him. He'd taken his time, lighting the cigarette and taking a puff of it, before turning it around in his fingers and slowly, very slowly, moving it downwards towards James's bare skin. James was crying, he didn't want to, he didn't want them to see him like that, but he couldn't help himself. Nigel lowered the cigarette until it was as close to James's skin as it could be, without it actually touching him. James could feel the heat and he knew what was coming. Then it came, The hiss, then the pain and the smell. The burning smell. James had closed his eyes, but he could hear Nigel and the others laughing.

'Did you hear the hissing sound?' one of them said. 'Do it again.'

And James felt a second stab of pain on the back of his hand as the cigarette was pressed onto it.

Nigel Harrison had definitely been one of the worst of the bullies, and James knew he needed to pay him back. He had to admit he'd enjoyed handing out the punishment to Stephen Jones, giving him a taste of his own medicine. After all these years, he'd finally started to fight back and get even, and it felt good. When he'd gone to Stephen's house, he hadn't known what was going to happen, what he was going to do, but suddenly it had just come to him. Do to Stephen what he did to me, James had thought. And it had turned out to be the perfect solution.

He was surprised that there had been no comeback from his visit to Stephen. He thought Stephen would have phoned the police straight away and told them what had happened, but so far James had heard nothing. Maybe they hadn't been able to track him down, or perhaps it just wasn't a priority for them. He'd heard stories about minor crimes not being investigated due to lack of police resources, and maybe this one fitted into that category. If that was the case, well even better. Stephen had deserved his punishment after all those years and now they were even, James didn't really feel he should be further punished for doing it, but he had expected that he would be. Maybe after the next one, he thought, then perhaps it would progress from a minor crime to something more serious. Something worth investigating.

James had taken some precautions as part of his overall plan for getting his revenge, which he had hoped would give him enough time to carry out everything he wanted to do before he was finally apprehended. He knew that was the likely end point, but if so, so be it, he'd decided. Perhaps he might have longer than the two weeks he'd planned it for, but he wanted to get everything done quickly, and so he still intended to stick to those original timescales.

James had booked a fortnight off work, much to the hospital management's disappointment, but they couldn't really say too much as it was his first proper break for over a year. As always, the hospital was short staffed and James not being there would mean a number of operations would have to be further delayed. James felt guilty about that, but this was just something he had to do. It wasn't his fault the hospital didn't have enough anaesthetists.

James had moved into a friend's empty flat for the two week period, hoping that would also help buy him a bit of time while the police tried to find him. However, he had popped back to his own flat twice already and there had been no obvious sign that anyone had been looking for him. No police cars sat outside his flat, and none of the neighbours coming out to tell him that the police had been around asking questions about him. So far it had all been very quiet.

Having given Stephen Jones a piece of his own medicine, James was now planning to do the same to Nigel Harrison too. It seemed appropriate. Let him see what it felt like to have a cigarette stubbed out on his arm. James would enjoy seeing him feel the pain, the helplessness, just like he had fifteen years earlier. He unconsciously looked down at his forearm as he thought about it. There was still a faint, dark round patch on his skin where Nigel had pressed the cigarette end, and they'd all laughed as James had sat there crying and helpless.

James had found out that Nigel Harrison worked from home most days, while his partner left the house every morning at eight am to walk to the nearby train station, where she boarded a train to London. She was never home before seven pm which meant that Nigel was on his own, in the house, for eleven hours. Perfect, thought James. He could pick any day and time to give Nigel a visit, knowing he'd be there on his own. James was confident he would be able to overpower Nigel and do what he needed to do. All those years down the gym meant that he was now a fit and strong young man, not the weak little boy he used to be.

James decided to visit Nigel the following Monday morning. He drove early to the street where Nigel lived and parked between his house and the end of the road that led towards the station. It was a cold morning, the sun still hadn't broken through yet, and James had to keep his window slightly open to stop the car from steaming up inside. At eight am, he watched Nigel's partner walk past his car on her way to work. She was smartly dressed, wearing a buttoned up, light, beige coloured raincoat and carrying a dark brown leather bag.

That's good, James thought. He wasn't normally an early morning person, but he had got there in time to make sure that Nigel's partner did leave the house as usual. He wanted to be certain Nigel would be on his own, and he didn't want to take any chances.

Ten minutes later James got out of his car and pulling up his jacket collar, he walked with his head bowed down towards Nigel Harrison's house.

There was no-one else around and James was soon standing on Nigel's doorstep. He knocked twice firmly, his breath rebounding back at him off the door in the cold morning air.

'Oh, what have you forgotten this time?' he heard a voice call from inside the house, and then the door was pulled open and there stood a smiling Nigel Harrison dressed in a baggy, dark blue sweatshirt and a pair of black tracksuit trousers. In an instant, his face changed from a smile to one of surprise.

'Oh, sorry, I thought....How can I help you?' he asked.

'It's Nigel isn't it? Nigel Harrison?' James said, smiling at his ex-classmate. Of course he knew it was him, but it was just one of those things you said. He hadn't changed much physically from his schooldays. He just looked older. It was funny seeing him like that. It reminded James of a software app he'd looked at once which purported to show how you would look as you grew older. Nigel seemed to fit that bill.

'Yes....who...oh wait.....it's you,' Nigel replied, a shocked look on his face as he realised who it was standing on his doorstep, and, on instinct, he tried to close the door. But James had seen what he was going to do and had stepped forward, managing to put his foot in the gap.

James was too strong for Nigel, and he pushed the door open and stepped into Nigel's house, kicking it shut behind him. He smiled at Nigel, who was standing a few feet in front of him, his back against the banister of the stair and all of the colour drained from his face. James was surprised by his reaction, but at the same time pleased that Nigel seemed to be scared of him. Just like he had been scared of them, fifteen years before.

'So you remember me then?' James asked him, maintaining his friendly smile. 'I know I've changed a bit, but it's still me, and I certainly remember you.'

'What, ….what do you want?' Nigel asked him and James could see that he was physically trembling. He really was frightened. How times had changed. James felt good. This was what he wanted.

'I…I know what you did to Stephen Jones and you won't get away with it. The police will find you out,' Nigel said, still trembling and glancing around, looking for any sort of weapon he could use to defend himself. There was nothing in his hallway.

'Ha-ha, I doubt it,' James replied, noting that what he had done to Stephen Jones had seemingly become public knowledge. 'He got what he deserved. I can't see him going to the police anytime.'

'They'll still get you though and then you'll get what *you* deserve, a long prison sentence,' Nigel replied, as he began to regain a small element of courage in the face of his adversary.

'Come on let's go and have a chat,' James replied, still smiling, and he took Nigel by the arm and walked him down his hallway, turning through a door on the right hand side which turned out to be the main sitting room. Inside there were two light brown couches with a coffee table in the middle and a large screen TV on the wall above a gas fireplace.

'Perfect,' said James and he sat down on one of the sofas, forcing Nigel to sit down beside him, before reaching over and pulling the coffee table closer to them.

James reached into his jacket pocket and took out a lighter and a packet of cigarettes. He placed them on the table in front of them and turned to face Nigel with a smile.

'Do you recognise these, Nigel? Do they bring back any memories?' James asked, not taking his eyes away from Nigel's face.

Nigel was staring at the two items on the coffee table and his face had turned a deathly white colour again. All his previous bravado had gone. He looked like a ghost, and James could feel him trembling beside him on the sofa. He didn't speak.

'Come on, you must remember, surely? James asked him. 'Maybe if I roll up my sleeve a little....would that help you remember what I'm talking about? I'll give you a clue. Think back, mmm...let's say...fifteen years. Anything come to mind yet?'

Nigel still didn't reply. His eyes seemed to be transfixed on the lighter and cigarettes. He was still trembling. James reached forward and picked up the packet of cigarettes, slowly sliding one out. He then picked up the lighter and was about to flick it open when he was suddenly interrupted by a voice from the doorway.

'Morning, how's.....oh sorry I didn't realise ....I was just going to make a coffee...do you...?'

James was distracted, and Nigel suddenly jumped up and moved around behind the settee. James looked across at the man in the doorway. He was about the same height and build as Nigel, similar face, but he looked a few years younger. He was wearing a t-shirt and jogging bottoms, with bare feet. It looked like he'd just got out of bed. Who was he, James was thinking, and what was he doing here? Nigel was supposed to be here on his own. This was just between the two of them, it wasn't right that someone else was here. It had nothing to do with this man. His appearing had ruined the moment, James's moment, and he rose from the settee and walked towards the man standing at the doorway.

'Sorry, I was just leaving,' he said, smiling at the man as he walked past him, down the hallway and out through the front door.

Back in the house, Nigel was still standing behind the settee, leaning on the back of it. His legs had turned weak, and he was frightened to move in case they gave way and he fell. The man in the doorway walked into the room and looked at his older brother.

'Who was that Nigel? he asked. 'He seemed a bit strange, he seemed very keen to leave? I'm sorry if I interrupted you. I didn't know there was anyone here, especially this early.'

Nigel made a great effort and moved back around the settee, holding tightly on to it as he slowly edged his way forward. He slumped back down on the seat, before replying to his brother.

'That, Nick. That was a ghost from the past. I....I think you might just have saved my life,' Nigel replied. 'It was lucky that you crashed here last night and came down the stairs when you did. I'm not sure what would have happened otherwise. I'm not sure what he was going to do.'

Nick walked across and sat down on the sofa beside his brother. Nigel explained what had happened that morning, and also, more reluctantly, what had happened when he and James Gray had been at school fifteen years before. He also told his brother what he had heard about his old schoolfriend, Stephen Jones just a few days ago. Nigel explained that he had lost touch with Stephen since they'd left school, but he'd met him again recently at their school reunion. Then, just last week, he'd seen a report on his death on the local TV news programme. The report had said it was an unexplained death at this point, and that the police were looking into it.

'When James Gray turned up on my doorstep today, it all just fell into place,' Nigel said. 'He must have killed Stephen and now he's come after me. I didn't recognise him at first. He's bigger now. I mean he's filled out. Muscly. He was just a chubby little fat boy at school.'

'Shit. You have to go to the police. This man is clearly dangerous,' Nick said to his brother. 'It looks like he's already killed somebody. He could have killed you. What if he comes back again?'

'Well, they didn't say Stephen had been killed just that he'd died in...., what did they say again? Something like an unexplained death… something like that,' Nigel replied, so I may be jumping to conclusions, but…'

'But why would he come here, to see you, unless he wanted some kind of revenge?' Nick interrupted him.

'Yes, I know, but, even so, I can't go to the police,' Nigel replied.

'Why not?' Nick asked his brother, frowning at his response. 'Surely you have to? He's…he's dangerous…he might try and get you again and I won't be here next time.'

'No, I can't. Don't you see. If I go to the police now, the whole story will come out,' Nigel pleaded. 'Everyone will find out about how I bullied this kid when we were young. I'll be ruined. I'll lose my job, Pattie will probably leave me….I'll lose everything. I need some time to think, and I need you to promise me that you won't tell anyone. Do you understand? You can't tell anyone, do you get it?' Nigel held his brother's arms and looked straight into his face.

Nick nodded his head, and he reached forward to give him a hug. He'd never seen his brother like this before. Nigel had always been the one who had looked after him, but now it looked like it was his turn to step up and help his big brother out for once.

'Of course, mate, don't worry, whatever you say,' he said, giving his brother a friendly pat on his shoulder as they separated from their hug. 'Look, thanks for putting me up last night, but I've really got to get ready to go to work now. Is that okay? Give me a call if you need anything, I'll keep my mobile on, or I can pop back later tonight if you want?'

'No, you're okay, I'll be fine,' Nigel replied. 'You get off, honest it's fine. Just don't say anything to anyone, okay.'

Nick left his brother's house twenty minutes later and headed off along the street towards the train station. He had his collar up and head down. He was in a hurry. James Gray turned away as the young man walked quickly past his car and disappeared around the corner. A photo of Miss Hardy's class and a red biro pen lay beside James on the passenger seat of his car.

Chapter 8

It was late in the evening and DI Strong had managed to escape the police station to spend a few hours at home. It was always like this when a major investigation was underway. You had to grab any free time when you could and get some rest. They hadn't made a lot of progress on the Stephen Jones case so far, and Strong thought that some time away from the office might give him a bit of space to clear his mind and let him think about things freshly again, before he met with his team in the morning. He had an idea forming in his mind around the school photograph, but he wanted to take some time and think about it first.

'I thought Sophie was going out with that Keegan tonight?' he asked his wife Catherine as she came into the living room carrying a cup of tea, which she set down on the table in front of him.

Strong had been watching TV. Well, not really watching it, but it was on, in the background, and he was catching bits of it. It was The News and Strong was thinking it should really be renamed The Bad News, as that was all they seemed to report on. Famine, floods, wars, heatwaves, all stuff like that. Surely life wasn't that terrible? Although having been a police officer for many years, Strong knew life wasn't all sweetness and light. Far from it. But surely there were some good things they could report on too?

'Yes, she was supposed to be, but Keegan called off, pretty much last minute I think,' Catherine replied, screwing her face up. 'Some friend's birthday do or something. It was a boys only thing apparently, Mo.'

'Oh, did she say where he was going?' Mo Strong asked his wife.

'No. I don't think she wanted to talk much about it, she was a bit upset I think, but I expect they'll be ending up at the Green Room Club. That's where they always go,' Catherine replied.

Strong picked up his tea and took a long sip. It tasted good. His wife knew how to make a proper cup of tea. Not too weak, but not too strong either. Just right. Much better than what he got at work.

He was glad he'd taken a break from the police station. Not just for the tea. It felt nice just to sit here, in his home, and relax. He could hear Sophie walking around in her room upstairs and his thoughts moved back to her. He was worried about his daughter, but maybe that was just part of the role of being a father. She would always be his child, even though she was now an adult woman. There would always be something to worry about. At the moment, Strong's main concern was around her relationship with Keegan Summers. In short, Strong didn't like Keegan. More to the point he didn't trust him. Keegan had let his daughter down once before, and although they were both older now,

Strong feared the same would happen again. Having spent a lifetime in the police force, Strong had an instinct for people, and he had a feeling about Keegan. Not a good one. Strong didn't want his daughter to get hurt again.

Sophie had returned home, back to the nest, just a few months ago. After graduating from Leeds University, she'd got a job in Leeds as a marketing assistant for a digital media company. From what he heard, mainly through his wife Catherine via the regular mother and daughter phone calls and chats, Sophie seemed to be doing very well, and she was enjoying living in Leeds. As well as having a good job, she had a very active social life, regularly going out to the city's bars and clubs.

But then, through a contact she'd made at a trade event she'd attended, she'd been approached by another company, a similar organisation, and offered a higher level position in London. The new job came with a much improved salary, and she couldn't resist the idea of having all of that extra money in her bank account every month to help finance her lifestyle. So, much as she loved living in Leeds, she packed her bags and headed back down South. Back home.

DI Strong and his wife had agreed that Sophie could move back in with them until she saved up enough money to be able to afford the deposit on somewhere to rent. Catherine was especially happy with that, and secretly hoped it might be a few months before Sophie found anywhere else to move to. It was good to have her little girl home again. However, she knew it couldn't be for ever and she and Mo had talked about the possibility of lending or giving her some money for a deposit on a small flat, just to get her started on the property ladder. Although Mo wanted to do that sometime, he didn't feel she was ready to take that step yet, especially while she was seeing Keegan. Mo definitely didn't want any of his money ending up in Keegan Summers's hands. He couldn't admit that to Catherine though and so for now the excuse he used for not giving their daughter a helping hand financially, was that Sophie wasn't ready to settle down yet.

'She's often spoken about going travelling,' Mo said to his wife. 'Let's wait a while and see, she's still young. We'll see how she gets on in this new job for a bit. Maybe in a year or so.'

Mo's arguments seemed to persuade his wife, although what he didn't realise was that Catherine was happy that Sophie was back living at home, and so she was content to go along with her husband on this one.

'Yes, okay, I think you're right. Maybe next year,' she replied.

Since coming back South to live with her parents again, Sophie had renewed some of her friendships with several of her old schoolfriends. They'd go out regularly to some of the local bars and clubs. The same places they used to go to when they were teenagers. When they used to con their way in, even though they were still too young, using fake IDs they'd got from older siblings. Of course she never told her parents that, although she suspected her mum knew. One day, Sophie had left her false driving licence on her bedside table and when she returned home later, she found it had been moved to her desk. Her mum had been in, tidying up her room, and must have seen it. She didn't say anything to Sophie though.

As a teenager, on nights out with her mates, Sophie had always been careful not to drink too much and to stay away from drugs and any potential trouble. She knew if she got into any bother, it wouldn't look good on her dad, with him being a police officer.

It was on one of those recent nights out that Sophie had bumped into Keegan Summers again. It was in Sophie's favourite place, The Green Room Club. Sophie hadn't seen him since she'd left to go to university, and she almost didn't recognise him as she made her way through the throng of people to the bar.

'Sophie,' someone said, grabbing her arm as she was walking past. 'What are you doing here?'

Sophie looked at the man who had taken hold of her arm, ready to tell him off, but something stopped her in time. He was smiling at her and, after a few seconds, she recognised him as her ex-boyfriend from school, Keegan Summers. But he looked different now. More grown up, more manly. He'd only been a boy when they had gone out before, but now he seemed to have stretched up and filled out. He looked like he'd been going down to the gym on a regular basis! Keegan had also changed his hairstyle and he now had much shorter hair, still dark brown, and it was now set off with a lightly trimmed beard.

'Keegan?' Sophie said, beginning to smile. 'Oh my God, I almost didn't recognise you. You've...you've...emm...changed.'

'Do you think? Well, you haven't,' Keegan replied laughing. 'You look just as gorgeous as I remember you. Before you deserted me and ran off to Uni,' he laughed. 'I'd heard you were back in town,' he added, before stepping forward to give Sophie a friendly hug.

The two of them chatted for a bit that evening, reminiscing on times gone by, and filling each other in on what they had both been up to the last few years. Keegan told Sophie he was now working as a customer account representative for a company that sold on-line software for education and training. He claimed he was one of their top performing sales people and had won a couple of awards. Sophie could imagine him doing that, being in sales, he'd always been a very charming character.

As he was speaking, Sophie's mind drifted back to their schooldays. Keegan Summers had been in the same year as her at school and when they were thirteen or fourteen, Sophie had fallen for him. They had soon become boyfriend and girlfriend, but the truth was that they were still very young and innocent, and Sophie laughed to herself as she thought about it now. But it had seemed real and important at the time. Her first real love, or so she thought. It seemed to be going well, until he started to ignore her. Suddenly he wasn't returning any of her calls or messages and seemingly avoiding her at school. Soon, Sophie found out he was seeing someone else. It was another girl from the year above them. Pauline Brass. Pauline looked older than she was and had a bit of a reputation. Sophie knew why Keegan had started seeing her. No doubt she would do things that Sophie wouldn't.

"Pauline Brass, she's a pain in the ass!" Sophie and her friends used to sing, but not to her face. Needless to say, Keegan's relationship with Pauline Brass hadn't lasted long. They both got what they had wanted from it and moved on. Sophie wondered what Pauline Brass was doing now. Probably a dentist or something like that.

At the time, Sophie had been heartbroken. Keegan had been her first proper boyfriend and to her it seemed like the end of the world. Why had he done it? Were all boys like that? She laughed when she thought about it now. She had been so young.

Her father, DI Strong, was upset at seeing his daughter crying, but he was realistic enough to know that those were the sort of things that happened when you were a young teenage girl. That had been a long time ago, but he still wasn't happy when he heard that Sophie was now seeing Keegan again. He tried to disguise it, but he guessed both Sophie and Catherine knew he wasn't pleased. He didn't trust Keegan Summers. It was as simple as that. Sophie had said that they were both adults now, more mature. But Strong believed in the saying that a leopard can't change his spots and so he hoped that their revived relationship would just be a short term thing. The sooner it finished the better. That was Strong's thinking.

His wife Catherine also admitted she had some reservations about Keegan, but her view was Sophie had to make that decision herself. She was a grown woman now.

'You know Sophie. She's very determined. If we say anything, it's more likely we'll just push her in the other direction,' Catherine said. 'She'll just dig her heels in and stick with him to spite us.'

Strong agreed with his wife. He knew that was how his daughter was. She had to come to her own decision on her relationship with Keegan Summers. But that didn't mean he couldn't nudge her in the right direction. As long as Sophie didn't know what he was planning to do, then it would all be fine. Strong's plan was that she wouldn't know.

Strong made a mental note to talk to Marsha Hughes in the morning. Marsha worked in the police administration support team, and he had another little job she could do for him. On the quiet, just like she had successfully done for him several times in the past.

Chapter 9

Detective Sergeant Knight was glad to be back in the police office, back on the job again, having returned from her stint at the annual police conference. She had learned a lot while she was there, some good, some not so good.

DI Strong had asked Knight how she had got on at the event, and she thought she had been able to convince him that it had been a worthwhile few days. She just didn't tell him about the constant innuendo, or the number of times she had been asked what her boyfriend or husband did for a living. Or what had happened with Detective Inspector Murphy. That was something she'd rather forget, and definitely wouldn't be sharing with DI Strong.

Despite what they all said on camera or to the Press, the police force was still a big men's club. But for now, DS Knight felt she was a strong enough woman to survive in it despite the extra barriers she had to overcome.

DI Strong had quickly brought her up to speed on the Stephen Jones case and he was happy to let her take over the lead on it, as ever offering his help if required.

'It's probably best I stay involved,' he said, 'for continuity. But of course it's your investigation to run. You'll be making the decisions, or we can make them together.'

He passed a file over to DS Knight and, as she took it, their fingers briefly touched, and they both felt a small static shock.

'Ow,' the two detectives said in unison and then they both laughed.

One strange thing about the case was that DS Knight had recognised some of the people in the school photo. She had also gone to Danesborough High School, and it was actually a photo of one of the classes from the same year as she had been in. It had been a big school and Knight didn't know, or at least couldn't remember, Stephen Jones. She did know a few of the girls in the class, although she wasn't in contact with any of them now. However, Knight had seen some of them again, fairly recently, when she had gone to a Danesborough High School reunion party in a local hotel.

'Yes, it's Miss Hardy's class. I remember her vaguely, that's her at the back on the right,' she told DI Strong. 'I think she taught Geography, but I wasn't very good at that. It was the flags that did me, I could never get them right. And the capitals, they were hard too.'

DS Knight hadn't wanted to go to the school reunion, and wouldn't have, but her good friend Alice Mountjoy had persuaded her otherwise. Alice was the only schoolmate she had kept in touch with.

It would be fun, Alice had said. But it hadn't been. Not really. It had been good to have a night out with Alice again, but the rest of it had been a bit boring. Just as DS Knight had imagined it was going to be. Most of her ex-schoolfriends had seemingly mundane lives. They didn't appear to have much ambition. They weren't like her and Alice.

Knight was making a career for herself in the police, one of the youngest female Detective Sergeants in the force, and Alice was working hard to become an actress. Knight had no doubt her friend would succeed. She'd seen her in a few productions, and she knew Alice had the talent and determination to make it big. They had that in common, unlike the rest of their old school friends.

Since Stephen Jones's mother had identified the school photo, the police now had a list of the names of everyone in it. Strong told Knight that he wanted to get the views of a police psychologist before they made their next move.

'I've used Doctor Sam Collins on a previous case, and she was very helpful, pretty good at identifying who the criminal was in that case, and why he was doing it,' Strong explained. 'He had some sort of medical condition, a type of PTSD and that was making him kill. However, with this case, we're still not a hundred percent sure that this was a murder, or even some sort of unlawful killing yet, so I'd like to get Doctor Collins's take on it, particularly around the significance of the school photo. I've sent her the information and she's coming to see us this afternoon. I've booked us a meeting room on the second floor, so let's see what she says.'

'Okay,' DS Knight replied, thinking what part of it being her "investigation to run" or her "making the decisions" did this fit into?

Despite that, she trusted DI Strong and she had heard him talk highly about Doctor Collins before, and so she was keen to meet her. Maybe she would be able to help them.

Chapter 10

Doctor Sam Collins opened the door and entered the second floor meeting room in the police station. There was a rectangular table in the middle of the room with six chairs messily arranged around it. She took off her coat and laid it over the back of one of the chairs, resting her briefcase on the floor beside it. Dr Collins was wearing a matching light blue jacket and skirt with a white blouse. Her long blonde hair lay smoothly over the shoulders of the jacket.

Detective Inspector Strong was sitting on the far side of the table and he stood up to greet Doctor Collins as she entered the room, with a welcoming smile on his face. The Detective Inspector shook Doctor Collins's hand firmly.

'It's good to see you again, Doctor Collins. Thank you for coming in,' DI Strong said. 'This is Detective Sergeant Knight,' he added nodding his head towards a young woman with short dark hair who was sitting beside him. DS Knight stood up and shook the Doctor's hand, not quite so firmly, but not limply either.

'Nice to meet you Doctor Collins,' she said, smiling at the Doctor. 'I've heard a lot about you.'

The police psychologist returned her greeting, and they all took their seats around the table.

Doctor Collins had never met DS Knight before, but she had heard a little about her from other police officers she had worked with. They had all said that Knight was a very good detective, very confident and ambitious too. Looking across the table, Dr Collins could also see that she was young and attractive, which she knew could be both an advantage and a disadvantage, depending on the situation you found yourself in.

Dr Collins opened her briefcase and took out a document which she put down on the table in front of her.

Across the desk, DS Knight was focused on the doctor. She'd heard quite a lot about her from DI Strong and others in the office, and she was keen to get to know her better. Although police psychologists didn't always have the best reputation around the police force, Dr Collins seemed to be regarded as an exception to that. And, in DS Knight's view, it was good to have another woman apparently doing well in her job. Knight could see that she would be popular with many of her male colleagues, due to her being very attractive. However, Knight expected there to be much more to her than just her looks, and she was keen to hear what the doctor had to say about the Stephen Jones case. At this point, Knight was optimistically hopeful that Dr Collins might be able to help them.

'Shall I make a start on Stephen Jones?' Collins asked DI Strong, as if she had just read DS Knight's mind.

'Yes, please go ahead, we're keen to get your take on this one Dr Collins,' Strong replied. 'See if you might be able to steer us in the right direction.'

'Okay, well firstly, thank you for sending me the information pack on the death of Stephen Jones. I've looked through it all carefully and here's what I think,' Dr Collins started, and she opened the document in front of her as she spoke.

DS Knight listened closely to what the doctor had to say. She came across as being very thorough and confident as she discussed her findings. She'd definitely done her homework and was able to answer any questions Strong or Knight had for her. Some of her ideas were based on assumptions which couldn't be fully proven at this point, but she always had good, solid reasoning behind these points. DS Knight was impressed. She was glad that Dr Collins had lived up to her expectations and she felt the two women had a lot in common, especially with them working in what was largely a man's world.

'So, my overall summary is that I think Stephen Jones was assaulted. An attack which may have led to his death,' Dr Collins continued. 'I'll leave that one to the pathologists though, not exactly my area of expertise,' she smiled, showing a perfect set of straight white teeth. 'I believe the school photo is significant,' she carried on. 'There is no reason for it to be there, other than it being left with the intention of sending out a message. In my opinion the message is that Stephen Jones is only one of a number of people from this school class who are being targeted in some way. I think the fact that his head was ringed in the photo with a cross through it, indicates he was a target, but probably just the first. Now the nature of the attack on Stephen Jones might indicate that the attack was some sort of revenge. Perhaps for something that Stephen Jones did to the assailant, or someone close to that person, when they were at school. If you can find out if there was any incident that Stephen Jones was involved in, it may help identify who else was there, and so who else might be in danger too. It is key that we speak to everyone in the photo and see what they can tell us about Stephen Jones's time at school,' Dr Collins paused for breath and to see if either of the detectives had any questions at this point. The room remained silent, so she carried on.

'However, I don't believe everyone in this photo is in danger or is a target for the assailant. My guess is that there will have been a small group of people from the class who were involved in something. Maybe a gang. We need to find out,' Dr Collins paused again, shrugging her shoulders and then looking down at her document.

'Now, the next key thing is that I think there may be a good chance that the person you are looking for is also in this class photo, Dr Collins said.

'Wait, why do you think that?' DS Knight asked. 'We've obviously thought that could be the case, but I'd be interested to know what your reasoning is to come to that conclusion.'

'Well,' Dr Collins replied, looking straight at DS Knight. From the short time they'd been together in this meeting room, Dr Collins could already see that DS Knight was a very confident young woman, not frightened to challenge her, but listening to what she said, and the doctor admired her for that.

'The whole situation seems to me, that what we are looking at is confined to this one group of schoolkids, or adults, as they now are,' Dr Collins explained. 'The fact that the attacker left a class photo and not an individual photo of Mr Jones, I think shows that it is the bigger group that is important, and I believe the person you are looking for must also be closely connected to that bigger group, which is this school class,' Dr Collins said as she held up a copy of the school photo. 'The most likely explanation would be that he, or she, is in this class too.'

'I can make some guesses as to how Stephen Jones and his attacker were connected, but I think it best that we keep an open mind at this point and find out what you can from the rest of the people in this photo. What can they tell you about Stephen Jones? Who were his closest friends? Who did he upset, if anyone? I think you'll get a much clearer picture, and perhaps a motive, after you've done those interviews. My one suggestion though would be to keep them as informal as possible, try and make it seem like a chat about their time at school generally before you focus in on Stephen

Jones specifically. I think that way they may tell you more and you'll be able to build up a bigger picture of what went on in this class. I'd be happy to help out in any way that I can,' Dr Collins said, smiling confidently.

'Thank you Dr Collins, we'll certainly discuss that,' DS Knight replied, smiling back at the doctor.

'I believe, DS Knight, you went to this same school, Danesborough High. Is that correct?' Dr Collins asked.

'Yes, that's correct. I was in the same year as Stephen Jones but a different class,' DS Knight replied. 'It was a big school though and I didn't really know Stephen. I knew a couple of the girls in his class, in the photo, but not that well. Thinking back, we tended to stick with the people in our own classes.'

'I see,' Dr Collins replied. 'What was the school like generally? Was there ever any trouble, was it well disciplined?'

'I think so, yes,' Knight replied. 'I can't remember there ever being any major trouble really. Probably a few fights and so on, but that was about it. The Headmistress was quite strict as I recall. I've been trying to think back, but there's nothing really that I can think of that would help. We'll talk to the Headmistress, Mrs King, assuming she's still around. She seemed quite old when we were there, but I don't really know.'

'Yes,' Dr Collins nodded. 'You should talk with her and also the teacher in this photo, this Miss Hardy. I think she could be a useful source of information for you. She'll have a different perspective on things, having been an adult at the time when everyone else was still young. Also she may be able to remember the class as a whole, how they interacted, stuff like that.'

DI Strong, who hadn't really been participating in the discussion over the last few minutes, suddenly stood up and took his phone out of his jacket pocket, looking at the screen.

'Sorry, I need to take this,' he said, and he walked out of the room with the phone pressed to his ear.

Dr Collins smiled across the table at DS Knight as the door closed behind her.

'He's a good DI isn't he? Strong. I hear a lot of positive things about him. I guess he must be good to work for?' Dr Collins asked.

'Yes, he's very supportive. He's clever and he's helped me a lot with how to get things done,' DS Knight replied, nodding her head. 'I'm always learning from him.'

'Yes, he's helped me too,' Dr Collins replied. 'To be honest, a lot of the police are pretty sceptical about us psychologists and what we can usefully do to help them with their cases. But DI Strong has always been very positive when we've worked together in the past. I like working with him, he makes me feel like I'm part of the team.'

'Yeh, he's good at that,' DS Knight replied, nodding her head. 'And he's told me that you really helped him before with the Anniversary Killer case, so I'm happy to involve you on this one too, as much as is useful.'

'Thanks, that's good to know,' Dr Collins replied. 'I think we could work well together.'

Just then, the door opened, and DI Strong walked back into the room. The two women fell silent.

'What did I miss?' he asked, looking at the two women sitting at the table.

'Oh, nothing really. We were just talking about other stuff, nothing important Guv,' DS Knight replied, before glancing across the table at Dr Collins with a mischievous smile on her face.

DI Strong sat back down at the table and looked at the two women. Neither of them spoke.

'Okay, well unless there's anything else then, I think we're all agreed,' Strong said. 'Our next step is to go ahead and have an informal chat with everyone in that school photo. I'm sure you'll get that moving,' he said looking at DS Knight.

'Yes, of course,' Knight replied nodding. 'Let's see what we can find out about Stephen Jones and anyone else in the class. What went on at Danesborough High School? Let's try and build a picture and see if we can find out why Stephen Jones was attacked,' DS Knight concluded.

'Can we meet up again when you have done that?' Dr Collins asked the detective. She was keen to stay involved in the case. It was one of the drawbacks of her role as an expert psychologist. She would often be called in for one meeting on a case and then not have any more involvement thereafter. She found that very frustrating.

'Sure, I don't see why not,' Strong replied. 'You okay with that?' he asked looking across the table at DS Knight.

'Yep, okay with me,' DS Knight replied. She wasn't exactly sure why, but she liked the psychologist.

'Good, here's my card,' Dr Collins said. 'Give me a call, it would be good to stay in touch, maybe we can do dinner one evening,' she said as she passed her business card across the table to Detective Sergeant Knight.

Later that day, Knight and Strong met again in the Detective Inspector's office.

'What did you think of our Dr Collins?' Strong asked Knight.

'Yeh, she was good,' Knight replied. 'She talked a lot of common sense, not too much scientific babble which I liked. She seems to know her stuff. You were right Guv,' she said smiling at her boss.

'Okay, good, so what's happening now?' Strong replied, smiling back at his colleague.

'Well, I've allocated out all of the class between the team, you included, as I know you wanted to stay involved. We've each got about two or three of the ex-pupils to see. I've also written a brief summary of what we want to get from the interviews, how to approach them etc., taking into account what Dr Collins said earlier today. It's all in an email which should have hit your inbox a few minutes ago.'

'Ah good,' DI Strong replied, turning to look at his computer and picking up his glasses as he did so. ‘Ah, yes, here it is. Right, good, let’s get on with it then,’ he said as he stood up from his desk.

DS Knight also stood up and nodded at her boss, before turning around and leaving his office.

Chapter 11

Detective Sergeant Knight walked up the pathway towards the green front door. There was a wooden porch at the entrance and on either side were two hanging baskets full of vibrant flowers. Oranges and yellows, lit up by the sun. DS Knight had never been a gardener and so she couldn't name them, but she had to admit they did look pretty.

Knight stepped forward and pushed the bell. It was one of those bells with a built-in camera that allowed the homeowner to see who was at the door, on their mobile, before they went to answer it. Or if they weren't at home, they could still see who was at their house. Being a police officer, Knight knew there were obvious security benefits with this type of bell, and she had considered getting one for herself. But, when she thought about it more, she realised that no-one actually ever came to her door. Well, no-one except the postman or the Amazon delivery driver and she didn't really need to see a video of them on her phone.

The door opened and Jenny Broughton stood there smiling. Of course she'd known it was going to be Laura Knight standing there before she opened it. That was one downside of these type of doorbells. They took away that moment of revelation. Jenny Broughton would never be able to open her door now and honestly say "Oh my word, what a surprise to see you!" because she'd already know who was there.

'Laura. Good to see you, how are you? Do come in,' Jenny said, stepping aside and allowing DS Knight to walk into her hallway.

The other reason why this particular visit wasn't a surprise for Jenny was that DS Knight had called her earlier that day and asked if she could pop round and see her for a few minutes, nothing to worry about, just a quick chat about one of their ex-school friends, DS Knight had explained. Jenny had organised the recent school reunion and so Knight thought it might be useful to give her a call, in addition to those in the photo. Having shown an interest in getting her old schoolmates together, there was the chance she might have some more knowledge on them, particularly Stephen Jones. Knight also knew that Stephen Jones had been at the reunion and so there was a chance Jenny might have spoken with him and found out something from that conversation.

The two women walked along the carpeted hallway. Clean and tidy, Knight thought, very well looked after. They carried on through the house to a large, open-plan kitchen and dining area which looked like it had been a recent extension to the original house. Again, everything looked perfect, not a thing out of place.

Jenny had one of those fancy looking coffee machines and she quickly made two lattes while telling DS Knight all about what they had done to the house.

'When we bought it,' she began, 'it was in a bit of a state, but we kind of wanted a place like that, so we could put our own mark on it. Do you know what I mean?'

DS Knight nodded her head as she took another sip of her lovely coffee. It was much better than the stuff she was used to drinking at the police station.

'And it was in the right location. That was important too. For the schools and that, you know? Anyway, we stripped it all out and we put this extension on,' she said, indicating the room they were now standing in, 'and we're really pleased with it. It's made such a difference,' she smiled vacantly as she looked around the room.

'Yes, I can see that, it's lovely,' DS Knight replied, wondering if she would ever get so enthused about some building work. Probably not.

The two women took their coffees and sat down on red, aluminium bar stools by a large island in the middle of the kitchen. They each took a sip of their drink before getting down to business.

'So, when you called me, you said you wanted to ask me about one of our old schoolfriends?' Jenny asked DS Knight.

'Yes, that's right. Stephen Jones. He was in our year I believe. He was in Miss Hardy's class. Do you remember him?' DS Knight asked.

'Stephen Jones, yes, yes, I do. Why do you ask? Has he done something? He was at the reunion. Did you see him there?' Jenny asked the detective.

'No, I don't think I did, but I didn't really know him at school. I can't really remember him,' Knight replied.

She took another sip of her coffee before putting her cup down on the counter and looking directly at her ex-schoolfriend.

'I take it you haven't heard, but unfortunately Stephen was found dead at his house, and we're trying to piece together exactly what happened,' DS Knight said.

'Oh no, I didn't know. I'm so sorry to hear that. He was so young,' Jenny replied with a shocked look on her face. She took another drink of her coffee.

'Yes. It's early days in the investigation yet and we're just trying to build up a picture of him, from when he was young up until now,' DS Knight said. 'Can you remember what he was like when he was at school?'

'Well, as far as I can remember about him at school, he was a nice enough boy. A bit of a prankster at times though. I think he, and a few of his mates, used to get up to things at school, you know? Just daft young boy things I think, nothing too serious, but they always seemed to get away with it,' Jenny replied.

'What sort of things?' Knight asked. 'Can you remember?'

'Well, you know, it was mainly just boys stuff. I think I remember the fire alarm going off once and someone said it was him that had pressed it, but I don't think it was ever proven,' Jenny replied. 'I think there was also something happened with another boy. They might have picked on him a bit, you know? I think he might have left the school, but I can't remember his name,' Jenny added. 'It was so long ago.'

DS Knight reached into her bag and took out a copy of the class photo, without the penned markings on Stephen Jones's head. She handed it over to Jenny Broughton.

'This is a photo of Miss Hardy's class, from when we were all about fourteen or fifteen. Do you recognise some of the people in it?' Knight asked.

Jenny held the photo up and looked at it, smiling as her eyes darted across the faces of the young pupils.

'Oh yes, I recognise most of them, I think. Quite a few of them, especially the girls. A lot of them came to the reunion party,' she said. 'That's Stephen Jones there,' she added, pointing at the photo. 'I can't believe he's dead, such a shame. How did he die?' Jenny asked DS Knight.

'I'm afraid I can't say at this point, it's an ongoing enquiry. What about the boy you were trying to remember. Is he there?' DS Knight asked.

'No, no,' Jenny replied, shaking her head. 'I can't see him. Maybe he'd left by then or he was in a different class. It's going to bug me now, not remembering his name.'

'What about Stephen's friends. Do you know who he hung around with at school?' Knight asked.

Jenny sat for a second thinking, before shaking her head.

'I'm sorry I can't think. I didn't know him that well really, him being in a different class and that. I'm really sorry,' Jenny replied.

'Well, don't worry, I'll give you my card with my mobile number on it and you can call me if you remember anything. We're talking to most of the people in this photo so I'm sure someone will remember things about him and who the other boy was,' DS Knight replied as she returned the school photo to her bag.

'I'm sorry I couldn't help you more,' Jenny called out as DS Knight walked down her garden path and she closed the front door.

Chapter 12

DI Strong was on his way to interview another of the pupils from the school photo. Between the team, they were working their way through them all, but so far, they hadn't uncovered anything that was of any great significance to their enquiry. This time the old classmate was a man called Bradley Smith and Strong was hoping that he might know something that would give them a breakthrough.

DS Knight knew Bradley Smith and had wanted to talk to DI Strong about him, but Strong had stopped her, telling his Detective Sergeant that he wanted to go in with an open mind so he could form his own opinion of the man. A preconception can be a misconception, he had said, and so the Detective Inspector had only read the most basic details about the man he was about to see. He preferred doing it that way.

Strong parked his car outside the address he had for Bradley Smith and pressed the buzzer at the entrance to the block of flats. It was a cold day and Strong stamped his feet on the doorstep to stay warm. There was a faint odour in the air coming from the nearby waste recycling centre. The intercom was soon answered by a man's voice and after DI Strong explained who he was, the door was buzzed open. Strong made his way to the flat and knocked twice, firmly on the door. It was answered by a man who, Strong thought, looked older than he actually was. The man had a high forehead with a shock of curly brown hair sitting on top of it. He was wearing a multi-coloured, patterned cardigan, pulled together tightly at the bottom, secured with a single button, straining to conceal a bulging stomach. If Strong hadn't known this man was the same age as DS Knight, he probably would have guessed that he was about ten years older than her.

DI Strong introduced himself, and Bradley Smith did likewise, before letting the detective into his home, guiding him along a narrow hallway, through into a sitting room.

'Would you like a cup of tea or a coffee?' Bradley asked the Detective, intimating he should sit down on a bright orange settee. 'It's cold out there. Oh, and please call me Brad by the way, most people do.'

Strong asked for a black coffee and Bradley left the room, returning a few minutes later with two steaming red mugs, one of which he handed to DI Strong. The Detective took a sip of his drink, immediately recognising it as a cup of instant coffee. It wasn't that he was a coffee snob, it was just that he was so used to drinking coffee made from ground beans now that anything else tasted less fulsome. Too weak and watery. Even the kitchen in the police station now had a coffee machine, which he'd mastered the art of using, after an initial bit of help from one of the ladies in the admin support team.

'This is a nice place you have here,' Strong said, looking around, trying to put Bradley Smith at ease. Experience had taught him that was the best way to proceed when interviewing someone in connection with a crime. If they thought you were their friend, they were more likely to tell you something useful. In reality though, in Bradley Smith's living room, Strong could still smell the odour from the local waste recycling centre, which he knew was just around the corner.

'So, can I ask you, what do you do for a living Mr Smith?' Strong asked him.

'Oh, please call me Brad. I'm the manager in the local supermarket,' Bradley replied, smiling. 'Do you live locally? You might have seen me in there, although I'm often in the office making sure things are all running smoothly, you know. I don't get out on the floor as much as I'd like to. These things don't just run themselves.'

Strong nodded and smiled. The truth was he didn't do much shopping himself. His wife Catherine was in charge of that. They were a bit of an old-fashioned married couple in that respect. The most DI Strong ever did was to walk down to the local corner shop for a pint of milk, or a newspaper.

'So, I guess you're here because of what happened to Stephen Jones then? Terrible business that. Am I right?' Bradley asked DI Strong with a knowing look on his face.

'Why do you say that?' Strong replied. Of course, Bradley Smith was right, but as far as Strong knew, none of the other pupils they had already spoken with had started the conversation in that way. Most of them hadn't known and had appeared genuinely shocked when they had learned about Stephen Jones's demise.

'Well, I read about it in the local paper and saw some other stuff on the internet. Social media stuff and that you know? It said he'd been found dead in his bathroom. Is that right? Do you know what happened yet?' Bradley asked, eagerly sitting forward in his chair. 'Have you had the report back from the pathologist yet on how he died?'

'I'm afraid I can't discuss any of that with you at this point. It's an ongoing investigation, I'm sure you understand,' DI Strong replied.

'Yes, yes, of course. I'm sorry,' Bradley replied. 'I watch a lot of crime dramas on TV, they're kind of my thing, and so to meet a real detective on a real case, well it's sort of interesting for me.'

'Yes, I understand,' DI Strong replied. 'Unfortunately, what you see on TV though, it's not so much like that in real life I can tell you. There's a lot more day to day stuff, lots of data to process. And it takes longer. We can't fit it all into one sixty minute episode,' Strong said, smiling at Bradley Smith.

'No, of course, I get that,' Bradley replied, returning the detective's smile and feeling a little embarrassed by his own enthusiasm.

DI Strong paused for a few seconds to allow a change in the topic of conversation, before carrying on.

'So, Mr Smith, we're trying to build up a picture of who Stephen Jones was, what he was like. I wonder, can you tell me what you remember about him?' Strong asked.

'Well, I hadn't seen him since we left school, but of course I bumped into him and the others at the school reunion recently. I assume you know about that?' Bradley stopped and looked at the detective.

'Yes, I do. Did you speak to him then?' Strong asked.

'Yes, just briefly, you know, like how are you what are you doing now. That sort of thing. I didn't spend a lot of time with him,' Bradley replied. 'He seemed fine, he didn't say, or do, anything unusual, as far as I know.'

'And did anything happen at the reunion at all? Any incidents, arguments, anything like that?' Strong asked.

Bradley sat still for a few seconds, his hands clasped together, apparently recalling the event in his mind.

'No, no…nothing that I can think of,' he replied. 'It all seemed quite peaceful to me. Just a …just a normal school reunion, I guess.'

'I see,' Strong nodded. 'And tell me, what do you remember about Stephen from your schooldays? Were you friends with him at school?' the Detective enquired.

'Emm…well I knew him. We were in the same class at school, but…I, he wasn't my closest friend, no,' Bradley replied.

'Who was your closest friend at school?' Strong asked him.

'I…emm…well, I didn't really…I had a number of friends. I'm not sure really,' Bradley replied, shifting uncomfortably in his seat.

'Okay,' Strong replied, noting Bradley's apparent unease at his question. 'And what about Stephen? Can you remember what he was like at school? Was he popular? Who were his best friends, can you remember? Was there anything he did at all that sticks out in your mind? Anything you can remember, no matter how small it seems, could be helpful,' Strong said.

Bradley was keen to help. He wanted to be the one who gave the police that vital piece of evidence that helped them crack the case. He'd seen it in so many of his favourite TV detective dramas. He knew there could be something that didn't seem much to him, but put together with other evidence the police would have gathered, it might just be the key to finding the guilty party. Even before the detective's visit today, he had thought really hard, read up all he could about the case so far and tried to remember Stephen from their schooldays. But the truth was Bradley had been a bit of a loner at school. He had been shy and didn't mix well with the other boys. Especially boys like Stephen Jones. As far as he could remember, Stephen had been one of the more confident boys and hadn't taken much notice of little Bradley Smith. Bradley felt more comfortable avoiding boys like that and his only friend at school had been a girl called Alison Kirkbride, but she was almost as shy as he was.

'I'm sorry, I can't think of anything much. I think he was quite a popular boy, quite confident, but…I didn't really know him that well,' Bradley replied, disappointed that he couldn't recall anything that might help the detective. Then a thought struck him, and he looked at the detective sitting across the room.

'Can I ask, why are you asking about his schooldays? Do you think his death was something to do with that? But what…?' Bradley asked, his mind racing as he spoke.

'No, we're just pursuing a number of lines of enquiry,' DI Strong replied, shaking his head. 'At this stage we're just trying to build up a picture of what Stephen was like, including talking to a number of people like yourself who knew him at some point in his life.'

'Oh, I see,' Bradley replied. 'And emm…they said he was found in the bathroom. Was he emm…drowned? Is that how he died, in the bath?' Bradley asked the Detective.

'I can't give you any details, Mr Smith,' Strong replied. 'As I said the investigation is ongoing and I'm sure everything will come out at some point in the future.'

'Of course, of course,' Bradley replied. 'I'm sorry, I'd just love to help. It would be my dream to help solve a murder case,' Bradley laughed nervously.

'Yes, well just to be clear, at this point it's just an unexplained death,' DI Strong replied.

'Oh yes, of course,' Bradley replied. 'Well, I'm sorry I haven't been much help to you today

Detective Strong. As I said I didn't know him that well really. But if there's anything you think I can do to be of assistance, please let me know. As I said before I'd love to help,' Bradley replied.

'Okay, thank you. Well, if you do remember anything about Stephen Jones. If anything comes to mind. Perhaps something that he did when he was at school, please just give me a call,' DI Strong replied, and he handed Bradley a card with his number on it.

'Just one final thing,' Strong said as he got up to leave. 'Can you tell me where you were last Tuesday evening?'

'Oh…emm…last Tuesday evening,' Bradley could feel himself starting to blush. 'Oh, I…emm…think I was here…in the house. Yes, I think so, last Tuesday, yes,' he replied.

'Okay. Is there anyone can confirm that? It's just for our records, you know?' Strong replied.

'Of course, emm…no, I, emm…live here on my own. I was just here myself, watching TV, I think,' Bradley replied.

'Okay, no worries,' Strong replied. 'As I said, give me a call if you remember anything else. Thank you for your time, Mr Smith,' Strong said as he walked out of Bradley Smith's front door.

As he made his way back to his car, Strong was thinking about what had just happened. Bradley Smith had been nervous, more nervous than he needed to be. And he seemed interested in the case. Too interested. Asking a lot of questions and making assumptions as if he knew stuff. Why was he so interested if he hardly knew Stephen Jones as he had claimed?

Then when Strong had asked him about Tuesday night, the evening that Stephen Jones had been attacked, Strong got the strong impression that he was definitely hiding something. Something wasn't quite right, Strong could sense it. He could smell when someone wasn't telling the truth and the aroma coming from Bradley Smith was even stronger than that coming from the nearby waste recycling centre. Strong would have to talk to DS Knight about his suspicions and suggest to her that they do some further investigation into Bradley Smith.

Chapter 13

'Oh my goodness, wait it'll come to me……it's James, isn't it? James Gray? I'm right, aren't I? It's been such a long time. How are you? Please come in out of the cold,' the old lady said, and she stepped to one side to let the face from the past enter her house.

Irene Hardy had spent her life teaching children the joys of Geography and English. She'd done it for forty three years before reluctantly retiring. It was a job she had loved and if she could have carried on, she would have. But the arthritic pains had built over the last few years until she had to concede that the role was now beyond her physical capabilities. Just standing up for more than a few minutes could be an effort on a bad day now. Having to do that for eight hours a day Monday to Friday was no longer possible.

The day she had stopped teaching at Danesborough High School had been a day of mixed emotions. She was looking forward to having a more relaxed life, but she knew she would definitely miss the children. Her children.

Irene had never married. How could she? There just wasn't enough time. Her teaching job took up all the hours in her day. The joy of educating children really was a full-time occupation. But she loved it. Seeing them developing, growing, teaching fulfilled her in all the ways that were important to her.

She had been a good-looking young woman, and she had many male admirers over the years. Some of them had tried to move things to a more serious level. A relationship. But Irene had to let them down. They just weren't as important as her children. And they never would be.

Patrick Morrison had been particularly persistent, and he was a pleasant enough man, but Irene just couldn't fit him in to her busy school schedule. There was always something needing done. Marking homework, preparing lessons, planning for events. If she was being totally honest, she'd found him a bit boring. Nothing wrong with him, just a bit mundane. She heard that he'd married a vicar's daughter from a neighbouring town and that they had three children. Good for them.

It hadn't been totally one way though. There had been one man, once. Someone she had admired and dreamt about potentially having some sort of relationship with. Maybe a future. But when she found out that he was already married, that was that. Irene wasn't the type of woman who would try and take someone else's man. That wasn't right.

When she was on her own at home, she did occasionally wonder if she would have been a good mother. She loved children, but did she need any of her own? Probably not. She had enough children to cope with at the school, and they were all hers in a way.

Since she'd retired five years ago, she'd gradually extricated herself from the school system. She'd resigned from the Board of Governors and over time had stopped attending the various school events she'd always gone to over the preceding decades. It just wasn't the same when she wasn't actually teaching the children. That had been the joy of the job. The exhilaration she got from seeing children develop, grow and learn new stuff. She didn't know the current set of pupils. She wasn't working with them every day and so she didn't get that same feeling of connection when she saw them.

Irene would still see many of her ex-pupils, "her children", when she was out and about. At the local shops, or perhaps when meeting a friend for a coffee. Statistically, it would be quite difficult not to after forty seven years worth of pupils. Of course some of them had moved out of the area, but many had stayed put and had children of their own. Indeed, there were families where Irene had taught a couple of generations. Mother and daughter, father and son. She was always happy to see any of her ex-pupils and find out what they were up to. How many children did they have now? Where were they working? Irene would always try and give them a positive word of encouragement, no matter what they were doing.

Irene had been in her kitchen when she'd heard the doorbell go. She'd looked at the clock. It was too early for her neighbour Joan, who would often pop round mid-afternoon for a cup of coffee and a gossip, mainly about the woman who lived four doors down from her and apparently had a lot of gentleman callers.

'I just happened to be out at the bins yesterday morning,' Joan had told her. 'Just putting some more junk mail in before they came to collect it. They never seem to come very early now. It's often after eleven o' clock. I remember when they'd always be there at six in the morning. You didn't need an alarm clock to wake you up on bin day. Anyway. as I was doing that, a car pulled up outside her house, you know the one. This man got out and he looked around before he walked up to her door and knocked. I swear she answered it in her dressing gown, although I couldn't say for certain as she let him in very quickly. He was in there for forty five minutes. I mean what would they be doing during that time?' Joan finished with a knowing smile, her head nodding.

Apart from Joan, Irene didn't get many callers. She wiped down her hands on the kitchen towel and checked her hair in the hall mirror before answering the door. It had taken her a few seconds to recognise the young man on the doorstep in front of her. He'd changed since he'd been in her class all those years before. He'd stretched up and built out too. He was now a solid looking young man. Maybe still not what you would describe as good-looking, but he was okay. When she'd known him as one of her pupils, he'd been quite a small teenage boy, and a bit chubby. But she still recognised his face. She was good at that. She could recognise most of her ex-pupils and remember their names within a few seconds of meeting them. She might be struggling mobility wise, but her mind was still sharp in that respect.

Irene ushered James Gray through the house and into the conservatory at the rear. She'd added the conservatory ten years ago and she now spent a lot of her time sitting in it, looking out to the garden.

Since she'd stopped working and when the weather was agreeable, Irene also spent a lot of her time in the garden. It was beginning to look like how she'd always imagined it could be but had never had the time to do it while she was still teaching. Outside the conservatory doors there was a small, paved patio area with a little round table and two chairs. That was where she and her neighbour Joan regularly sat with their coffees, chatting about nothing and everything. Joan was particularly good at that, and Irene was happy to just sit and listen to her. She found Joan's rumour mongering funny. It passed the time. If the weather wasn't good, they'd just do their thing in the conservatory.

Beyond the patio there was a small, rectangular, neatly manicured lawn, resplendent in a dark shade of green. Irene was proud of that. She'd found a "weed and feed" fertiliser on-line which seemed to have worked miracles on her grass. After the lawn, at the bottom of the garden, there was a small wooden shed, painted light green with two climbing roses growing up either side of the door. One with yellow flowers, the other orange. Irene's two favourite colours. When both roses were in full bloom she could just sit there and milk in their resplendence. On either side of the lawn there was a border with an assortment of plants, bushes and flowers, seemingly randomly placed, but giving Irene the wild, country garden look she'd always wanted.

Today there was a slight chill in the air, so Irene had the conservatory doors closed. She showed James into the bright room and he sat down on the cushioned wicker sofa, placing his green rucksack on the floor beside him. Irene took a seat on the matching chair across the room.

'So this is a pleasant surprise. How are you? What have you been doing since you left school?' Irene asked him, but before he could answer she added, 'Can I get you a drink? Tea, coffee….anything else?'

'Oh, no thanks I'm fine,' James replied.

'Okay. So come on then, tell me all about yourself. Start at the beginning and don't leave anything out or I'll be upset!' Irene laughed.

'So, you do remember me then? I was only at Danesborough for a couple of years,' James replied.

'Oh really? Oh yes, I remember now. You moved on to another school, didn't you?' Irene replied.

'Yes, that's right. Can you remember why I did that though?' James replied, he was leaning forward, his hands interlocked on his lap, looking directly at Irene.

'Emm…no…not exactly,' Irene replied, trying hard to remember. So many children had passed through her classroom over the years, she used to be able to remember them all, not just their names but their characters too, but now her memory wasn't quite as good as it used to be. Although she was good with names, quite often now she'd find herself in a room in the house not sure why she had gone there in the first place.

'Oh, maybe I can help you with that,' James said. 'How about Fatty, Podgy, Fatboy….Porky, Pigface? Does any of that ring a bell?' James said, with a steely look on his face.

Irene shifted uncomfortably on her seat. When she'd opened the door to see James standing there, this wasn't how she'd expected the conversation to go. She always loved seeing her old pupils again after all these years and, without exception, they'd all been happy to see her too. Up till now that was. She sensed there was something different here. Something wrong. This boy, James Gray, wasn't acting the same as all the others. It seemed like he was here on some kind of mission, like he had something he needed to get off his chest. Irene wasn't sure how best to respond and she needed to buy some time to think.

'I'm just going to get a tea. Are you sure you don't want anything?' she asked as she rose from her seat.

James shook his head and Irene left the room and went through to the kitchen. She pressed the switch on the kettle and leant against the worktop, waiting and thinking as the water heated. There was no sound coming from the conservatory and so she assumed James had stayed where she had left him. She felt that was a good thing, although she didn't quite know why, other than it gave her a few minutes on her own to think. Why had this boy come to her house after all these years? In fact, how had he known where she lived? She hadn't thought about that when he'd turned up on her doorstep. Although she guessed that would have been relatively easy to find out if he'd wanted to. She was in the phone book, or at least she thought she was. She hadn't actually seen a phone book for years – had they stopped making them now? A lot had changed in the last few years. He'd probably be able to easily find her through Google now. You could find out just about anything with a few taps on your mobile phone.

Her mind was brought back to the current situation by the sound of the kettle switch clicking off. She poured herself a cup of tea and added a dash of milk, taking her time to stir it. The few minutes break had helped her. Irene was feeling more relaxed again. James probably just wanted to talk to her, to get some stuff off his chest and get some reassurance from her. That had happened with Irene once or twice before. Even though her ex-pupils were now all fully grown adults, and Irene had been retired from teaching for five years, most of them still saw her as some sort of mentor, someone they could ask for advice, and invariably they still called her Miss Hardy. She liked to help them where she could and, of course, she would do the same with James Gray.

Irene walked back through to the conservatory with her cup of tea and was relieved to see James was still sitting where she'd left him. She wasn't quite sure why she felt relieved, but that was certainly her immediate emotion. She put her cup down on the side table and retook her seat.

'Now then where were we?' she asked, smiling across the room at James. 'You must tell me what you've been up to since you left school. Have you been working? You look well.'

'We were talking about why I left Danesborough High School,' James replied. 'Do you remember, Miss Hardy?'

'Oh, okay,' Irene replied. 'You weren't getting on too well were you?' Miss Hardy took a sip of her tea. 'I remember your mother coming in to see Mrs King, the headmistress, and then I think you transferred to another school not long after that. Is that right?'

'Yes, that's some of it,' James replied. 'Do you remember me coming to see you at the end of lessons one day though? It was a Monday, end of the day. I remember it was heavy rain outside. You were in the classroom, and I came in and asked if I could talk with you. Do you remember what happened next?'

'No, not really. The thing is James, I was always very busy, and I just didn't have the time to do everything I wanted to,' Irene replied. 'I'm afraid that's the reality of being a teacher. There's just not enough hours in the day to do everything.'

'I wanted to talk to you, and you just sent me away,' James replied. 'You said, could I come back tomorrow, but I wanted to see you then, don't you see? I *needed* to see you,' James emphasised. 'And you sent me away. Like you didn't care.

Nobody cared,' James said, clenching his fists hard by his side.

'No, you're wrong James,' Irene replied, sitting forward. 'People did care. I cared. But we couldn't do everything. There was too much. I didn't know what you were going through. I still don't. Why don't you tell me, I know it was in the past, but I'm listening to you now.'

'It's too late now,' James replied angrily. 'I needed to talk to you fifteen years ago. Not now. What good is it now!' he exclaimed.

'Okay James, just take your time and tell me what happened,' Irene replied, calmly. 'I'm listening now, and I promise it'll help, and I'll do anything I can for you. You were getting bullied, yes? Is that what was happening?'

'Yes,' James replied, nodding his head and letting it drop forward. Irene could see tears starting to roll down his cheeks.

'And that was why you had to leave the school, yes? It got too much for you?' Irene asked quietly.

'Yes,' James repeated, still nodding his head, looking down at the floor, his hands clasped in front of him, prayer-like.

James began to tell Miss Hardy about his two years at Danesborough High School. How he had been bullied relentlessly, both physically and mentally, day after day. And how no-one seemed to be able to stop it. Once he'd started talking, he couldn't stop, and everything just came tumbling out, along with the tears flowing down his cheeks. Miss Hardy sat and listened, not interrupting once, sensing that she had to let him tell her the full story. He needed to get it all out, even if it was fifteen years later. It was a terrible story, and Miss Hardy felt desperately sad for him. Sad for what he'd had to go through, and sad that she hadn't seen it, and been able to do something about it at the time. If only she could have put a stop to the bullying. If only she had listened to him then, like she was listening to him now. Maybe things would have turned out differently.

James had come to the end of his story, and he paused to take a deep breath, wiping his cheeks with the back of his hand.

'I'm so sorry James,' Miss Hardy said sympathetically. 'You shouldn't have had to go through that. It's not right. And has something happened now, lately, to bring it all back to you?' she asked him softly.

'Yes,' he nodded again and then raised his head slightly to look at Miss Hardy. He felt calmer now he'd spoken to her.

'There was a school reunion a while back. I'd decided to go. I thought it might help me move on, you know? But they were there, in the pub, still joking about me, still laughing. About what they had done to me. They thought it was funny. Just a laugh. Even after all these years.'

'I see,' Irene replied. 'I can see why that would have been hard for you, after all this time, bringing back these horrible memories. Did you say anything to any of them?'

'No, I emm…I couldn't go…I just left and…emm…I went home,' James replied. 'I don't think anyone saw me.'

'Okay, that was probably a sensible thing to do, going home, I mean. But I can see that you're still very upset about it all,' Irene replied.

'Yes…that night, it was then I decided I needed to do something about it,' James said. 'You know, after all these years and seeing them again. Nothing had changed. I just needed to get back at them somehow. So, I emm…made a plan.'

'What sort of plan?' Irene asked him with a quizzical look on her face.

'Well, just how I could make them pay for what they'd done, get my own back somehow, you know,' James replied. 'That sort of thing.'

Something was stirring in Irene's head, but she couldn't pin down what it was. It was connected somehow to what James was saying, but she didn't know how.

'So…what…this plan…what have you done? Have you done something? Is that why you're here?' Irene asked him.

James let out a big sigh and sat back in his chair, looking upwards towards the conservatory ceiling.

'I came here to see you Miss Hardy because I needed to talk to someone, just like I did when I was at school, and I thought you might be the only one who would understand,' James said. 'When I saw them still laughing at me that night, I knew I needed to do something, otherwise it was going to be the same all my life. It would never change. They would always be laughing at me. So, I found out where they lived, and I've started paying them visits to remind them what they did to me, and how it affected me.'

'Wait…wait,' Irene interrupted him. It was all coming back to her now. The connection between what he was saying and what was in her mind. 'Did you go and see one of the boys…Stephen… Stephen Jones?' she asked, fearing she already knew the answer.

'Yes, he was the worst, so I chose him first,' James replied, still lying back and not noticing that Mrs Hardy's face had turned white, and her mouth was hanging open.

'When we were at school, he flushed my head down the toilet and so I went round to his place and did the same to him,' James said. 'It was so cathartic,' he added, breaking into a big smile as he sat up again, but then stopping as he noticed the look on Miss Hardy's face.

'Are you okay?' he asked. 'You look a bit…pale.'

'You…killed…him,' Irene replied slowly.

'What? What are you talking about?' James replied. 'I told you, I put his head down the toilet, just like he did to me. That was all'

Irene rose from her chair and walked across to a table in the corner of the room. She looked through a pile of documents on the table-top before she found what she was looking for. She picked up a newspaper and walked back across the room to where James was sitting.

'Well, what's this then?' she said as she thrust the local newspaper into his lap.

James looked at the paper. Miss Hardy had opened it and folded it back to show the top half of page seven. James picked it up and held it in front of him. There was a picture of a man who he recognised as being Stephen Jones and beside it the headline read,

"Local Man found Dead. Police Appeal for Witnesses."

James sat staring at the paper, not being able to comprehend what was there in front of him. It wasn't right. Stephen wasn't dead, James had only seen him a few days before. The day he'd flushed his head down the toilet. He wasn't dead then, just a bit wet and sad and angry and humiliated. All the things that James had felt fifteen years before.

'I…I…don't understand,' James said, finally finding his voice and looking at Miss Hardy, shaking his head. 'Stephen's not dead. He's not dead. There must be some sort of mistake.'

'There's no mistake. Read what it says,' Irene replied. 'He was found dead on the bathroom floor in his flat.'

'But he can't be. I didn't kill him. I told you what happened. I did to him what he did to me. Nothing else. I told you everything,' James pleaded. 'That was all I needed. After that I just left him. It was justice. Revenge. Call it what you want. I didn't kill him. Of course I didn't. It's just not….'

Irene Hardy had spent a lifetime listening to kids stories and she was very confident that she could tell when someone was telling the truth and when they were telling a lie. She could see that James Gray was telling the truth. His reaction to the newspaper report on Stephen Jones's death had been one of genuine disbelief and shock. He couldn't fake that, and she knew immediately that James had not killed Stephen Jones.

'Oh shit, what am I going to do?' James said out loud, his head in hands. 'They'll think I killed him.'

'Okay, don't panic, let's sit down with a cup of tea and have a think about what we're going to do,' Irene replied. 'I may have let you down fifteen years ago, but I'm not about to do the same again now.'

Chapter 14

Just as Miss Hardy handed James a freshly made cup of tea, the doorbell rang. James looked up at Miss Hardy and raised his eyebrows.

'Are you expecting anyone?' he asked her.

'No, but it's probably one of my neighbours, Joan Branson. She often calls around for a cup of tea and a chat in the afternoon. A bit of a gossip. If we just ignore it, she'll guess I've gone out and just go back home,' Miss Hardy replied.

The doorbell rang again and then it was followed by a loud knock on the door.

'She sounds a bit persistent,' James said. 'It doesn't look like she's going to give up.'

'No, I don't think it's Joan then,' Miss Hardy replied. 'She wouldn't normally knock as loud as that.'

They then heard the sound of the letterbox being opened and a man's voice called out,

'Hello. Is there anyone in?' There was a slight pause and then the man's voice continued.

'Miss Hardy, are you there? Can you come to the door please. It's the police, I just want to ask you a few questions.'

The letterbox banged shut again and James and Miss Hardy looked at each other.

'Why would the police come here?' he whispered to her.

'I don't know,' Miss Hardy replied quietly. 'Maybe I'd better answer it. They'll only come back if we don't.'

'Okay, I'm just thinking…it might be something to do with the school photo, I guess,' James replied. 'You were on it too.'

'School photo?' Miss Hardy replied, confused, but James wasn't listening.

'I've got an idea, let me deal with them and see what they want,' and he marched out of the room before Miss Hardy could ask him anything else.

Standing at the door, Detective Constable Harris was just about to put a cross against the sheet of paper with Irene Hardy's name on it, when he heard someone approaching from inside the house. He stepped back on to the pathway to allow some space. The door opened slightly, and a man's head poked around the gap. He was a young man, with a slightly odd looking face.

'Hello,' he said. 'Sorry I was on the phone.'

'Ah, yes, right,' DC Harris said. 'I'm Detective Constable Harris,' and he held out his warrant card so the man, half-hidden in the doorway, could see it. 'Does a Miss Irene Hardy live here?' he asked, looking down at a document he was holding in his other hand.

'Yes, yes she does,' James replied. 'But I'm afraid she's not too well at the moment and she's just having a nap. Just a little rest, you know.'

'Ah okay…emm…I wonder, would you be able to maybe wake her up? I just have a couple of questions for her. It shouldn't take too long,' DC Harris replied. Harris was keen to get his job done and get back to the station.

'Emm…not really,' James replied to the policeman. 'She's not very well and really needs her rest. What's it about? Is there anything I could help you with?'

'No, I don't think so. It's just something we want to ask her about when she was a schoolteacher,' the detective replied. 'One of her old pupils has been involved in an emm… an incident, and we're just talking to people that knew him in the past. Just to build up a picture.'

'Oh, I see,' James replied, still holding the door only slightly open, so that his head and one hand were his only visible parts. 'I think we saw something about that in the paper. Was he called Stephen Jones or something?'

'Yes, that's right. Did you know him at all?' DC Harris enquired.

'No, I'm afraid not, I'm not from around here,' James replied. 'But Miss Hardy did tell me that she had seen the newspaper report.'

'Oh right, did she say anything about it?' DC Harris asked, getting slightly irritated that the man hadn't made any move to open the door properly.

'Yes, she just said she didn't remember him at all,' James replied. 'I'm afraid her memory isn't as good as it used to be, you know?' he said with a rueful smile.

'Oh, okay, I see.' Harris replied. 'Well perhaps you can get her to give us a call sometime? When she's feeling a bit stronger. It should only take a few minutes.'

The policeman fished around in his jacket pocket before producing a card and handing it over to the man at the door. 'Just ask her to give us a call on that number there and ask for the Serious Crime team. Any of us there can take her call, they'll know what it's about.'

'Okay, I will do, thank you,' said James. 'How is the investigation going by the way? Do you know what happened yet, the newspaper report was a bit vague. I think they called it an unexplained death.'

'Yes, well it's still early days yet, but we are pursuing several lines of enquiry,' the policeman replied with the standard answer.

'Do you think he was killed then?' James asked him.

'I'm afraid I can't discuss that with you sir,' DC Harris replied.

'Oh, okay,' James said glancing at the card and starting to close the door.

'Oh, just one last thing,' DC Harris said. 'I…emm…I didn't get your name sir, are you a relative of Miss Hardy?'

'Yes, that's right. I'm…emm…James Hardy, her nephew,' James replied through the now even smaller gap in the doorway. 'I'm just staying with her for a few days. She hasn't been very well lately, so I'm just helping her out. Hopefully she's on the mend now,' he said smiling as he finally closed the door.

'James Hardy,' DC Harris repeated the name as he wrote it down in his notebook.

Back in the house James had re-joined Miss Hardy in the conservatory.

'You made me out to sound like an old lady at death's door,' Miss Hardy said, with a mock look of indignation on her face. 'I'm not there yet. There's still some life in this old dog,' she added, smiling.

'Did you hear everything then?' James replied, smiling back at his old teacher.

'Yes, most of it,' Miss Hardy replied. 'But remember I am old, and my hearing is not so good…' she laughed.

'No,' James smiled. 'But it sounds like they've made the connection between what happened with Stephen Jones and it being something to do with his schooldays. No doubt because of the school photo I left in his flat. They're probably working their way around everyone in that photo to see if they can find anything out.'

'Ah, so that's the school photo connection. I guess they'll be calling on you too then, if they haven't done already,' Miss Hardy said.

'Well maybe, the thing is though, I wasn't in that photo. I wasn't at school the day it was taken and so I missed it. Maybe that means I won't be on their list of people to visit,' James replied, thinking about what that might mean for him.

'Well at least that might buy us some time,' Miss Hardy replied. 'Now let's have that cup of tea and discuss what we're going to do next.'

Chapter 15

'Actually, there's something else I ought to tell you,' James Gray said to Miss Hardy as they both sat in the conservatory, each with a cup of tea and a chocolate éclair on a side plate.

'Oh yes, what's that then?' Miss Hardy replied, pausing mid-bite of her pastry, sensing that it was going to be something interesting, but perhaps not necessarily something good.

'It's Nigel Harrison,' James replied, before taking a mouthful of his own éclair.

'Nigel Harrison…oh yes, I remember him,' Miss Hardy replied. 'He was good friends with Stephen Jones, wasn't he?'

'Yes, that's right,' James replied, looking at what was left of his cake. Not much. It had looked bigger when Miss Hardy had brought it in a few minutes earlier, on the white side-plate. But two, or was it three, bites later and now it was almost gone. It had just seemed to melt away while they were sitting there.

'What about him?' Miss Hardy asked. James noticed she still had half of her pastry left. She'd been taking smaller nibbles, making it last, savouring it.

'Well, he was…he was another of those that, you know…'

'Another of the bullies?' Miss Hardy asked and James nodded his head, then looked down at the floor, feeling his eyes getting moist. He felt embarrassed and ashamed. It was still difficult to talk about, even to Miss Hardy.

'What did you do? Another flushing?' Miss Hardy replied, seeing that James was feeling uncomfortable and trying to lighten the mood.

'No, it wasn't that,' James replied. 'He…he once stubbed a cigarette out on my arm and so that's what I decided to do back to him.'

'Ooh, that's nasty…and how did that go?' Miss Hardy replied sensing it hadn't been totally straightforward.

'Well, I went to his house, and it was all going well, well you know what I mean,' James replied. 'I had him set, his sleeve rolled up, all ready to do it, when another man suddenly walked into the room. I thought Nigel was on his own, I was sure he was, but it turns out he wasn't. I managed to get out and back to my car and I sat there for a bit, just thinking.'

'Okay, what did you do then?' Miss Hardy asked, intrigued to find out what happened next.

'Well, as I was sitting there, the other man walked past,' James continued. 'He looked like he was on his way to work. So, I thought, that means Nigel is on his own again and I'd come all this way, I mean in my mind and…well… I went back in.'

'Oh my. What happened?' Miss Hardy asked, her éclair frozen mid-way between the plate and her mouth.

'Well, I forced my way in and grabbed him and I pushed him back into the living room, but before I could get him onto the sofa, he managed to slip out of my grasp, and he made a bolt for the door. I ran after him and managed to grab his arm just by the doorway. He spun around and then, I think, somehow, he caught his foot against the doorframe. The next thing I know, I'd let go and he's on the floor, screaming in pain. I looked down at him and his foot was turned at an odd angle. It looked nasty. I thought he might have broken his ankle. I sat him up against the edge of the stairs and his ankle didn't look good. He was screaming at me and screaming in pain. I thought he was probably suffering enough so I called an ambulance and went back to my car, leaving his front door slightly open. About ten minutes later the ambulance turned up and I watched the paramedics go into his house before I left and drove home.'

'Wow, that's a story,' Miss Hardy replied, before finally taking another bite of her éclair just as the cream was about to drop out of the end.

James briefly wondered if she had taken the bigger pastry for herself. It seemed to be lasting much longer than his.

'So, you didn't actually manage to burn him then, like he did to you?' Miss Hardy asked.

'No, I didn't. It didn't seem right to do it when he was lying there already screaming in pain,'

James replied. 'That was probably just as good. Enough, I thought.'

'Yes, well he deserved it, after what he'd put you through,' Miss Hardy replied. 'But I guess that means the police will now be looking for you. He'll have told them.'

'Yes, well, I guess so,' James replied, with a frown on his face. 'Although that policeman at the door didn't say anything, but I guess maybe they wouldn't. You'd have thought he would have mentioned my name or something though.'

James stopped to have another bite of his éclair. There wasn't much left, so he just popped the whole lot in, savouring the rich taste before it quickly melted away in his mouth. He looked across enviously at Miss Hardy's plate. She seemed to have at least half of her cake still uneaten. How could that be? James swallowed the last of his pastry and carried on talking.

'The thing is, I always assumed the police were going to be looking for me as soon as I started this. You know, right from Stephen Jones. I didn't try to disguise myself. I wanted them to know it was me, and why I was doing it. I wanted them to know what they'd done to me, how it had affected me, you know? I figured I just needed a couple of weeks to get it all done, before they caught me, and then… whatever happened after that…well,' James shrugged his shoulders.

'So that's two done, but apparently you caused two accidents!' Miss Hardy said laughing. 'You're not very good at this are you?' she said, laughing even more, and James, seeing the funny side of it, also joined in until the both of them were crying with laughter.

The truth was Irene Hardy was really enjoying this sudden input of excitement into her life. Things had all become a bit boring lately. She'd somehow sunk into a weekly routine of repetition. Shopping, gardening, housework, washing, tea with Joan…it had all become the same, week after week. Month after month. For the first time since she retired, she'd begun to miss the excitement, the uncertainty of being a school teacher, where every day threw up something different, a new challenge. She didn't want to go back to being a school teacher again but she knew she needed something new to focus on. James turning up on her doorstep could just be what she needed. It was like the switch marked "excitement" had been turned on again. For the first time in many years. Miss Hardy's head was full of ideas. Ideas of how she could help James fulfil his mission and get his deserved revenge on his erstwhile bullies. She'd let James Gray down once before, but she wasn't going to do it again. Besides, apart from helping James, she was having a lot of fun!

'So, what's next?' she said, looking at James Gray, rubbing her hands together, with a big smile on her face.

Chapter 16

DI Strong and DS Knight were sitting in Strong's office, having another discussion on the Stephen Jones case. Strong had given Knight a summary of his visit to Bradley Smith. He told her of his suspicions about him.

'He came across as being really nervous. And he asked me lots of questions about the case, like he was trying to find out what I knew, what we had so far, that sort of thing,' Strong recounted. 'In my book, that's always a sign of something not quite right. Then when I asked him where he was on the night of Jones's death, he claimed that he hadn't been out, but I could see that he was lying. He was hiding something, that was obvious. I think he's definitely someone we need to investigate further,' Strong concluded.

DS Knight had listened closely to her boss, as she always did, nodding in the appropriate places. If DI Strong believed Bradley Smith was hiding something, then she had little doubt that he was correct. In her experience, DI Strong was right more often than not. But she was finding it difficult to picture Bradley Smith as a killer, or even someone who would hurt another person in any way. She knew him from school, and although he had always been slightly odd, a bit different, she just couldn't imagine him going to the extreme of attacking someone. But she knew she had to be careful in what she said, she didn't want to be seen as disagreeing with her boss. She knew she owed DI Strong a lot, and if he said there was something suspicious about Bradley Smith, then there probably was. But was he really a killer?

'I get what you're saying Guv,' she said to her boss. 'I just don't know, he just…I guess he just didn't seem that sort at school. Not someone who would go that far. I might be wrong, but he was just one of those boys who you never really noticed,' DS Knight said, struggling to find the right words.

'Well, they're often the ones that turn out that way,' Strong replied. 'I think we should give Dr Collins a call and see what she makes of him. Let's see if she thinks he fits the profile.'

'Okay, I guess that might help us, but from what I remember of him, he was just one of those…I don't know. He wasn't anything really. I can't think of anything that he did or said, or any story about him while we were at school. He was just a quiet boy that never stood out for any reason. The only thing I do remember about him was that he went out with one of the other girls, Alison Kirkbride. She was pretty quiet, and timid as well. They were a strange pairing. I would never have him down as someone who would…..' DS Knight stopped talking as her thoughts took over.

She remembered meeting Bradley Smith at the Danesborough High School reunion. It was the first time she'd seen him since they'd both been at school. It had been a strange meeting. Bradley had tried chatting her up at the bar, telling her he'd fancied her at school, conveniently forgetting all about Alison Kirkbride, who wasn't at the reunion. Then, later that night, DS Knight found out that he'd tried the same chat up line with a few of the other girls there, including Knight's best friend Alice. At least he'd given them a good laugh. But overall, he'd always seemed pretty harmless.

'It's often the quiet ones. They're usually hiding something,' Strong said, interrupting her thoughts, and aware that he was making a sweeping generalisation, but confident it was something he could safely say between himself and DS Knight.

Strong had worked closely with DS Knight on a number of major cases over the last few years and had watched her develop into a very good detective. He was pleased that she was progressing well, as he had spotted her early on. It was soon after she had joined the Serious Crime team that he had concluded she had the potential to progress in his team. She worked hard and had a pragmatic outlook, similar to DI Strong. She liked to get things done. Complete. Strong felt he could trust her, and on the odd occasion where he had needed to manipulate things to help deliver justice, she had always supported him.

'Okay Guv, I'll set up a meet with Dr Collins and see what she thinks,' DS Knight said as she rose from her seat.

DI Strong stood up and walked with her to his office door.

'Let me know about Dr Collins,' he said. 'Keep up the good work,' he added, smiling, and he gave Knight's arm a slight squeeze as she left the room.

DS Knight walked back to her desk thinking that she knew her boss well enough to know that he wasn't going to be easily swayed from his current line of suspicion with regard to Bradley Smith.

Chapter 17

DI Strong took the small mobile phone from his briefcase. It was the one he only used for specific purposes, and he'd had it for many years. It was so old that all it did were calls and texts. Only a few, select people knew the number and it would only ever be used to communicate with them. He switched it on and waited. A minute later, it buzzed, indicating that he had a voicemail message. He pressed a few buttons and listened, surprised to hear a voice from the past. It was from someone who used to provide him with information when he had been a young detective, but he hadn't heard from her for many years. Strong had never met this person, and didn't know who she was, but the information she had provided at the time had been very useful to him, and had certainly helped him advance up the ranks in his career as a police officer.

The woman had only ever been known to him by the name "The Social Worker" and she had insisted it had to stay that way. She had threatened Strong that if he tried to find out who she was, then the information would immediately stop. Strong had been desperate to find out her identity, largely because he always wanted to be in control, but the information she was feeding him on local criminals was too valuable to risk losing, and so after a while he just grew to accept that was how it was going to be. Besides, none of his other contacts seemed to know who she was.

Not having heard from her for a long time, Strong couldn't help wondering why she was calling him now. The message she'd left hadn't helped much, she'd simply said who it was, and given him a number to call her back on. No doubt a burner phone, and so Strong knew there was no point in trying to trace it.

The detective sat still for a few minutes just trying to make some sense of it. Why was she calling him now? Did she have some new information? But she hadn't called for at least ten years, Strong thought. She'd been really useful in his early days as a detective, but as he'd moved into more serious crime, her input became less relevant to the cases he was working on. He couldn't think what she wanted now, but he was intrigued to find out, and so he dialled the number she'd given him.

After a few rings the phone was answered and Strong immediately recognised her voice, a voice from many years ago, and he smiled, while, at the same time, a shiver ran down his spine.

'Hello, this is a surprise,' Strong said.

'Yes, I guess so,' the woman replied.

'Are you still doing your social work then?' Strong enquired.

'No, not so much,' the woman replied.

'Okay, but I'm guessing you've got something for me. I mean, it must be a big one after all these years,' Strong said, laughing.

'Well, no…actually, I was hoping to get something from you this time. Maybe something in return for all the help I gave you?' she replied.

'Oh yes, what's that then?' Strong asked, intrigued by her request, but feeling wary at the same time.

'I just want to know what you can tell me about Stephen Jones and Nigel Harrison,' the woman replied. There was a short silence before Strong replied. Stephen Jones, he knew about, but not Nigel Harrison. Had something happened to him too? He quickly did a search on the case database on his computer and speed read through the document that came up on his screen.

'Why are you asking about them?' he asked as he finished reading.

'Just out of interest. They're two boys I used to know, from my area, and I'd heard some stuff about them lately. I know you can't tell me the details, but maybe you can give me the headlines?' the woman asked.

Once again there was a pause as Strong glanced at his screen before answering.

'Okay, I guess I owe you something for all the help you gave me,' Strong replied. 'The overall headline is murder and accident,' Strong replied.

'Murder? Are you sure?' the woman asked.

'We believe so. It's not straightforward. I can't say any more at this point. It's an ongoing case,' Strong replied.

'And do you know who did it yet? This alleged murder,' the woman asked.

'I can't tell you that,' Strong replied.

'Okay, thank you,' the woman said, and she ended the call.

Strong looked at his phone in surprise.

'Well, nice to talk to you too after all this time,' he said out aloud, smiling, as he shut the phone down and put it back into his briefcase. He hadn't been able to control The Social Worker in the past and it appeared that was still going to remain the case.

Irene Hardy was smiling too. It had been fun to talk to Mo Strong, a Detective Inspector now no less, after all these years. She couldn't deny she had got a thrill from it. However, that aside, the main thing was that she'd found out what the police were thinking, how they were treating this whole thing that James had started. A murder and an accident.

Firstly, an accident. That was a good thing. It suggested that Nigel Harrison hadn't said too much, if anything at all. He might not even have mentioned James Gray. Maybe he didn't want to drag up the past again and admit to what he'd done to James Gray when they were at school. That was certainly a possibility.

The murder wasn't so good though, but Irene believed that when the facts all came out, they'd see it wasn't a murder at all. Not if it had all happened the way James had told her. And she believed he was telling the truth.

Also, Irene felt that if Strong knew who was responsible for this, then he would have said so, without necessarily naming the person. DI Strong would have wanted to show her that they were on top of it. That he was in control. But he didn't, and so Irene surmised that they didn't know about James Gray yet. That was a positive. At least it bought them some more time.

Chapter 18

There was a soft tap on DI Strong's office door, and it opened slightly, with Marsha Hughes tentatively poking her head into the gap.

'Sorry Guv, have you got a minute?' she asked her boss.

'Sure, come in Marsha,' DI Strong beckoned her forward into the room, from behind his desk.

Marsha Hughes was one of the police support and administration team and DI Strong had got to know, and trust, her over the years, so much so that he often asked her to carry out jobs he wanted to keep private, without letting any of the rest of the Serious Crime team know what they were doing. Well, what he was doing really. Marsha had proved herself to be very efficient at carrying out these activities, without anyone else knowing. On top of that Marsha really enjoyed doing them, it made her feel a bit like a real detective and she'd always liked working for DI Strong. He'd been very good to her over the years, especially so when her son had died. He'd helped her get through what had been a very difficult time.

'I've been looking into that man you asked me to, Keegan Summers,' Marsha said as she took a seat in front of Strong's desk. 'Well, he's never been charged with anything, but his name has popped up a couple of times as being on the fringes of some minor crimes. A disturbance of the peace and a drug bust. But as I say, it looks like he just happened to be in the area in both cases, without him having actually been involved.'

'Mmm...nothing else? No family issues, any relatives involved in anything criminal? Nothing like that?' Strong asked.

'No, I haven't been able to find anything like that,' Marsha replied. 'I did a search on all his immediate family, but nothing came up. Looks like they're all clean. Do you want me to do any more searching Guv?' Marsha asked. She was disappointed that she hadn't found out anything for DI Strong this time, and keen to see if she could do any more.

'No, thanks Marsha,' Strong replied. 'I think you're good for now. I'll let you know.'

Marsha got up from her seat, turned and left DI Strong's office, closing the door quietly behind her. Strong stayed behind his desk, just sitting there and thinking. So, they had nothing on Keegan Summers yet, but he was on the edge. Strong had seen that happen many times before, over the years he had been in the police force. It was like a structured career path for criminals. Firstly, you'd start off by just being associated with other criminals. You'd get picked up by the police a couple of times, but nothing would happen. You hadn't been directly involved. You didn't actually do anything. But you were there and so your name was now on the PNC system. You were on the first rung of the ladder. Soon, maybe a few months, or even a year later, you'd get arrested. This time you'd been more involved, not on the outside any more, but part of it. A fight, or you'd handled some stolen goods. That time you'd probably just get a warning, if you were lucky, but you were now on the second rung. It was getting harder to turn back. After that, the time periods between misdemeanours became shorter, and you became more deeply involved, graduating into some more serious criminal activities. You were now a few more rungs up the ladder, and it was now almost impossible to turn back. The drop was too far. It wouldn't be long before you were in prison and the likelihood then was that became a regular thing.

The other key thing, Strong knew, was that going up this ladder didn't just affect that one person, the person climbing, it also had a hugely negative impact on their family and friends. It dragged them into situations they never wanted to be in, causing them pain and heartbreak.

Keegan Summers was on that ladder, sure he was still only on the first rung, and some people did manage to step off at that stage, but DI Strong had a feeling about Summers, a gut instinct that told him he would carry on climbing the ladder, and that simple fact meant he would only bring hurt and pain to everyone close to him, including Strong's daughter Sophie.

DI Strong decided he wasn't going to let that happen. Not to his daughter. He picked up his briefcase, took out his little mobile phone and made a call.

Chapter 19

There was a knock on DI Strong's office door, and it opened to reveal the ginger haired head that belonged to Detective Constable Morgan.

'Guv, have you got a minute?' he said as he stepped forward towards DI Strong's desk with a serious look on his face, and a piece of paper in his hand. 'DS Knight isn't around anywhere, and she's not answering her phone, so I thought I should bring this to you.'

'Yes, what is it?' Strong asked him from the other side of his desk. 'DS Knight is tied up in court all day today.'

'Well, you know you asked me to have a look at Bradley Smith's movements on the Tuesday evening of Stephen Jones's death. There was nothing on CCTV, nothing we could find nearby, but when we did an ANPR check on his car, Smith's car, we picked it up on the Newham Road at seven fourteen pm,' DC Morgan said, standing in front of Strong's desk.

'Okay, that's interesting,' Strong replied. 'So Smith did lie to us then. He said he hadn't gone out. Anything else? Any idea where he was going?'

'No Sir, nothing definite,' Morgan replied. 'But of course, if you carry on down that road a mile or so further then you hit the Red-Light district.'

'Mmm…I see,' Strong replied and he brought up a map on his computer screen. 'That's not in the same direction as Stephen Jones's house, but not a million miles away, assuming of course that it is Bradley Smith driving the car,' Strong said, frowning as he looked at his screen. 'He would still have had time to go to Jones's house, kill him and then be picked up on the ANPR later, or even before I guess.' He turned his head back towards DC Morgan.

'Did we get any photos of the car driver from the ANPR?' Strong asked.

'I'm afraid not sir, it was only captured from behind, so we really only caught the plate' DC Morgan replied.

'Okay, I'll talk to DS Knight when she's back in later. The fact is he lied to us about his movements on Tuesday night, so we need to find out why, and what he was actually doing, where he was going. We need to get him in here and see what he's like when we put him under a bit of pressure,' Strong said, voicing his thoughts out loud.

'Can you recheck the area around Stephen Jones's house, all the CCTV you can find, go over it again and see if there is any sign of Smith's car,' Strong said. 'If we can pick it up anywhere in the vicinity of Jones's place then we'd have a much stronger case.'

'Yes Guv,' DC Morgan replied, and he left the room, not looking forward to having to spend the next few hours reviewing CCTV footage that he'd already been through earlier that day, but that was part of the job of being in the police. It wasn't all exciting and glamorous. In fact, very little of it was like that. Most of it was routine, just sitting at a desk, looking at a screen, or filling in forms.

Bradley Smith was excited to get a call from Detective Inspector Strong asking if he could come into the police station and meet with him again. This was like his best dream coming true, him helping solve a major crime. He hadn't thought to ask why DI Strong wanted to see him again, he hadn't been able to help him much the last time. Bradley could only assume Strong had seen that his interest in these types of crime meant that he could be a useful help in the investigation. He agreed to go in that afternoon and when the call ended, he'd immediately retrieved his scrapbook of the case and started to read through it again. Although, in reality, he practically knew everything in it by heart.

Bradley turned up ten minutes early at the police station reception. He wasn't sure if that was the correct etiquette, but he'd hung around outside for the previous five minutes and he was beginning to feel the cold. It was a grey, overcast day with the sun struggling to break through the thick clouds. Aside from that, Bradley didn't like some of the suspicious looks he'd been getting from the police officers as they left the building and walked past him towards the car park. He was acutely aware that he was the only person standing outside the police station, and no doubt they were wondering what he was doing there. He was slightly surprised none of them had spoken to him. If he had been a policeman, he felt he would have checked the person out. You never know what someone might be hiding.

It was warm in the police station reception and Bradley unbuttoned his overcoat, revealing a dark blue jumper, as he approached the reception desk. The police officer behind the desk looked up as Bradley stepped forward to the counter. They were separated by a plastic screen, with a small gap at the bottom.

'Good afternoon sir, how can I help you?' the policeman asked in a neutral voice.

'Good afternoon,' Bradley replied, bending his head down towards the gap. 'I'm here to see Detective Inspector Strong. My name is Bradley Smith.'

'And is he expecting you sir?' the police officer asked.

'Yes, yes he is,' Bradley nodded, smiling, remembering that he was here to help solve a major crime. Maybe they'd give him some sort of reward if it all went well?

The police officer asked Bradley to wait, while he dialled a number into his desk phone. He picked up the receiver and Bradley could see the police officer's mouth moving through the plastic screen, but he couldn't hear what was being said. After he'd finished his call, he wrote something down on a pad and then told Bradley to take a seat in the waiting area.

A few minutes later the door to the right of the reception desk opened and a man stepped into the room, holding the door open with his foot. He was a big man, probably around forty years old, with short brown hair, wearing a dark brown suit and a white shirt, without a tie. The man looked around the waiting area and his eyes stopped on Bradley Smith. He called out Bradley's name, and Bradley nodded and stood up. He walked across the room to where the man was standing and followed him through the door and along a dark corridor. The man didn't speak, and the only sound was that of their footsteps, echoing on the grey tiled floor. Halfway down the corridor, the man stopped at a door on his left and opened it, indicating that Bradley should enter the room with the man following closely behind him.

The room looked like the typical police interview room Bradley had seen on many of the crime dramas he'd watched on television. Although it was basic, the familiarity of the room made Bradley feel more comfortable. It was what he'd expected. A table with four plastic chairs and some shiny looking recording equipment. Nothing else. The man indicated to Bradley that he should sit on one side of the table before taking a seat himself, diagonally opposite.

'My name is Detective Constable Morgan,' the man said, and Bradley immediately detected a Welsh lilt in his voice. 'Thank you for coming in today. Detective Inspector Strong will be joining us shortly, would you like a drink? Tea, coffee or a water?'

'No, I'm okay thanks,' Bradley replied, pleased that the detective inspector would be joining them. Bradley was sure that indicated how important this meeting was.

'It's good to meet you Detective Constable Morgan,' Bradley said. 'I've seen your name before and it's nice to put a face to it.'

'Where have you seen my name before?' DC Morgan asked, with a quizzical look on his face.

'Oh, just in various crime reports, that sort of thing,' Bradley replied. 'Crime's my thing…I don't mean I'm a criminal,' he laughed. 'I mean I find the whole criminal and police thing really interesting. I watch a lot of stuff on TV, you know, Real Life Crimes, that sort of stuff. I love trying to solve the cases. I should have been a detective really,' Bradley laughed again.

DC Morgan was watching Bradley Smith closely, trying to read him. He seemed excited, a bit hyper, maybe it was just nerves, he thought. He did seem a bit strange though.

Meantime, Bradley was thinking about who else had been in this room. How many criminal masterminds had sat in the same seat he was now sitting in? Maybe Tony Fleming, the gangland boss or even Andy Austin, the Anniversary Killer. Wow, just to think he was now sitting in the same seat as them. He began to wonder about what they had been thinking when they were sitting here, facing the detectives across the table? Bradley imagined they had been super cool, taking it all in their stride. "No Comment" or some smart answer. Of course, they would have had a clever lawyer sitting beside them, advising them on what to say and, equally importantly, what not to say. That was often the key thing. Bradley noticed a chip in the corner of the table, and he wondered how that might have happened. Maybe a fight? An upset suspect suddenly standing up and turning the table over, crashing it into the floor. He guessed if that happened, all sorts of alarms would go off and the room would be flooded with police officers.

As Bradley's mind wandered, the door opened again, and DI Strong walked into the room, interrupting his thoughts.

'Ah, Mr Smith, good to see you again. Thank you for coming in so quickly,' DI Strong said, shaking Bradley's hand before sitting down, directly across the table from him.

'Oh, that's no problem, please call me Bradley by the way. Mr Smith seems so formal. Some of the younger ones at work call me that and it makes me feel so old,' Bradley replied. 'But anyway, I'm glad to come in. I'd be pleased to do anything I can do to help with the investigation. I've been keeping up with it as much as I can, mainly through social media and the like.'

'Okay, that's interesting,' Strong replied. 'And what's being said on social media about the case?'

'Well, a few things,' Bradley said, sitting forward in his chair, encouraged that they seemed to be getting straight into the detail. 'Some of it is a bit rubbish of course, but sifting that stuff out, Stephen Jones was found dead by his partner. It looks like he was assaulted, but they say he had heart problems and may have just died of a heart attack. Is that right?' Bradley looked across the table at DI Strong, waiting for his response.

'Keep going,' Strong said. 'What else have you found out?'

'Oh, well. It seems the police think there's a link to his schooldays and they're interviewing all of the people that went to school with him. There are also a few references to the recent school reunion that Jenny Broughton had organised, but that's about it,' Bradley replied.

'Mmm…interesting,' Strong replied. 'Anything on why we are talking with his school-friends? Are there any comments on anything that might have happened involving Stephen Jones when he was at school?'

'No, nothing on that really…well…' Bradley hesitated.

'What is it?' Strong enquired.

'Well, nothing really. There was just a couple of comments on there from people saying that he deserved it. That he had been a bully. What goes around comes around, that sort of thing. Trolls, you know? Happens all the time on social media. But they got deleted quite quickly,' Bradley replied.

'Do you know who they were from?' Strong asked.

'No,' Bradley replied shaking his head. 'People don't usually use their real names, just made-up names.'

'Okay, I see,' Strong replied. 'What name do you use?'

'Oh, emm…, my on-line name is emm…Poirot90. It's just a name I came up with. I like watching Poirot on the TV you see, he's one of my favourite detectives and ninety was when I was born, nineteen ninety,' Bradley explained, feeling himself beginning to blush.

'Right,' Strong replied. 'And these trolls, did they say anything at all about what Stephen Jones might have done? The bullying. Why they thought he might have deserved his downfall?'

'No, nothing,' Bradley shook his head again. 'The thing is though they might not even have known him. Some people just seem to get a kick out of posting stuff like that about anyone. It's terrible. I remember when you guys were looking for the Anniversary Killer, there was all sorts of stuff posted on-line. People claiming to be him, that sort of thing. And it was the same when you came across those two bodies in that deserted farm. Tony Fleming and Dylan Hughes. People were posting comments suggesting that had been set up and they hadn't really shot each other.'

'You seem to know a lot about the cases we've been working on over the last few years,' Strong commented.

'Ah, yes, sorry,' Bradley laughed. 'I get a bit carried away sometimes. I just love the real life crime mysteries and so I read everything I can about them. Especially when they're local ones. Obviously, you and your team have been involved in those ones. I know a lot of the on-line stuff is rubbish though. There are some weird people out there.'

DI Strong nodded his head slowly. He'd met many strange people in his line of work, and he knew it was easy to waste a lot of time trying to understand them or trying to rationalise why they had done whatever they were being questioned about. Early on in his police career, Strong had come to understand that not everyone's brain was wired in the same way, and something that seemed wrong to one person could be seen as being perfectly normal to somebody else. Strong quickly began to work on the basis that the key wasn't to try and get to some logical explanation for every crime, it was simply to deliver justice. And that was what he believed he was good at doing.

Strong decided it was time to move the conversation with Bradley Smith onto a different track. He picked up a piece of paper from the table and began to study it carefully.

'So, Bradley, when we met before, you told me that you hadn't left the house on the Tuesday night, the evening when Stephen Jones died,' Strong said, putting the paper back down and looking directly at Bradley. 'Is that true?'

Bradley was taken aback by this change in the conversation. He'd been enjoying the discussion up to this point. It had been like he was working with DI Strong, maybe as some sort of special crime consultant they'd brought in to help them crack the case. Special Agent Bradley Smith. No, Special Agent Brad Smith. It sounded good. But now the atmosphere in the room had changed. It was as if someone had turned the thermostat up a few notches. Bradley suddenly felt warmer. His cheeks were flushed, and he could feel the palms of his hands start to get sweaty. He was aware DI Strong was still looking at him, waiting for an answer.

'Yes…yes, I guess so. I think so,' came his stumbling reply.

'You said you stayed in all night and watched television. Is that correct?' DI Strong asked him.

'Yes, I think so,' Bradley replied.

'What did you watch?' Strong asked him.

'Emm…I don't know. I can't remember,' Bradley replied. 'I think it might have been a movie, but…emm…I think I might have fallen asleep. I often do that if it's not a good one,' he added, trying to force a laugh but it wouldn't come.

DI Strong picked up the piece of paper and slid it across the table to Bradley.

'The thing is, Bradley,' he said. 'We picked up your car on ANPR being driven on Newham Road at quarter past seven on Tuesday evening. How do you explain that?'

'What…emm…I…I don't know…emm…' Bradley stammered, looking at the black and white photo of a car on the table in front of him. He recognised the number plate. It was his car.

'Maybe someone else was driving it Bradley? Is that what it was?' Strong suggested. 'You'd loaned it to a friend perhaps?'

'No…emm…no, I think I remember now,' Bradley replied. 'I'd run out of milk and popped out to get some. I'd totally forgotten about that.'

'Okay, so how long would you say you were out for, getting your…emm…milk?' Strong asked.

'Oh, not long…just a few minutes,' Bradley replied.

Strong picked up a second piece of paper, one that DC Morgan had given to him, just ten minutes before Bradley Smith had arrived at the police station. He placed it in front of Bradley, laying it carefully on top of the first piece.

'This is a second photo of your car, also on Newham Road, coming back the other way,' Strong said. 'It was taken two hours after the first one, at around nine thirty pm. That's a long time to get a pint of milk Bradley. Do you want to explain where you'd been? Had you been visiting an old schoolfriend perhaps? Stephen Jones? Did something happen Bradley? Something between the two of you?'

'What?...No,… you don't think. I…of course I. Stephen Jones…that had nothing to do with me. Of course not,' Bradley exclaimed. 'I came here to help you. You can't…I need to get out, I need some air,' he said, and he pushed his chair back and stood up abruptly.

DC Morgan also stood up, but DI Strong remained sitting at the table.

'Sit down Bradley,' Strong said calmly, but with a firm tone, and Bradley immediately complied.

'Good. Now take a deep breath and tell me what you really did on Tuesday night,' Strong began. 'And this time make sure you tell me the whole truth, otherwise I'll have you done for wasting police time. I'm sure you've seen that happen before on your police TV dramas.'

Bradley was sitting down again, with his head bowed and his hands clasped tightly, resting on his knees. He was breathing quickly. After a few seconds he raised his head slightly and began to speak very quietly.

'I went to meet someone,' he said.

'Who did you go to meet Bradley? Was it Stephen Jones?' DI Strong asked him.

'No, no. It was emm…a woman friend. Just someone I know,' Bradley replied.

'Okay, I'll need a name Bradley. What was her name?' Strong asked forcefully.

'It's Jane,' Bradley replied. 'Her name's Jane.'

'Okay and surname?' DI Strong asked, with DC Morgan poised to write it down on his pad.

'I…emm…I don't know. I just know her as Jane,' Bradley replied, his head bowed down again so that he was speaking directly into the floor.

'Okay, and where does this Jane live?' Strong asked him.

'I don't know,' Bradley said shaking his head as he spoke. The room stayed silent for a few seconds before DI Strong spoke again.

'You're going to have to help me out here Bradley. I'm confused. Who is this Jane and where did you meet her?' DI Strong asked as he leant back in his chair, his hands locked behind his head.

'She's…she's just a friend. Just someone I know. We just meet up sometimes and…and go for a drive and have a chat and stuff,' Bradley replied, his head still bowed downwards.

'Is she a prostitute Bradley? Do you meet her for sex?' Strong asked softly.

Bradley didn't reply, but he nodded his head slowly and his whole body had started shaking. Strong could see tears dripping from his face onto his lap. Strong decided to give him a break and he instructed DC Morgan to terminate the interview. The two detectives left the room, with Bradley remaining sobbing quietly at the table.

DC Morgan was tasked with tracking down Jane, the sex-worker, so that they could check out Bradley's story. DI Strong returned to his office and as soon as he sat down, his door opened.

'Guv,' DS Knight said as she entered the room. 'I caught the end of the Bradley Smith interview from the observation room. I'm not surprised,' she said as she took a seat in front of Strong's desk.

'No, well, Morgan's going to check it out and see if he's telling the truth this time,' Strong replied. 'I don't like him though. I don't trust him. Even if this is true, he might still have gone to Stephen Jones's that evening. He's got something creepy about him.'

'Yes, he's always been a bit like that,' DS Knight replied. She still didn't believe Bradley Smith could be the killer, but she sensed now wasn't the time to say that to her boss. He was on a roll.

'Have you managed to get a hold of Dr Collins yet? I'd really like her take on Bradley Smith,' Strong asked DS Knight.

'Yes, I spoke to her,' Knight replied. 'She was away at some conference in Brighton, but I sent her an email with everything we know about Bradley attached. She said she'll get back to me tomorrow.'

'Okay, great,' Strong replied. 'I'll send her a brief email now on what we learned today, and we'll see what she has to say about our young man, Bradley Smith. Just hang on a minute here, there's something else I've got to tell you.'

Chapter 20

'So, the next one on the list is Daniel Blake, is it?' Miss Hardy asked James Gray.

The two of them were sitting in Irene Hardy's conservatory again, the usual two cups of tea in front of them. James had temporarily moved in to Miss Hardy's house, and although it had felt strange at first, living with his old school teacher, he had begun to get more comfortable with it. Even though she must have been around forty years older than James (he didn't like to ask her real age), he was actually finding her very good company. She was very knowledgeable and had a mischievous sense of humour which he really liked. And she was really supporting him in his mission of revenge.

For her part, Irene Hardy was really enjoying having James stay with her. It was great to have some good company, other than just her gossipy neighbour, Joan, and what she and James were doing was the most exciting thing she'd done in years.

'Yes, Danny Blake. He was a bit of a thug at school and from what I've found out recently, he doesn't seem to have changed much since he left,' James said to Miss Hardy. 'He's been in court a few times, having been involved in fights, breach of the peace, that sort of thing. He works as a doorman at a club in town, Club Extream it's called. Pretty appropriate name. So, all in all he still seems a bit of a nasty piece of work.'

'Yes, so you'll have to be careful with him James. Do you have a plan for what you're going to do to him yet?' Miss Hardy asked.

'Well, sort of,' James replied hesitantly. 'The one thing I remember most about him, is him punching me in the playground one lunch time. He just came up to me and, for no reason, he just punched me in the face. It was in front of everyone, and I started crying. It bloody hurt, but it was also the shock of it. I knew he was a bully of course but I wasn't expecting him to punch me just like that. Then he just laughed and walked away. That was it. So, the plan now is to do the same back to him. Just punch him as hard as I can, just once, and then walk away.'

'Mmm…you could be putting yourself in danger, especially if he has a reputation for getting into fights,' Miss Hardy replied. 'He might hit you back. Have you ever actually punched anyone before?'

'No, I haven't,' James laughed.

'Well, you ought to practice then. You might just get one chance and you don't want to mess it up. Knowing how it's gone so far with the others, you'll probably miss him! Here try hitting this,' she said holding up a cushion.

James couldn't help laughing at Miss Hardy taking such a practical approach, but she was right.

Out of the three of them, Stephen, Nigel and Danny, Danny was likely to be the trickiest one. The one where it could backfire on him. Despite James's many hours in the gym, building himself up, he knew Danny would still be a physical match to him. James stood in front of Miss Hardy and threw a punch at the cushion, but she moved it before the punch landed and James found himself just hitting fresh air.

'See what I mean?' Miss Hardy said from behind the cushion. 'You can't let him see it coming or he'll just duck out of the way. Remember he's done this before. You need to get close to him and give him a short sharp punch, a jab, so that he doesn't have the time to react to it. Try again,' she said, holding the cushion up.

James stepped forward so he was now directly in front of Miss Hardy and this time he threw a shorter punch, catching the edge of the cushion as Miss Hardy moved it to her left.

'That was better, keep trying, you'll get it,' Miss Hardy said smiling at James. 'I think also maybe distract him in some way just before you punch him. You know? Ask him something or shout out, or maybe point at something to the side. Try that now.'

James threw some more punches at the cushion, shouting just before he raised his arm. After a few attempts, he found he was regularly connecting with the middle of the cushion.

'I think you've got it,' Miss Hardy said, lowering the cushion again. 'If you do it like that, that's probably your best chance of getting him. The only other thing I'd say is that it'll probably hurt you too. Your hand, I mean. So you need to be ready to try and ignore that so you can get away from him quickly. But, all in all, I think you're almost ready. Now, how quickly can you run?'

Chapter 21

Detective Inspector Strong hit the send button and his email disappeared off into the ether, hopefully arriving in Doctor Sam Collins's inbox just a few nano-seconds later. He looked up at Detective Sergeant Knight who had been sitting on the other side of his desk, patiently waiting.

'Right,' DI Strong announced. 'That's that done. So, how did it go in court today. All good?' he asked.

'Yes, I think so. You know what it's like,' Knight replied. 'Lots of hanging around, waiting to be called, before you get your five minutes in the box with some smart defence counsel grilling you on this and that.'

'Who was it today?' Strong enquired.

'Alan Bately,' Knight replied. 'He was up to his usual fun and games, trying to catch me out but I think I managed to hold my own. I tried to stick to the facts, despite his best efforts to divert me.'

'Ah, good…good,' Strong replied, as he shuffled some papers around on his desk.

He stood up and walked around from behind his desk to stand in front of DS Knight, towering above her. He perched on the edge of his desk, his long legs stretching out in front of him. The two detectives' feet were almost touching, with Strong's being twice the size of Knight's.

'Well, emm, it looks like you made a good impression at the annual conference,' DI Strong said with a smile on his face.

'Oh…right…why do you say that?' DS Knight replied. Her stomach lurched as she feared she already knew the answer.

'Well, did you happen to meet DI Murphy from the Merseyside region?' DI Strong asked.

DS Knight felt her stomach go again and she took hold of the back of the chair in front of her. She tried to keep her face as normal as possible and hoped that DI Strong couldn't see how she was feeling inside.

'Emm…yes, I think I did…why?' DS Knight managed to reply, forcing the words out and trying to sound as casual as possible. Underneath the water she was paddling hard.

'Oh, I was speaking with him yesterday, after we'd finished the monthly regional review conference call,' DI Strong replied. 'We were catching up on a few things and he asked about you. He said he'd met you in Birmingham. Said he was very impressed and that he might have a DI role coming up later this year which he'd definitely consider you for. So that's good news,' Strong looked down, smiling at his DS.

'Yes…I guess,' DS Knight replied.

'Super, well I knew sending you there was the right thing for you,' DI Strong replied. 'Of course, I told him you weren't available, but let's see what happens I guess. If he did take you on, you'd be one of the youngest female DIs in the country, if not *the* youngest. That would be some achievement.'

'Yes, okay….is that all sir?' DS Knight replied. 'I ought to get on…'

'Yes, that's it. I just wanted to let you know,' DI Strong replied. 'Its good news, but let's see if anything comes of it. Meantime let's crack on with Bradley Smith. Keep it going, you're doing well.'

Almost before DI Strong had finished talking, DS Knight was out of his office and walking quickly down the corridor towards the ladies toilet, her head bent down so she didn't make eye contact with anyone as she walked. She pushed the toilet door hard, banging it against the wall and headed straight for the nearest cubicle. She locked the door behind her and leant over the toilet, pulling her hair back behind her head with one hand. DS Knight coughed once then threw up into the toilet. There goes lunch, she thought as she coughed again before standing up and wiping her mouth with a piece of toilet paper. She threw the paper into the toilet and flushed it away along with her lunch.

DS Knight left the cubicle and walked across to the row of washbasins. She looked in the mirror and saw that all the colour had disappeared from her face. She turned the tap on and splashed some cold water onto her face, the shock of it reviving her somewhat. She dried herself off and walked along to the office kitchen where she made herself a cup of strong coffee. As she sipped the hot liquid, she began to feel better again. The shock of hearing about DI Murphy's interest in her was beginning to fade slightly.

After DS Knight had left his office, DI Strong had been sitting, plotting. An idea had formed in his head, and he'd developed it into a plan. Bradley Smith had lied to him, and he didn't like that. He still didn't know if Bradley was telling him the whole truth now. He might be, but there was still something not quite right about Bradley's story and Strong wanted to catch him out. He wanted to pin something on him, even if it wasn't for the death of Stephen Jones.

Strong went through to the main office and found DS Knight again. She was back sitting at her desk. He placed his hand lightly on her shoulder and Knight felt a slight shiver run through her body.

'Have you got a minute?' he asked her. 'I need you to do me a favour.'

Please don't let it be anything to do with DI Murphy, was all Knight could think of as her boss stood by the side of her desk, still with his hand on her shoulder. She just couldn't handle that right now.

'I'm going to let Bradley Smith go in twenty minutes, but I want you to bump into him as he leaves and take him to the local pub for a drink,' Strong began to explain his idea to his colleague.

He stepped to the side, taking his hand off her shoulder, and Knight looked up at him.

'Make it look like you're just coming into the station and it's all just a spur of the moment thing,' he told her. 'Keep it informal. See if he'll open up to you a bit, with you being an ex-classmate and that. I think there's more to him than what he's telling us. Maybe he won't see you as a cop, more as a friend. I'm sure he'll be happy to have a drink with you. Anyway, see what you can find out and we can catch up again in the morning. Is that okay?'

Knight nodded her head in response. She hadn't really been listening fully, but she was just relieved it was nothing to do with DI Murphy.

With that, DI Strong turned and walked back to his office, satisfied that part one of his plan to nail Bradley Smith was now starting to take shape.

Chapter 22

Bradley Smith emerged from the police station. It was only early evening, and it was still light, but he was already feeling tired. It had been a long day, a very intense day.

When the police had contacted him again and asked if he could come in for another chat, of course he'd been delighted. He'd watched so many police dramas on television, and now he was actually taking part in a real life one. He'd imagined maybe he'd be the star of the show. The one who helped crack the case. He'd always dreamt of being a detective, but he'd never even been inside a police station before. Bradley had been excited just to see what it looked like, and it hadn't disappointed him.

To begin with, everything had just been what he'd expected. They'd taken him into one of the police interview rooms and it looked exactly like those he'd seen in some of his favourite programmes on TV. He'd met with Detective Inspector Strong and another detective, a Welsh man. Bradley couldn't remember his name. The Welsh detective had just sat there silently, seemingly letting DI Strong do all the talking, while occasionally jotting something down in his notebook. He'd seen that happen on TV before too and had thought that might be a commercial decision with the detective with fewer lines being paid less. But now it seemed it was real, that was how they did it.

The conversation with DI Strong had started off just exactly as Bradley had imagined it was going to. Strong asking him questions about Stephen Jones's death, and Bradley trying to help him as best he could. The detective had asked him about social media stuff, Bradley could remember that. Strong probably wasn't in to all that sort of modern thing, Bradley guessed. At that point, they were like a team, working together. Bradley was the man on the inside. The man that had known Stephen Jones, albeit fairly remotely, but there was obviously some sort of connection to their schooldays that Bradley could help him with. But before Bradley had been able to ask the detective what that connection was, the mood had changed.

Apparently, they'd found out that Bradley had gone out on Tuesday night when he'd told them that he hadn't. A stupid mistake to make. He should have known. But that was all it was, just a mistake. It had nothing to do with Stephen Jones, which is why he hadn't told them in the first place. That, as well as him being embarrassed to admit to the real reason he had gone out. But they seemed to be inferring that he had some involvement in the crime, that was where he had gone, which of course, was ridiculous.

DI Strong, being the great detective that he was, soon made Bradley confess to the real reason that he had been out that night. He'd been visiting a prostitute. Something that had become a regular event for him over the last few months. Bradley had felt hugely ashamed, and he broke down, unable to stop the tears coming. The two detectives had left the room, presumably to give him some time to compose himself. He was surprised, but at the same time relieved, when some time later another police officer had come into the interview room and told him he could go home. All Bradley could think was that they'd been able to track down the sex-worker woman, Jane, and that she had corroborated his story. He didn't know whether to feel happy, or even more ashamed that it was real, and Detective Inspector Strong now knew.

Now that he was out, the whole idea that he had somehow been involved in Stephen Jones's death was laughable, but it hadn't been only a couple of hours ago. Now all he wanted to do was get home and curl up on his sofa. He wouldn't be watching any TV crime dramas tonight, he wasn't in the mood for that.

As he turned to walk down the street, Bradley heard a voice call his name. He turned around to see Laura Knight, or Detective Sergeant Knight as he now knew her, walking towards him.

'Hey Bradley. Sorry I missed you. I guess you've had a long day,' DS Knight said. 'You look like you could do with a drink, come on,' she said, and before he could reply, she took hold of his arm and guided him along the road.

Knight hadn't been overwhelmingly convinced by DI Strong's idea to do this, but her mind had been elsewhere, and she just decided to go along with it anyway. It couldn't do any harm and after a day in court and the mention of DI Murphy, she could do with a drink herself.

Two floors above, DI Strong watched them go from his office window. Great, he thought, now he had a couple of hours to carry out his own part of the plan.

Chapter 23

Although DI Strong had his suspicions about Bradley Smith, that there was something not right about him, he felt confident enough that DS Knight would be safe with him in a busy bar. He wasn't going to try anything there and, besides, DS Knight knew how to handle herself. He'd asked Knight to keep Smith occupied for a couple of hours, which would give him enough time to carry out the second part of his plan.

As soon as he saw DS Knight and Bradley Smith disappear down the road, Strong grabbed his coat and left the office. He walked quickly to his car and punched Bradley Smith's address into his SatNav. Ten minutes later, he pulled up outside the entrance to Bradley's block of flats. He sat in his car for a few minutes until he saw a young woman approaching with a pram and another child walking hand in hand, by her side. Strong got out of his car and followed her to the entrance to the block of flats. The woman typed a code into the keypad on the wall and the entrance door clicked open.

'Here let me get that for you,' Strong said, easing his way past the woman to hold the door as she manoeuvred her pram and accompanying child through the gap.

'Thank you,' she smiled at DI Strong as she moved past him and headed towards the grey elevator doors.

Strong waited by the door until she'd disappeared into the elevator, before speedily bounding up the stairs to the first floor. He quickly found the door he was looking for and, making sure no-one was watching him, he took out a tool from his pocket and inserted it carefully into the door lock. A few seconds later he felt the lock give and he pushed the door open, stepping inside and closing it quietly behind him. He put the tool back in his pocket, Eddie's tool he called it.

Eddie Clarke was, or at least had been, a house burglar. He had died about ten years ago, after a sudden heart attack. Apparently, the doctors had warned him about his lifestyle, but Eddie had ignored them. Eddie liked a drink.

Although he had been a lifelong criminal, Strong had been sorry to hear of his demise. He had encountered Eddie Clarke on a number of occasions over the years, usually to arrest him, and although he didn't agree with his choice of profession, they had come to develop a mutually friendly relationship.

'I never rob from my own kind, Mr Strong,' Eddie had told him many times. 'Only from the rich. Those that have too much and don't know what to do with it all. I just help them out by taking some of it away and giving it to people that need it.'

'Yeh, Eddie,' Strong replied. 'That all sounds good, except the only people you give it to is yourself and the barman at the Kings Head!' Strong would reply laughing.

One time, when Strong was visiting Eddie at home to question him about another burglary, Strong had asked him how he managed to break into people's houses so easily.

'Let me show you Mr Strong,' he said, and he led Strong to his front door.

They stepped outside onto the doorstep and Eddie closed the door behind them. He took a tool out of his pocket, inserted it into the lock and just a few seconds later he pushed the door open again.

'This is the magic tool,' Eddie said. 'This can get you in anywhere. If you know how to use it.'

He passed it over to Strong and the detective looked at it carefully. It wasn't in fact one tool. It was a number of pointed pieces of metal, all varying shapes, sizes and lengths. Strong examined them closely.

'Can I have a go?' he asked.

'Sure, go ahead, Mr Strong,' Eddie replied, pulling the door closed again. 'Look at the type of lock first, see how big the opening for the key is and then pick the rod that just snugly fits it.'

Strong looked at the lock, then the different rods, then back to the lock, before making a choice. He stepped forward, towards the door.

'Okay, now do it slowly. It should slip in, but only just. It needs to be a tight fit or it's not the right one,' Eddie said as he smiled, watching Strong in action.

Strong inserted the rod into the lock and it felt tight, just as Eddie had suggested. He began to push it forward very slowly.

'Now, slowly does it, that's good,' Eddie said, leaning in to watch closely. 'Now as soon as you feel a slight resistance at the end of the rod, stop. Then very slowly turn it anti-clockwise. Very gently. You should feel it begin to click, then gradually give way.'

Strong was following Eddie's instructions and he felt the resistance. He turned the rod slowly and he could feel it giving way. There was a soft click.

'You've done it!' Eddie exclaimed with a beaming smile as he pushed the door open again. 'You can be my apprentice from now on, Mr Strong,' Eddie said laughing.

Strong laughed along with him and went to hand the tool back to Eddie.

'No, no, you keep that one Mr Strong. You're a natural. You never know when you might need it, and I've got plenty more.' he said still smiling from ear to ear. 'If your career in the police force goes down the pan, then you know what you can do!' Eddie said and he roared with laughter, his cheeks turning pillar box red.

Strong had kept the tool and over the years he had used it when he had needed to. When it helped him deliver justice. Sometimes he had needed to get into a building to find a piece of critical evidence, without him having the time to go through the official route of obtaining a search warrant. That was such a painful process. At other times, on a few exceptional occasions, he'd needed to gain access to plant some evidence that would lead to the conviction of a known criminal. A criminal who would otherwise still be free to walk the streets and cause more misery to his victims. The tool, and Eddie Clarke's guidance, had certainly helped DI Strong over the years.

Inside Bradley Smith's flat, DI Strong took a few seconds to get his bearings and he slipped on a pair of disposable plastic gloves. He'd been here once before to interview Bradley Smith and so he could remember roughly how the flat was set up. It was just like most flats really. Strong was standing in the hallway and, looking along it, he could see various, similar, white doors leading into the other rooms. Kitchen, Bathroom, Bedroom and Lounge. Strong walked a few steps along the corridor until he reached the first door on his left. He opened it and saw that it was the bathroom. Inside, there was a white coloured bathroom suite and a shower cubicle with a silver glass door. He had a quick look around, opening the mirrored cabinet above the sink, but there was nothing of any interest in there.

Strong went back into the hallway, closing the bathroom door behind him. He opened the next door along and walked into Bradley Smith's bedroom. Untidy, was Strong's immediate thought, but that was probably a bit unfair as Strong was married to a woman who kept their own house very clean and tidy. If Strong had lived by himself, then the bedroom might have looked a bit more like the one he was now standing in.

In the middle of the room there was a double bed, with a dark blue duvet spread across it, ruffled up in various random places. There was also a dark brown, rumpled up towel lying on top of the duvet near to one of the two white pillows. On either side of the bed there were small, matching wooden tables, each with two drawers underneath. Strong walked towards one of the bedside tables and opened the drawers. Both of them were full of clothes, what appeared to be underwear and socks. He felt around inside the drawers but there didn't seem to be anything else there. Nothing concealed. Strong walked around the bed and opened the drawers in the other cabinet, but this time both of them were empty. On top, there was a bedside lamp.

Strong returned to the first bedside table and looked at what was on it. It was busier. This must be the side of the bed Bradley Smith sleeps on, thought Strong. There was also a lamp on this side, but in addition there was an alarm clock, a pair of glasses and three books stacked up in a pile.

Strong picked up the books and looked at them closely, one by one. He placed two of them on the bed, but kept hold of the third one, reading out the book title.

'How to Commit the Perfect Murder,' he said quietly to himself.

He flicked through the book, occasionally stopping at a random page and reading a few of the paragraphs. He read the blurb on the back cover of the book which described it as a "part fact, part fiction" story, based on real life crimes, about how to commit a murder and get away with it. Strong turned back to the contents page and scanned down the list of chapter titles. He stopped on one entitled,

"*Tip 2 - Make it look like an Accident.*"

He had a quick read of the chapter before carefully replacing the books just as he'd found them. He then began to explore the rest of the bedroom. Five minutes later he was back in the hallway. There had been nothing else to see in there, just what you'd expect in a young man's bedroom, but that book had been interesting. Had Bradley Smith been researching it, or even using it as some sort of guidance for what he was now doing?

The detective had a quick, uneventful, scout around in the kitchen, before entering the lounge. Again, it couldn't be described as the tidiest of rooms, but once more, Strong gave Bradley the benefit of the doubt. A single man living on his own, he probably only made an effort to tidy up when he was expecting a visitor. In Bradley's case, Strong thought, that would probably most likely be his mother.

Strong's attention was immediately drawn to a set of shelves on the far wall, to the left of the TV, between that and the window. There were three shelves, and they were full of books and, what looked like, other assorted documentation. Strong scanned the book titles. There were a lot of, what appeared to be, crime related books. Mostly fiction by the looks of things, but there were also a couple of real life crime books, and one or two written by ex-policemen. Strong briefly wondered if that's what he might do when he retired from the police. He certainly had a lot of stories to tell, but, for his sake, most of them would have to remain secret. The detective ran his finger across the book spines, occasionally pulling one out to have a look at the front cover. Suddenly he heard a noise from the front door. It sounded like someone was coming in. Strong froze and looked around the room, trying to work out if there was anywhere he could hide. There was another noise from somewhere down the hallway, a bang, and then a softer sound and Strong realised that it was just something being posted through the letterbox. He breathed a sigh of relief, he didn't want to be disturbed when, technically, he had broken in.

His mind drifted back to the only time that had happened before. He had been looking around a well-known criminal's house, a man known as Bobby Forest, when Bobby had returned home unexpectedly. He had caught Strong in the act and things had got a bit messy. There had been a fight and Forest had pulled a gun on the detective. Strong had tried to wrestle it off him and, in the melee, the gun had gone off and shot Bobby Forest in the face. He died on the floor and luckily Strong had been able to clean things up and make it look like a suicide, before quietly leaving the house. When the call came in, the case was assigned to him, and it was quickly confirmed as a suicide. Everyone knew Bobby Forest was a violent criminal and there were few tears when his death became public. DI Strong was satisfied that, although it hadn't been how he intended it, justice had been delivered.

Strong turned his attention back to the current job in hand, in Bradley Smith's flat, and he crouched down to have a look at the bottom shelf. It was laden with piles of documentation. Strong pulled one of the bundles out to get a closer look and, on examining it, he saw that it was all paperwork to do with music. As he looked more closely, he realised that it was more specific than that. In fact, it was all documentation, press cuttings, magazines and other paperwork, all about the Eurovision Song Contest. It appeared Bradley Smith was a big fan of the event. There was even a programme from the previous year's event, held in Copenhagen, along with some Danish newspaper clippings, suggesting that Bradley might have been there.

Strong wasn't a big Eurovision fan and he gave it only the briefest of scans before putting the event documentation back in place. He pulled out the adjacent pile. This time it appeared to be a number of print outs from the internet covering various conspiracy theories, mostly to do with China. Strong flicked through them quickly, but there was nothing of interest to him. He put them back and pulled out the next load which was a number of scrapbooks, it felt like around ten in total. Strong opened the first one and flicked through it. Surprise, surprise, it was all about Eurovision again. He placed it to the side and started on the next one. This one caught Strong's interest immediately. It was full of press cuttings about a case he'd worked on. Andy Austin, the Anniversary Killer, as the Press had dubbed him. There was even a photo of

DI Strong and his sidekick at the time, DS Campbell, as they were coming out of the police station.

Strong quickly looked through all the other scrapbooks and found they were all similarly related to a serious crime case, usually a murder. Some of them, DI Strong had worked on. Others had been before his time in the Serious Crime team or were related to crimes that had taken place in other parts of the country. Strong put them all back carefully in their place on the shelf. His knees were beginning to ache, and he stood up to give himself a stretch. Feeling better, he crouched back down in front of the third, and final pile, on the bottom shelf.

There was one single scrapbook on top of a collection of old newspapers. He picked off the scrapbook and stood up again, opening the book as he stretched himself upwards. He stopped halfway, leaving himself in a strange, semi-crouch position, as he began to realise what this particular scrapbook contained. It was all about the Stephen Jones killing. As he flicked through it, Strong saw items that Bradley must have printed off the internet, as well as newspaper clippings and two photos. One was the school photo, the same one that had been found at Stephen Jones's house. The other photo looked like a cutting from that class photo, showing a blown-up version of Stephen Jones on his own. There was a circle drawn around Stephen Jones's head. DI Strong let out a whistle as he looked at the photo.

He looked around the room and walked over to a grey sofa where he sat down and proceeded to go through the scrapbook, page by page, checking that he hadn't missed anything else. Apart from the photos, it was all publicly available information, either from newspapers or the internet. When he was satisfied that he had seen everything he needed to see, he stood up and walked back to the shelving unit, placing the Stephen Jones scrapbook carefully back where he had found it. He looked at the shelving unit, satisfying himself that it looked just as it did when he'd entered the room.

Strong spent the next ten minutes looking around the rest of the lounge, but he didn't find anything else of interest. Apart from the scrapbooks it was just like anyone else's lounge with a sofa, a chair, a television and a coffee table. There was also a unit with a couple of drawers which held a variety of items, including some letters and other documentation. Strong had gone through it all but found nothing of relevance to the case he was working on. Still, that scrapbook, and Bradley Smith's obvious obsession with violent crimes was pretty damning in Strong's mind. There was definitely something not quite right about Bradley Smith.

After one last general look around the flat, ensuring that everything was as he had found it, DI Strong left the building and walked back to his car. He got in and looked at his watch. The whole visit had taken him less than an hour and he hadn't yet heard from DS Knight who, he assumed, was still in the pub with Bradley Smith. He wondered if she would get anything out of him. He'd seen before how people talk more when they are in an informal setting. It was like they forgot the person sitting across the table from them was a police officer. Over the years, Strong had obtained as much information over a few beers in the pub, as he had when interrogating a suspect in the police interview rooms. Strong briefly considered calling DS Knight but decided not to. He remained sitting in his car for a few minutes longer. He had a lot on his mind.

At the same time, a few miles away, DS Knight was also looking at her watch, but trying to do so without Bradley Smith noticing. DI Strong had asked her to spend a couple of hours with Bradley to see if she could get anything more useful from him. Anything that would implicate him in the death of Stephen Jones. But so far she'd not got anything and she was beginning to think that she was wasting her time. Having had a few drinks, Bradley had loosened up, but instead of talking about Stephen Jones, he seemed to be acting more as if they were on a date.

'This is nice,' he said. 'I haven't been out for a drink with someone for a while. It's…emm…nice,' he said, and he took a drink from his glass of beer.

Knight still couldn't see Bradley Smith as being a killer, but DI Strong seemed to believe he might be and so she had no option but to go along with his plan. So far it had been fruitless.

After an hour of conversation with him, nothing had come out and she was starting to get really bored. He had told her all about his trip to Copenhagen to the Eurovision song contest. He had said it was amazing and Knight nodded and smiled along with him. She never watched Eurovision, it was too cheesy. In truth, Knight just wanted to go home and put her feet up, but to keep her boss happy she decided she would keep the conversation going for another fifteen minutes.

When she'd first "bumped into" Bradley outside the police station, she could tell that he was tired, and a bit shaken by what had gone on during his interview inside the building. He told her he'd thought he was being asked to help the police, but it turned out that Strong seemed to be accusing him of the crime. Of killing Stephen Jones. He couldn't believe it and he talked freely and at length to DS Knight about it. Listening to him only further convinced DS Knight that Bradley Smith was not the man they were looking for. In her estimation he was an innocent man. As he began to relax more, half-way through his second pint, he started to talk about other things. Apparently, one of the most exciting things he'd done lately had been to buy a new wastepaper bin.

'It's brilliant,' he said grinning at DS Knight. 'When you throw something into it, a light flashes and it gives off a cheering sound. It's really funny.'

DS Knight could imagine, as she glanced at her watch.

'Yeh, it's great. I had to get a new one and I'm glad I did now,' Bradley carried on. 'It's similar to the last one I had, but I made sure this one wasn't made in China.'

'Why, did the last one break or something?' Knight replied, not really interested in his bin, but just wanting to keep the conversation going for a bit longer.

'Well, no, but they were listening in,' Bradley replied, with a serious look on his face.

'Who was…listening in?' Knight asked with a frown.

'The Chinese. It was a Chinese bin, and they were listening to everything we said,' Bradley replied.

'What…through the wastepaper bin?' Knight asked, still frowning.

'Yep, it's a thing. I read about it on the internet. There's a chip built in to it. In fact anything that's Chinese, they can hear what you're saying. And then I proved it,' he said raising his glass and taking a drink.

'You proved it…how?' Knight asked, thinking she might have drifted into a parallel universe. She'd always thought Bradley Smith was a bit odd, but she hadn't realised he was this odd.

Bradley put his pint down and smiled triumphantly at the detective sat across from him.

'Well, my mum was around one night, and I didn't have much in, so we decided to get a Chinese takeaway. I phoned them up and right away they knew who I was, without me even saying. And then, even more. They knew what we wanted to order! Can you believe it? That's when I knew they'd been listening,' Bradley said, and he raised his pint and took a long drink.

'Had you used that Chinese restaurant before, for a takeaway?' Knight asked him.

'Yeh, once before, with my mum around again,' Bradley replied. 'She likes a Chinese, prefers it to Indian, but they didn't know who I was then and that was before I had the Chinese bin. So, there you go,' he said lifting his glass and finishing off his drink.

The clock seemed to move round slowly, but eventually DS Knight decided it was time to finish this little charade. She made up some excuse about having to get home to finish some work, and she could see the look of disappointment in Bradley's face. This was probably the nearest he'd been to a proper date with a woman for a long time and DS Knight had sensed that was what he thought it was. A date. He didn't realise that he was really still being investigated on suspicion of committing a serious crime. As they left the bar and stepped outside, Bradley leant towards DS Knight to give her a kiss on the cheek, but she neatly sidestepped him, saying goodnight and she started to walk back towards the police station where she had left her car.

'Oh, shall we swap numbers?' Bradley called out.

'No, it's okay, I've got yours already,' DS Knight called back over her shoulder, as she carried on walking away.

Knight waited until she was back home drinking a cup of tea before texting DI Strong. The message read,

"Finished with BS. Nothing new to report."

She decided she wouldn't mention Bradley's

theory of him being spied on by the Chinese to DI Strong. It would only make him more certain that Bradley Smith was an oddball and add to his suspicions of him being the potential man they were after.

A minute later, her phone buzzed, and she picked it up to read the reply from DI Strong. It simply stated,

"Okay thanks. See you at our meeting with Dr Collins tomorrow."

Chapter 24

'Hi, I saw you watching me. Want to have a drink with me?' the woman who was now standing by Keegan's side asked him. She had a hint of an accent, but Keegan couldn't place it. Maybe Scandinavian?

He could feel her thigh lightly pressed against his own and as she smiled at him, he could see how beautiful she was. He hadn't been watching her as such, well maybe the odd glance. She was very pretty and a good dancer too. Very sexy. Her tight red dress looked like it had been made specifically to show off her slim body. Like it had been painted on. Most of the men in the club had probably noticed her at some point, but here she was now, standing close to Keegan asking him if he wanted to have a drink with her.

'Sure, what do you want?' Keegan replied smiling, but not quite sure what was going on. This sort of thing had never happened to him before. He reckoned he was a good-looking guy, but…well, …she was just different class.

'Come with me,' she replied and before Keegan could say anything, she had taken his hand and was leading him across the dance floor, her long blonde hair swinging behind her in rhythm with her stride. Her hand felt warm and soft. Comforting. The woman continued walking up to a roped off area where a bouncer seemed to nod at her before raising the rope and letting them pass. Beyond the rope there was a small, secluded area with a few bright, comfy looking sofas and several low-level tables. The area was dimly lit, and the woman sat down on one of the sofas, pulling Keegan down beside her. She picked up two glasses of champagne from the table in front of them and handed one to Keegan.

'Cheers,' she said smiling at Keegan and clinking her glass against his.

Keegan took a long slow sip of his champagne, taking time to think about what had just happened. It tasted good, but just a few minutes ago he had been at the bar in the Green Room Club with some of his mates, celebrating his friend Charlie's birthday. They'd been having a good time. They always had a laugh when they were out together. Lots of banter. Keegan had a few drinks and he was in a good mood now. It was amazing what a bit of booze could do for you.

He had been feeling a bit down at the beginning of the night. He knew he'd let his girlfriend Sophie down. Again. They were supposed to have been meeting up that evening, but when Charlie had arranged a last minute thing for his birthday, he knew he couldn't say no. He'd known Charlie since they were kids, and the bond was too strong. He'd make it up to Sophie though. Somehow. He always did.

But right now, he found himself sitting on a sofa with a beautiful woman, maybe Swedish, drinking champagne. Just the two of them. What had happened? Maybe he was dreaming?

'So, what is your name?' the girl asked, leaning towards him, with that beautiful smile, and Keegan felt her leg pressing against him.

Keegan took some time to answer. Now that they were sitting close together, he found himself mesmerised by her beauty and the aroma of her perfume was also intoxicating. She was looking directly into his eyes, and he knew he needed to break her spell.

'Keegan, it's emm...Keegan,' he said reassuring himself that he'd got it right. Nothing seemed real at this point. 'What's emm… yours?' he asked trying not to look directly into her dark brown eyes. Those eyes.

'My name is Layla,' she replied, and she casually placed her hand on Keegan's knee.

Keegan took another gulp of the champagne, and as soon as he'd finished, Layla had already picked up the bottle and started topping up his glass once again. He glanced down at her legs, hoping she wouldn't notice. Her dress had ridden up slightly and he could see the top of her leg. Her skin looked so smooth, and he was tempted to reach out and touch it….

'You like my legs Keegan?' she said, following his gaze. 'Why don't you touch them?' she added, and she took his hand and placed it just above her knee.

'You've got sexy eyes Keegan,' she said, interrupting his thoughts, and she leaned in closer to him, her lips brushing lightly against his ear. 'I think you are very handsome,' she whispered to him.

Keegan moved his head back and, somehow managing to lift his hand from her leg, he took another drink from his glass of champagne.

'Look, I should tell you,' he said, looking down at his feet. Anything not to look at her. 'You're very beautiful Layla, but I've got a girlfriend and well, I wouldn't want to two-time her, you know? It wouldn't be right,' he said shaking his head and frowning, but still unable to bring himself to look at her again.

Layla pressed her hand more firmly on Keegan's knee. He'd forgotten it was there and now he felt her moving it, very slowly, but gradually, a little further up his thigh.

'I don't want to be your girlfriend Keegan. I just want to have some fun with you tonight,' Layla whispered into Keegan's ear, her mouth so close he could taste her sweet breath. He could feel her breasts pressing against his arm. They felt so soft. He glanced at her body quickly, hoping she wouldn't notice again. Her whole presence seemed to be enveloping him, taking over all of his senses.

'Look, your girlfriend's not here, is she? No-one else is here. It's just you and me. No-one else needs to know. We can have some fun, what do you say?' she asked, and Keegan felt her tongue gently touch the bottom of his ear lobe, or had he just imagined it? Her mouth felt so close, and he unconsciously licked his lips.

'All we're doing is having a drink or two and making friends with each other. What can be better that that?' she laughed, and she reached forward and took a drink from her glass.

Keegan was in a state of turmoil. If this had happened a few months ago, it could have been one of the best nights of his life. There would have been no question about it. He could imagine exactly how it would have gone. They'd chat for a bit in the club, finish the champagne, and then get a taxi back to her place. She would have a nice flat, she was a classy girl, Keegan had no doubt about that. As soon as they were inside the door, they'd be all over each other, frantically kissing and ripping off each other's clothes. Then they'd spend the night together. There would be no sleep that night though. Layla had a gorgeous body and Keegan would explore every inch of it. He could imagine it all now as he looked at Layla sitting beside him. He was teetering.

He shook his head, trying to clear it. What about Sophie though? Since he'd got back together with her again, he found he really liked her. He was surprised by *how much* he liked her. He'd never felt like that about anyone before. Of course, he'd let Sophie down once before when they were younger, and still at school. That had been a mistake, but they were only kids then and things were different now. They'd both grown up, Sophie had gone to university and now she was back home. And they were back together. And it was different this time. It was more serious. They weren't just messing around. She wasn't just a little girl anymore, she was her own woman, independent and clever. And funny.

And Keegan liked all of these new-found things about her. He'd always fancied her, but now she had become really interesting too. How crazy was that? He loved the times when the two of them were alone together, and they would just lie there chatting about anything and everything and nothing. He'd never done that with a girl before. Although he wouldn't admit it, he'd learned all sorts of things from her. And she'd definitely helped to keep him on the straight and narrow. A few of his friends had made good money from becoming involved in some dubious activities. Nothing serious, but technically illegal. Well, not *technically* illegal, just straightforward illegal. Keegan had been tempted a few times. It seemed easy money. All you had to do was deliver a parcel or change a number plate. Something like that. Simple, quick, easy money. No-one got hurt. But he knew Sophie would disapprove, and on top of that her dad was some sort of senior cop. Keegan sensed that her dad didn't like his daughter seeing him. He didn't want Sophie's dad to be proved right. That he wasn't good enough for her, and so he avoided doing anything that wasn't completely above board.

'Look, I know you're very beautiful Layla,' Keegan said, leaning back, slightly away from her. 'But….in another time, maybe….maybe we could get to know each other. But, right now, I've got a girlfriend and she means a lot to me…so I emm…I don't think we can do this right now.'

'Oh, babe, you're so sweet,' Layla said smiling directly at Keegan and she leaned forward, taking his head in her hands and kissed him firmly on his lips.

Keegan felt himself unable to resist, she was drowning him again, and he couldn't stop her, but after a few seconds she pulled away and slyly glanced at the bouncer still standing at the entrance to the roped off VIP section. He gave her the slightest of nods and she turned back to Keegan. He hadn't moved. He felt like he was in a trance. That kiss had been so soft, so perfect.

'Have some more champers babe, I'm just going to freshen up, I'll be back in a minute,' she said, and she stood up and walked to the rear of the roped off area, disappearing through a red, velvet curtain.

Layla wasn't her real name, but she liked the song with that same title. It was one of her favourites, and she'd got into the habit of using the name Layla when she needed to do these types of jobs. It suited the part. Her real name was Erica, but it was best to have a bit of anonymity, making it more difficult for anyone to trace her afterwards, in case they tried to. She would often imagine the Layla record playing in her head as she acted out the role required. More often than not it was some type of honeytrap. That was what they called it. She had always found it to be really easy money. Men always thought with their dicks, not with their brains. There was occasionally a bit of a risk involved if the man got too frisky and expected more, but she always had someone close at hand, on standby, to help out if needed. But that had never happened yet. She knew what she was doing, and she knew how to handle herself. She could read situations pretty well. And, most importantly, she knew how men were.

As usual, this one had been fine. The boy, Keegan, had played his part to perfection. Just what she'd expected. That was all he was really, just a boy. He couldn't resist her and who could blame him? She'd put on one of her sexy dresses and she knew no man could ignore her when she had that on. He'd mumbled something about a girlfriend, but Erica knew that wouldn't be a problem. Most of the men she worked with were married, but that didn't bother her, and when she was with them it didn't seem to bother them either.

On her own in the Ladies, she checked her phone and clicked on a message from Claude the Bouncer. That was the name she had him stored under on her phone, "Claude the Bouncer." Not that she knew any other Claudes, it was just something she did. Her way of categorising people she knew. There was Mick the Plumber, Dave the Barman, Phil the Fireman and Mo the Cop. It was just her way of organising her life.

She scrolled through Claude the Bouncer's message, checking that he'd got enough good, clear photos of her and Keegan in the VIP area of the club to do the job. They looked perfect. It was like a little picture book. Firstly, they were drinking the champagne. Then they were sitting together. Then they were closer, his hand on her leg, until finally, they were kissing. Perfect. Her client would be pleased. That was as much as he'd asked for, she didn't need to take it any further than that, although she would have if needed, and the client paid her the appropriate rate. This particular one was a good, regular customer. He always paid well, and promptly, allowing her to slip Claude an extra twenty, although he didn't seem to care. It was easy money for him too. All he had to do was stand guard in case of trouble and take a couple of photos.

She put her phone in her bag and walked back through the curtain to where she'd left Keegan sitting. He still hadn't moved but she noticed that his glass was now empty.

'Come on babe, let's go and see what your friends are doing,' she said, and she took his hand and pulled him to his feet. She led Keegan back across the room to where Charlie and his other friends were, still celebrating Charlie's birthday. Erica was smiling as she walked. Keegan felt like a little puppy dog as they went hand in hand across the floor. As they re-joined Keegan's mates, Erica quietly slipped away, leaving the club through a "staff only" side door. It was unlikely that she would ever see Keegan again.

Later that night, back at her flat, Erica sent the photos on to her client before climbing into her bed alone. Five minutes later she was fast asleep.

The next morning DI Strong was sitting on his own in his office at the police station. He'd arrived a few minutes earlier and, after switching on his computer, he reached down into his briefcase and took out a small mobile phone. He switched it on and placed it on the desk in front of him, waiting for it to fire up. He entered his security code and a minute later it pinged that he had a message, as he'd hoped it would.

He smiled to himself as he picked up the phone and flicked through the photos of Keegan and a beautiful woman. They should do the trick, he thought, and he printed off six photos and put them into a brown envelope. He sealed it down before applying a sticky label, typed with the name and address of his daughter, Sophie Strong.

Chapter 25

Carter the Mailman picked up the brown envelope from the office post tray and glanced at it briefly, before adding it to his basket along with the rest of the office mail. Carter had been the mailman at the police station for as long as anyone could remember. No-one knew if Carter was his first name or his surname. Everyone just knew him as Carter. In fact, although everyone knew him, no-one really knew much about him at all. How old was he? Where did he live? Was he married? Nobody seemed to know. He was just Carter the Mailman. He'd always been there, and always would be, as far as anyone could predict.

Twice a day he'd do his rounds, appearing from his little office, "The Post Room" proudly emblazoned on the door, heading around the building, collecting post and dropping off post. He'd always go the same route now. He'd tried different ways over the years, before settling on this one a few years ago. If anyone had asked him, he wouldn't be able to explain why, but this route just felt like the right one. Not that anyone was likely to ask him anyway. After he'd finished, he'd disappear back into his little office, and no-one would see him again until it was time for his next round. Carter the Mailman loved his job.

Having finished the afternoon round and returned to his little office, which was no bigger than a broom cupboard really, Carter began to sort out the mail. He organised it quickly into three piles. There was internal mail, external mail, which was already stamped and finally there was unstamped, external mail which would need to go through his franking machine. That machine gave Carter some status, it was the machine that only he was allowed to use. Apart from when he was off sick, or on holiday, when someone from the admin team would use it. But that wasn't very often.

As he sorted through that afternoon's post, he picked up a brown envelope and noticed that it wasn't properly sealed. Some of the contents were poking out slightly and Carter thought it looked like the edge of a photograph. His curiosity got the better of him and he carefully undid the rest of the lightly sealed envelope with his finger and pulled out the papers from inside. There were six separate sheets, and as he flicked through them, he saw that they were all photographs of a young couple, probably in their mid-twenties, sitting in what looked like a bar or a night club. The woman was very attractive, with long blonde hair and she was wearing a short, tight fitting red dress. Carter gazed at her for a while, wondering if she was somebody famous. He then took a closer look at the man in the photos. He had short dark hair and was dressed in a blue-patterned, open-neck shirt and dark coloured trousers, with a pair of black shoes. Suddenly Carter realised that he knew him. It was Keegan Summers! Carter had been at the same school as Keegan Summers, a couple of years above him, and although he hadn't seen him for a few years, it was definitely him! Wow what was he doing, and who was that beautiful woman he was with? He'd done well!

Carter flicked through the photos, all of which seemed to show the couple being very close and affectionate. There were a couple showing them kissing. and touching each others' legs. He briefly considered photocopying them so he could take them home and add them to his collection, but he decided it was too risky. The police photocopier was notoriously temperamental, and he could imagine it stalling mid-copy leaving him in an awkward position.

Carter stared at the photographs, going through each one slowly, taking in the detail. He felt envious of Keegan Summers. Why couldn't he get a woman like that? But he knew the reason why. He was a nobody really. Just Carter the Mailman. That was all he'd ever be. Women like that wouldn't even notice him if he was standing right in front of them.

Carter looked at the address label on the envelope and saw that it was addressed to a Sophie Strong. That rang a bell. Wasn't that the name of DI Strong's daughter? He was sure he'd heard people in the office talking about her before. That must be the woman in the photos, he guessed. Her and Keegan Summers. That made sense, they must be around the same age. Did she go to the same school as them? He couldn’t remember.

He took another close look at the woman in the photos. If it was Sophie Strong, she was certainly a stunning young woman, the Guvnor must be very proud to have such a beautiful daughter.

Chapter 26

DI Strong and DS Knight were in Strong's office waiting for the arrival of the police psychologist, Dr Sam Collins. They were at the long table, sitting diagonally across from each other, both drinking a cup of coffee.

'Look I ought to tell you, I might surprise you with a couple of the things I bring up with Dr Collins today, just go with me on it, Laura,' Strong said to his Detective Sergeant.

'What do you mean Guv, what sort of things?' Knight asked him, puzzled by his statement, and surprised that he'd used her first name. He rarely did that.

'Oh, nothing much, just a couple of things to do with Bradley Smith. Just some theories I want to try out with her. I just want to see what Dr Collins thinks of him overall. Just trust me on this one, okay Laura?' Strong replied, looking directly at DS Knight. 'Also let's not tell her about you having a drink with him yesterday either. As you said there was nothing came out of that and so there's no need to bring it up with Dr Collins.'

'Yes of course Guv,' Knight replied, still surprised by his use of her first name, but sensing from her boss's tone that agreeing with him was the correct response. For whatever reason, this was obviously how Strong wanted to play it and, although Knight was surprised, there wasn't any time to discuss it any further, and so she decided not to say any more and just wait for the upcoming meeting with Dr Collins.

A few minutes later, Strong's phone rang. It was the officer on reception letting him know that Dr Collins had arrived. Strong and Knight left Strong's office and made their way, walking silently, side by side, to the second-floor conference room where they had arranged to meet with the police psychologist. The two detectives arrived first and made themselves comfortable on the far side of the table. Shortly afterwards, Dr Collins walked into the room.

'Thanks for coming in again Dr Collins,' DI Strong said, standing up, as the police psychologist took a seat on the nearside of the table. Detective Sergeant Knight, sitting next to DI Strong, smiled, and nodded at the police psychologist. Once Dr Collins was settled, DI Strong opened the meeting.

'Okay, so as you know we are working on the Stephen Jones case and we've been interviewing everyone in the school class photo, as we'd previously discussed with you,' he said. 'Most of them, as you might expect, seem like normal every day, living people. Nothing particularly unusual has popped up in most of the discussions we've had so far. There's still a couple we haven't been able to track down yet, however we believe both of those may have moved abroad some years ago. So, on the whole, that's where we are,' Strong said, taking a deep breath.

'There is one character, however, who, as you know, we would like to get your opinion on. His name is Bradley Smith and I believe DS Knight sent you some information on him,' DI Strong said as he slid a copy of the class photo across the table, pointing to the young Bradley Smith as he did so. 'I interviewed him yesterday and also sent you a summary email on my findings from that.'

He looked through his file again before extracting another photo, which he also handed over to Dr Collins.

'This is a more up to date photo of Bradley Smith,' he said. 'He now works as a manager in a local supermarket.'

Dr Collins looked carefully at both of the photographs. DS Knight watched her closely and could see her eyes flicking back and forwards between the two. She wondered what the police psychologist was thinking. Something clever, or perhaps simply that Bradley Smith hadn't aged very well. He'd certainly put on weight and lost a bit of hair since DS Knight had known him at Danesborough High School. After a few seconds studying the photographs, Dr Collins looked up, flicked back her long blonde hair, and looked directly across the table at DI Strong.

'So, I've read what you sent me, but I'd like to hear it directly from you, if that's okay,' Dr Collins said. 'Sometimes there's things that don't come out as clearly in the written word. Things can be interpreted differently. So, what can you tell me about Bradley Smith?' she asked, sitting up straight, her face blank, and hands crossed, resting on her lap.

'Okay, I'll start, and DS Knight here can chip in with any of her thoughts, anything I might have missed as we go,' Strong replied, looking sideways at his fellow detective. 'It appears at school, Bradley was a bit of a loner,' DI Strong began, sitting back in his chair and stretching his long legs out underneath the table. 'Bradley didn't seem to mix particularly well with any of the other boys. Kept himself to himself. He wasn't in any of the sports teams or anything like that. He just seemed to get through school without anything major to note about him, neither good nor bad,' Strong looked at Knight and she nodded her confirmation.

'Since leaving school,' Strong continued, 'he got a job in a local supermarket and over the years he has worked his way up to a management level. His exact title is Retail Store Manager, which seems to mean that he is in overall charge of the shop,' DI Strong paused, before carrying on.

'He's thirty years old, lives in a flat, on his own, in a new development near the waste recycling centre, I don't know if you know it?' he asked Dr Collins.

The Psychologist screwed her face up, indicating she wasn't sure.

'Okay,' Strong continued. 'He doesn't seem to have a partner, although I believe he did have a girlfriend when he was at school,' Strong looked towards DS Knight.

'Yes, that's correct. Alison Kirkbride, but I don't think it was anything serious,' DS Knight chipped in. 'Certainly, when we spoke with Alison, she played it down, saying it was just an innocent school thing. She's married now with two kids.'

Just like most of them, DS Knight thought to herself. That seemed to be the extent of their achievement since leaving school. That, and getting married, and taking out a big mortgage to buy a house. Very few of them seemed to have moved on and done anything different or made something of their lives.

'I don't think I'd seen Bradley since we left school, but he was at the recent school reunion,' DS Knight added.

'Oh, that's interesting, did you speak with him there?' Dr Collins asked, looking directly at DS Knight. The detective felt a shiver run down her spine at the police psychologist's gaze and she sat up, straightened her spine, before answering.

'Emm…yes I did, but just briefly,' DS Knight replied.

'Okay, what did you talk about?' Dr Collins asked, still staring at the detective.

'Well…nothing really,' Knight replied, sitting forward in her seat. 'He…emm…he just told me a bit about what he was doing now, where he worked and lived. You know, just general stuff.'

'Uh-huh, anything else? No mention of any of the other schoolmates or partners or girlfriends? Anything like that?' Dr Collins asked.

'Well…,' DS Knight could feel herself start to blush. She didn't really want to have this conversation, especially with DI Strong being in the room. It was too personal, but she knew she'd have to carry on now. 'Well, he did try and chat me up, saying he'd fancied me when we were at school,' she forced a laugh. 'I reminded him about Alison Kirkbride, and I think that threw him off his stride.'

'Really, he tried to chat you up?' DI Strong asked, looking sideways and laughing at his colleague. 'You didn't tell me that!'

'Yes…yes he did. I think he tried it on with a few of us girls there. Sad git,' DS Knight replied, feeling strangely embarrassed and wondering why her Guvnor should think it was so funny.

'Mmm…interesting,' Dr Collins broke the silence, and she picked up a pen and made a note on her pad, which was now resting on her lap.

'What about the school teacher, Miss Hardy, did she have anything to say about Bradley Smith?' Dr Collins asked the detectives.

DI Strong flicked through the papers in the file in front of him until he came to the page he was looking for.

'Let me see,' he said. 'No, it doesn't look like we got much from her yet. Maybe we should give her another visit,' he added, looking at DS Knight sitting beside him.

DS Knight nodded and wrote it down in her notebook as a follow up action.

'And then of course the other thing was that Bradley Smith lied to us about his movements on the night of Stephen Jones's death,' DI Strong continued. 'At first he said he hadn't gone out, but then when we picked up his car on ANPR, he changed his story.'

'Ah yes that's correct,' Dr Collins replied, looking down at her notes. 'He then said he'd gone to see a woman called Jane? Is that right?' the doctor asked.

'Yes, well, it turns out Jane is a prostitute, but his story does seem to check out in that respect,' Strong replied. 'She said they'd spent a couple of hours together and that he was a regular. Apparently, they usually drive to a hotel car park, and he likes to just sit in the car most of the time and talk to her. She thinks it's sweet, and then at the end she does her bit, a happy ending, and he drops her back where he picked her up from.'

'So does that rule him out from being at Stephen Jones's hose, time wise?' Dr Collins asked.

'Not necessarily,' Strong replied. 'He could still have done it and, also, we only have her word for how long they actually spent together. I think he's still a strong suspect. He seems obsessed with murders, a little too much for my liking,' Strong paused for a second before continuing.

'What would you think if we found out that his flat was full of books on crime and he kept a scrapbook, full of information on the Stephen Jones murder?' Strong asked the police psychologist.

'Well, that would certainly be interesting, of course. It's not unusual to find that type of acute interest in similar types of crime in the lives of other murderers,' Dr Collins replied.

'Mmm...and what if he also had a copy of the same class photograph that was found at Stephen Jones's house,' Strong asked.

'Well, again, that would certainly be interesting, indicative perhaps,' Dr Collins replied, raising her eyebrows as she spoke. 'Why, have you found these things in Bradley Smith's house?' Dr Collins asked.

DS Knight was keen to hear her boss's answer to that question. She'd been dying to ask herself, but she'd remembered DI Strong's preamble to the meeting where he'd warned her that he might surprise her with a couple of things and that she should trust him. She guessed this was it, but she couldn't understand why he had gone down that track. No doubt all would become clear when he answered Dr Collins.

'Not specifically,' Strong answered. 'We haven't searched Bradley Smith's flat as yet, but I have received information from another source which suggests that we might find that type of evidence, were we to carry out a search. As I said, we haven't gone down that route yet.'

The room fell silent for a moment. DS Knight was trying to work out exactly what Strong meant. Did he have an informer, someone that knew Bradley? Someone that had been in his house? That didn't seem likely. But then why would he say that? Her thoughts were interrupted as DI Strong started speaking again.

'So, what do you think Dr Collins?' DI Strong asked. 'Do you think Bradley Smith could be our man? With all you've heard now, does he fit the profile of the man we are looking for?'

'Mmm…well…from what you've told me so far, I think he certainly has a number of characteristics which would tend to fit the profile of the type of person we're looking for, yes,' Dr Collins replied, slowly, thinking as she was talking.

'He certainly seems a lonely guy with very few friends,' she continued, 'and with difficulties in forming relationships. He also seems to have an acute interest in crime and perhaps this one, more specifically, but that could be explained by the fact that he knew the victim from his schooldays.'

Dr Collins paused, thinking about how best to phrase what she was going to say next. She liked working with DI Strong, and also with DS Knight now too, and she didn't want to make it look like she was disagreeing with them or, even worse, telling them how to do their jobs. She was worried they might not want to use her again.

'The main problem I have with Bradley Smith though is that I still can't see what his motive would have been, 'Dr Collins said. 'I don't know why Bradley Smith would have attacked Stephen Jones. There doesn't seem to be any reason for him to do that, unless I missed something?'

'No, you're right,' Strong replied. 'We haven't nailed that down yet, but we are still working on it.'

'From my viewpoint,' Dr Collins continued, 'I was hoping that the class interviews would have thrown something up, some sort of incident or something like that. From what I've read of the case, Stephen Jones did seem to get up to a few things, a few pranks, some of the other pupils mentioned. I think maybe you need to ask more questions of his closest friends at school and see if they can tell us anything more specifically. Did one of the pranks go too far? Did someone get hurt? There has to be something that would make Bradley Smith, or someone else, seek some sort of revenge so many years later.'

'Yes, we can do that,' DI Strong replied. 'And with Bradley Smith specifically, I think we need to look further into him too. Do you agree?'

'Yes,…I think so,' Dr Collins replied, nodding her head slowly.

DS Knight was watching the psychologist closely and, to her, that last, very hesitant answer to DI Strong's question indicated that she didn't really believe what she was saying. Like herself, Knight believed that Dr Collins also didn't really think Bradley Smith had killed Stephen Jones. But also, like herself again, it seemed the police psychologist hadn't wanted to disagree with Detective Inspector Strong and so had gone along with his thinking.

Chapter 27

DS Knight hadn't been able to get hold of DI Strong since they'd had their meeting with Dr Collins. That was frustrating. She'd wanted to discuss it further with him and get a better understanding of his thinking around Bradley Smith, and specifically what he had meant when he'd talked about Smith having a scrapbook and the school photo. That had really confused DS Knight. Despite DI Strong's misgivings about Bradley Smith, DS Knight still wasn't convinced that he was the man they were looking for in this case. He just wasn't the type.

It was Sunday afternoon, and it was still bugging her. She just couldn't get the case out of her head. She'd tried reading, watching television, even cleaning, but it was no good. As she had nothing planned for the rest of the day, Knight decided she might as well go into the police station and re-review all of the case information they had gathered so far. She wanted to see if they had missed anything. It would be nice and quiet on a Sunday, and she would be able to get through it all reasonably quickly, without anyone interrupting her.

Knight arrived at the police station, made herself a strong cup of coffee and sat down at her desk with the file in front of her. She started to read through all of the documentation, page by page, making notes as she went. Doctor Collins had seemed fairly sure that the answer to the downfall of Stephen Jones would lie in the school photo, or at least from something to do with someone in that class. Something that had happened at school, so Knight kept that idea in mind as she reviewed the file, looking for any clues. Anything that might have been missed first time around. She decided to look at all of the statements they'd taken from the ex-pupils again, and she extracted them from the file, making a pile on her desk. One by one, she read through them all, her pen poised over a notepad, ready to make any notes that came to mind.

Most of the statements were pretty straightforward, leaving her pen still poised, and the notepad blank. Many of the ex-pupils interviewed couldn't remember much about Stephen Jones from their schooldays and hadn't had any contact with him since they had left school. Of the few that did remember him to some extent, a couple had mentioned that Stephen Jones's best friend had been a boy called Nigel Harrison. Stephen, Nigel and one or two of the other boys had been a bit naughty on occasion, but it didn't seem to have been anything too bad. What was it Jenny Broughton had said? Pranks, just boy's stuff. Knight could vaguely remember some of the sort of things they did, but nothing serious. No-one had added anything more to Jenny's faint memory of the other boy who she couldn't put a name to. By all accounts, Danesborough High had seemed to be a fairly normal school, which was pretty much DS Knight's recollection of it too.

She finished reading the statements and sat back in her chair to look at the notes she'd made. There were two things that needed following up. The first was that it seemed no-one had actually spoken to Miss Hardy yet. The note on the file said that she was unwell when called upon by DC Harris. Harris had spoken with her nephew, a James Hardy, and he had asked if Miss Hardy could give them a call when she was feeling better, but there was nothing in the file to indicate that she'd done that yet. The second thing that DS Knight had noted was that Stephen Jones's best friend from schooldays, Nigel Harrison, had given his statement from a hospital bed. Apparently, he'd been in some kind of accident at home and broken his ankle. He hadn't given any useful information about Stephen Jones or their time at school and the interviewing officer had noted that he seemed reluctant to talk about it.

DS Knight sat thinking for a few minutes, staring at the notebook in front of her, before making her mind up on what she was going to do. She decided she would definitely go and see Miss Hardy and Nigel Harrison herself. They were a couple of loose ends that needed clearing up and she wanted to be there first hand to see if they had anything useful to say. She glanced at her watch and put the case file away. Although coming into the police station had taken up a few hours of a day off, she was glad she'd done it. The Stephen Jones case was only going to be nagging away at her all day if she hadn't and now, at least, she had two positive actions to focus on and follow up the following day.

On the drive back to her house, Knight stopped at a local takeaway and bought an American pepperoni pizza and a single portion of garlic bread. At home, she ate them straight from the box, curled up on her sofa, listening to Adele playing on her smart speaker.

Chapter 28

The phone rang again. That was the second time in just the last few minutes. Whoever was trying to get hold of Miss Hardy wasn't going to give up easily.

'It's probably Joan Branson, one of my neighbours. She often pops in for a coffee and a chat,' Irene said. 'If I don't answer it, she'll only worry and probably come around to see that I'm okay.'

When the phone rang the first time, James and Miss Hardy had been in deep discussion about how he was going to get his revenge on Danny Blake. They were on a flow, and they didn't want to stop that, so they just ignored the phone. When it rang again though, that just broke the roll they were on and they knew at some point Miss Hardy would have to answer it, otherwise it would just cause them problems further down the line.

The issue they had was that with it most likely being the neighbour, Joan Branson, she'd want to come over and then they'd have to explain James's presence. Irene didn't want to have to lie to Joan.

'Although she can be a bit of a gossip, her heart's in the right place,' Irene explained. 'I don't think I could sit here and chat with her as if everything is perfectly normal, while what we're planning is in the back of my mind.'

James had also been thinking about what to do about the phone. The less interference they had, while he was living at Miss Hardy's, the better for both of them. He'd hoped by not answering the phone that the caller would just give up. But not Joan Branson, apparently. Bloody nosy neighbour. He didn't want to answer it himself in case he had to explain who he was and why he was there. He had a story prepared but in truth he wasn't totally confident about it.

'Okay, what about if it rings again, answer it with a croaky voice,' James said. 'Tell her you've got the flu, or tested positive for Covid or something, and that you can't see her for a few days. Tell her you don't need anything, but if you do, you'll call her, but right now you just want to rest.'

The phone rang.

Irene Hardy picked up the handset and answered.

'Hello, Irene Hardy here,' she said with her best croaky voice.

'Irene, it's Joan. Oh, you don't sound too good. Are you all right?' she asked.

'No, I'm not too good Joan. I think I'm coming down with some fluey type thing,' Irene replied, maintaining her hoarse sounding voice.

'Oh, that's not so good,' Joan replied. 'I was thinking of popping over for a coffee. I've got a couple of cakes, might help you feel a bit better?' Joan suggested.

'Oh thanks Joan, but I think its best you stay away until I'm over this,' Irene replied. 'I wouldn't want you catching it. I'm sure I'll be fine in a couple of days. I'll give you a call then,' Irene replied.

'Oh, okay, if you're sure,' Joan replied. 'Have you got any Lemsip in? I think I've got some here. I can pop it over if you like?'

'No, it's okay Joan, I've got some,' Irene replied quickly. 'Thanks, I'll call you if I need anything, bye for now,' she added and ended the call.

She looked at James and smiled.

'I don't like lying to Joan, but it was just a little one and hopefully that'll be it,' she said.

'Yes, we only need a little while longer and I'll be out of your hair. Your flu should be better by then,' he laughed. 'Although actually it did seem to be getting better during the call. You forgot to put on the raspy voice towards the end,' James said, laughing.

'Oh did I? Oh no,' Irene replied, and she laughed along with him.

Chapter 29

Detective Sergeant Knight walked into the bright reception area of the main hospital building. She took the elevator to the eighth floor, before exiting and following the signs towards the Brownlee-Hughes Orthopaedic Unit. Knight walked along a long corridor until she arrived at the entrance door to the ward. She turned and went in, walking up to the glass-fronted reception desk. A young woman behind the screen raised her head from a mound of paperwork in front of her and smiled at DS Knight.

'Good morning. I'm here to see one of your patients, a Nigel Harrison,' DS Knight said brightly.

'Ah, okay,' the receptionist replied. 'Are you a relative of Mr Harrison?'

'No, actually I'm a police officer,' Knight replied, showing the young woman her warrant card.

The receptionist sat forward to look at the wallet the police officer was holding out in front of her. She'd never seen a warrant card before but this one did look like it could be official. The card said Detective Sergeant Laura Knight on it and there was a photo of the police officer who was now standing in front of her. She didn't want to appear awkward and immediately thought about her car parked in the car park, and how the exhaust had started making a funny noise. She definitely didn't want them looking at that and finding something wrong. She couldn't afford anything extra at the moment. There were just too many bills to be paid.

'He's in bay number five, just through there on the right,' she replied, smiling as sweetly as she could, hoping that she hadn't upset the police officer in any way.

DS Knight walked in the direction indicated by the young woman and soon came across a section with a number five pinned across the top. She went in and looked around. There were six beds in the bay, but four were empty. Of the other two, one was occupied by an elderly man, and the final one by a man who looked about the right age she was looking for. She walked to the end of his bed and picked up his notes. Nigel Harrison, she saw at the top of the page. She tried to read what else had been written about him but found it too difficult to understand. It was mainly medical terms, which was to be expected, but they meant little to DS Knight.

Nigel Harrison had been snoozing. It was pretty boring being in hospital, especially when you had some pins and screws in your ankle, and you couldn't walk without someone helping you get up and assisting you as you shuffled along the corridor to the toilet. There wasn't much to do, other than lie around or read a book – and he'd never been much of a reader. One of his visitors, maybe his mum, he couldn't remember who, had brought in a book of Sudoku puzzles, but he'd got bored with them, and lost patience after his first few failed attempts. He couldn't understand why people liked doing Sudoku, there didn't seem to be any point to it. All he could think about now was getting home and being able to walk by himself again. And what a stupid idiot he was.

Nigel's eyes sprung open, aware that someone was at his bedside. It was an attractive young woman with short dark hair. She looked about the same age as him and somehow familiar, but he couldn't recall where he might have seen her before. Since being in hospital, he found his mouth was often very dry and it took him a few seconds before he was able to speak so he just smiled at his visitor and mouthed hello.

'Hello, Mr Harrison,' DS Knight replied. 'My name is Detective Sergeant Knight. I wondered if I could ask you a few questions?'

Another police officer, Nigel thought, disappointed. He'd already spoken with the police and had no desire to do so again. He just wanted to forget all about what had happened and get on with his life again. Why had all this come up again now? It was all in the past and should have stayed there. Nigel eased himself up on the pillow, feeling the stiffness in his back and legs as he did so.

'Do you mind?' he asked with a rasping voice, pointing at the jug and glass which were sitting on his bedside cabinet.

'Of course,' DS Knight replied, and she poured half a glass of water and handed it carefully over to him, making sure none of it spilled onto the bed.

Nigel took the glass from her and had a couple of long gulps of the water, sighing with satisfaction as the cool liquid trickled down his throat. He licked his lips and moved his mouth around to try and get it back to feeling normal again. He took another drink before reaching over and placing the almost empty glass back on the bedside cabinet.

'I'm sorry but do I know you?' he asked. 'Have we met before somewhere? You look familiar somehow,' Nigel said as he sat up further on his bed, pushing the pillow up behind him and hoping that what he'd said hadn't come across as an inappropriate chat up line.

'Yes, you might do. I believe we both went to the same school, a while ago, Danesborough High,' DS Knight replied. 'You might remember me from there as Laura Knight?'

'Ah, yes that's it, Laura Knight, I remember now,' Nigel replied, involuntarily shivering as Knight said the name of the school. 'You were in one of the other classes in the same year as me, weren't you?'

'Yes that's right, fifteen years or so ago, a long time,' Knight replied, smiling. 'You've got a good memory.'

'Well, I don't know about that,' Nigel smiled back. 'As you say it was a long time ago. So what brings you here today?' Nigel asked the detective. 'I've already spoken with one of your colleagues and explained that this was an accident. I tripped and fell. That was it. Nothing else. I'm just a clumsy idiot I'm afraid,' Nigel added, forcing a laugh.

'Yes, I know. I did read that,' DS Knight replied. 'I'm sorry about that, it must have been very painful for you, breaking your ankle like that.'

'Yes, it was, I must admit, at the time. I've been operated on now though, a few screws and bits of metal inserted, and hopefully I'll be out at the end of the week,' Nigel replied.

'Oh, that's good. It's amazing what they can do nowadays, these doctors,' Knight replied, pausing for a second before changing the subject.

'I won't keep you long. I just wanted to ask you a few questions, and my apologies if you've already been questioned by another police officer, but as you will appreciate, we are dealing with a serious situation here.'

'You mean with Stephen Jones…and…do you know…what happened to him?' Nigel asked hesitantly, his face unable to hide his obvious nervousness at bringing up his old friend's name.

'Yes, as you know, unfortunately he was found dead in his own home. We're not sure exactly what happened yet, but we're just trying to build up a picture of what Stephen was like,' Knight replied. 'You were good friends with him when you were both at Danesborough High School, weren't you?'

'Yes, we knew each other at school but I haven't seen him much since then to be honest,' Nigel replied, before reaching across and taking another sip of his water. DS Knight noticed that his hand was shaking slightly.

'You saw him again at the recent school reunion though, didn't you?' Knight asked him.

'Yes…yes, he was there, along with a lot of other people from the past. Did you go?' Nigel replied.

'Yes, I went along. It was good to catch up with everyone again,' Knight lied, with a forced smile on her face. 'Did the two of you talk that night?' she asked.

'Emm…a bit, I guess. Not much, just a little, you know?' Nigel replied.

'Oh. Okay. I thought I'd heard that you met him in the pub beforehand. The one across the road from the venue?' Knight asked.

'Oh, yeh, you're right.' Nigel replied, nodding his head. 'He was there. I'd forgotten about that. There was a crowd of us in there. Just had a quick pint before we all went over,' he replied, shifting uncomfortably on the bed.

'What do you remember about Stephen from your schooldays? What was he like?' Knight asked, changing the subject quickly.

'Schooldays? Well, not much really,' Nigel replied. 'I guess we used to hang out a bit together, you know, play football and stuff. We lived near each other at that time.'

'Mmm…I've heard he used to like getting up to stuff at school, playing pranks, that sort of thing. Is that right?' DS Knight asked.

Nigel took another drink from his cup and shifted himself upwards again, against the back of his bed, his head resting on the iron frame. He looked uncomfortable, and even though he had just been through an operation, it seemed more than that to DS Knight. He paused a bit longer before replying.

'Well…no, not really…he was just like any other teenage boy, I guess. We all were,' Nigel replied, his eyes avoiding the detective's because in his head, Nigel could see himself stubbing out the cigarette on James Gray's arm.

'So, there is nothing you can remember that he did at school which might have got him into any sort of trouble?' Knight asked, looking directly at Nigel lying in his bed.

Nigel looked away again before replying, shaking his head as he did so.

'No, nothing I can think of,' he said.

'What about bullying? Was there anyone he, or any of the others, picked on? Maybe called them names or anything like that?' DS Knight asked.

'No,' Nigel replied, shaking his head again. 'No, I don't think so. I'm sure there were lots of nicknames, but I don't remember anyone being bullied. It was different times then though.'

'Okay,' DS Knight replied, not believing him for one second, but deciding to change the subject again.

'How did you break your ankle exactly?' she asked.

Nigel was taken aback by the sudden change in topic again.

'I…emm…I told you already. I fell and it emm…I caught it, twisted it,' Nigel replied, but DS Knight could tell from his body language that he was lying.

'Where were you? Talk me through it.' Knight replied, maintaining her look directly on him.

'I was in the house, walking towards the stairs and I must have caught it on the skirting board or something as I went through the lounge door and twisted it around and I fell down on it,' Nigel replied, his face beginning to flush.

'Were you on your own?' Knight asked.

'What…emm…yes…yes I was,' Nigel replied. 'My partner had gone to work.'

'Okay and what happened next?' Knight enquired.

'Well, the ambulance came, and they brought me here and I've been here ever since,' Nigel replied.

'Mmm…okay. And who called the ambulance?' Knight asked.

'What…emm…I'm not sure. I think it must have been one of the neighbours. They must have heard me calling out,' Nigel replied. 'I was in quite a bit of pain.'

'Okay, so they came to your door, did they? This…emm…neighbour?' Knight asked him.

'What…emm…no, I can't remember,' Nigel replied, his face now bright red. 'Why are you asking me all these questions. I told you it was just a stupid accident. I tripped and fell.'

DS Knight bent down and took her mobile phone out of her bag. She placed it on the bed in front of her and pressed a few buttons before looking up at Nigel who was now staring wide eyed at the detective.

'I just want to play you this,' DS Knight began. 'It's a recording of the emergency call made from your house. I want you to listen and see if you can recognise the voice.'

DS Knight pressed her phone and after a few seconds a man's voice began talking. He was asking for an ambulance, telling the operator that he was with another man who appeared to have broken his leg. There was the sound of another man screaming in the background, presumably Nigel, but the man on the phone seemed perfectly calm. After giving the address of the house he was calling from, he ended the call. DS Knight played it a second time, watching Nigel as the recording ran. He was definitely uncomfortable with it, he couldn't stay still, moving his arms, his legs, scratching his head. The recording came to an end and DS Knight paused for a second before looking at him lying on the bed in front of her.

'Who was that making the emergency call Nigel?' she asked.

'I…I think it must have been a neighbour,' he replied softly. 'I…I don't really remember. I was in a lot of pain.'

'The thing is Nigel, we've spoken with all of your neighbours, and it wasn't any of them,' Knight replied, shaking her head.

'Well, I don't know. It could have been anybody. Just a passer-by maybe. I don't know. Why are you asking me all this?' Nigel replied, getting visibly agitated, his cheeks bright red.

'Think really hard now Nigel, before you answer this. Are you sure no one was with you when you broke your ankle?' DS Knight asked him.

Nigel shook his head and mumbled "no" a few times. Knight pretended not to hear and asked him what he had said.

'I said NO,' he shouted angrily, raising his head and looking at DS Knight. 'Look I don't know why you're asking all of these questions. I told you. I fell down and broke my ankle. Can't you just leave me alone, please,' he exclaimed, and he turned his head to the side and closed his eyes.

DS Knight picked up her phone and sat looking at him. He was definitely lying, definitely hiding something, possibly the identity of the man who attacked both him and Stephen Jones.

DS Knight felt there was nothing more to be gained by asking him any more questions at this point. She'd learned enough from him for now. She knew that Nigel Harrison was lying. She knew that there had been someone with him when he broke his ankle, and that person also made the call for an ambulance. Maybe that person attacked him and that was how he got his ankle broken? She surmised that the person could be the same man who attacked Stephen Jones, and that again it was connected with something that had happened when they were all at school together. But she also knew that, for whatever reason, Nigel Harrison was too frightened to tell her. Finding out whatever it was that had happened, and who the other man was, would appear to have negative consequences for Nigel Harrison. So much so that he would rather keep it all a secret. Yet Knight knew that could be the key to solving this case. If she could find out what Stephen Jones and Nigel Harrison did at school, maybe that one thing, then she was sure that would lead her to finding their attacker.

Chapter 30

James left Miss Hardy's house, pulling the door closed behind him. He walked down the short garden path and turned right onto the street, heading off in the direction of his friend's vacant flat. The flat he had planned to use for the fortnight he needed it. However, Miss Hardy's offer of staying with her was an even better option. If the police or anyone else were looking for him, no-one would ever guess that's where he would be staying. It was the perfect hiding place until it was all over, and he could end it in his own way. In the way that he wanted to. Right now, he was on his way to pick up some clothes and toiletries to bring back to Miss Hardy's house.

Across the street, there was a small, almost imperceptible, movement of a curtain. Behind it sat Joan Branson, on her comfy armchair, by the window. She watched as James left Irene's house and made his way, off down the street. Joan had never seen that man before. Who was he and what was he doing at Irene's house?

She'd had tea and a cake with Irene in her conservatory only last week. They'd both had a nice custard tart from the bakers. Much better than the pre-packaged ones they sold in the local supermarket. Much fresher tasting. Irene hadn't said anything about a man visiting her then. Surely she would have mentioned it to Joan. There were no secrets between the two ladies, or certainly not any minor ones anyhow.

Irene had sounded strange on the phone when Joan had called her. She had sounded like she had a bad cold at first, but by the end of the call her voice was back to normal. And if it was just a cold, why wouldn't she want to see Joan, or let Joan do anything for her? That's what friends were for.

And who was this mysterious man in her house? Why had she not said she had someone there?
Joan knew he wasn't a doctor, he just didn't look like one and besides, she knew Irene's doctor, Doctor Khan. It definitely wasn't Doctor Khan who had just come out of Irene's house. Joan thought long and hard, but it just didn't make any sense. Maybe she should just go over there, but Irene had told her not to and she didn't want to upset her.

Joan couldn't stop thinking about it and all the scenarios that she ran through her head were of Irene in some sort of trouble. And each one was getting worse and worse. Perhaps she was being held hostage by this stranger in her house. Now that he'd gone out, maybe she was tied up and locked in her bedroom. Oh God, Joan thought, he could be doing all sorts to her. The stuff you saw on the News nowadays, there were lots of evil men out there. Joan never opened her door to anyone she didn't know, unless it was a relief postman.

Then she remembered she'd seen, what had looked like a policeman, at Irene's door a few days ago. He'd stood at the door for a few minutes, obviously talking to someone, but Joan couldn't quite see who it was. She'd moved her armchair and stood right at the corner of her window, but she still couldn't get a proper view across the street. Irene's door was only open a little and Joan couldn't see her. She was going to ask Irene about it when they next met, who he was, and what he was asking, and why hadn't he come to Joan's door too? But now she began to wonder if it actually had been Irene at the door. Maybe it had been this mysterious man that the policeman was talking to. And if so, what were they talking about? Joan's mind was in a turmoil.

Joan decided she needed to call the police. She knew one of the police officers, he'd been around a few times when she'd complained about cars speeding up and down the street. Using it like it was a race track. Just having a policeman there seemed to stop it happening. Why didn't they have Bobbies on the beat again like they used to when Joan was young? That had kept everyone in check. There was less trouble in those days.

The last time the policeman had come out to see Joan, he'd given her a direct number to call. He said that would get her through to someone quicker. If she called now, maybe they'd be able to tell her why they had been there and who the strange man was. That would set her mind at rest, and she already felt better, having made a decision that she was going to do something. She made herself a cup of tea and then sat down in her armchair with the tea and her phone on the little round coffee table by her side. She took a drink of the hot tea for a bit of courage, and then picked up the phone and dialled.

'Hello,' a man's voice answered. 'This is the police, how can I help you?'

'Hello, it's Joan Branson here,' Joan replied. 'I'm phoning about my neighbour, Irene Hardy. There's something strange going on with her, at her house, and I'm a bit worried about it.'

Joan went on to explain her concerns to the policeman about Irene's unusual behaviour and the strange man she'd seen leaving Irene's house. As she was talking, the policeman on the other end of the line was typing information into the PNC system on his computer. As he entered the name "Irene Hardy", a commentary box flashed up on his screen and he clicked on a link which took him to the summary note of Detective Harris's visit to Irene Hardy. The policeman quickly scanned it and read that Irene Hardy hadn't been well and DC Harris had spoken with her nephew, James Hardy.

'Hello, Mrs Branson. I'm just looking at some notes here. One of our detectives visited her and I believe her nephew James is staying with her as she's not well at the moment,' the policeman told her. 'I guess that's the man you've seen.'

'Her nephew?' Joan replied, quizzically. 'But she hasn't got a nephew.'

'Are you sure,' the policeman replied, stifling a yawn and looking at his watch. His shift would soon be over.

'Yes, well, she's never mentioned having a nephew to me. I don't think she has,' Joan replied. 'She would have told me, especially if he was coming to see her. I had coffee with her just last week and she didn't say a thing.'

'Okay, well I'm sure she's fine and there's nothing to worry about,' the policeman replied. 'But, if you like, I'll make a note on the system for someone to call round to see her and check that everything is okay.'

The policeman looked at the screen and sighed. He knew the right thing was to enter the details of the call into the database, but he was so tempted just to forget it. It was just more damn admin. No-one told him it would be like this in the police. He thought it would all be about catching criminals, but sometimes he felt like he was more like a social worker helping old ladies with their worries.

He sighed again and continued to enter the details of the Joan Branson call into the PNC system. As he typed in the name Irene Hardy, it turned green, indicating that the name was connected in some way with a current, ongoing case. He'd seen DC Harris's note and it hadn't said much. The truth was, he wasn't bothered. He just wanted to get it finished. Leave someone else to pick it up and make any connection there was. He doubted there was anything of any importance anyway. He just wanted to get home in time for his dinner and the eight o'clock football match on TV. It was Arsenal against Liverpool, he didn't want to miss that.

Chapter 31

DI Strong had told DS Knight that there was a regional meeting taking place and it was his turn to host it. Of course that meant that DI Murphy was going to be in town and so when the call came she'd been half expecting it. At first she'd been nervous about meeting him again, after what had happened in Birmingham, but after she'd done her homework and thought it all through, she was confident that she could do what she planned to do.

Murphy told DS Knight that he was staying on for a night after the regional meeting, before travelling back North the following day. Murphy suggested that they meet for dinner and a chat that evening. That was how he put it. He said he had some work to do first, but he'd booked a table in the restaurant of the hotel he was staying at for eight pm. A bit presumptuous, Knight thought, but she knew it was a nice hotel and the food would no doubt be very good. Also, she wanted to meet him again.

'I can tell you all about the Merseyside scene,' he'd said on the phone, 'and we can get to know each other a bit better. After that we can see where we go.'

DS Knight had felt a bit shaky after the call, but she soon recovered. She knew what she was going to do. She left the police station late-afternoon and headed home where she had a long relaxing shower. After that she spent a long time getting her hair just right and then donning a sexy black dress. The one that best showed off all of her curves. She looked at herself in the mirror and smiled. Who could resist that, she thought, and her smile grew into a laugh. Satisfied she was ready, Knight went through into the kitchen and poured herself a glass of wine, which she knocked back quickly. A bit of Dutch courage, and it made her feel good.

The taxi turned up on time and fifteen minutes later she was being dropped off outside the hotel. A doorman, dressed in a long red coat, stepped forward and opened the taxi door, allowing Knight to step out. He then held the hotel door for her, and she stepped through into the bright reception area. Knight glanced at her watch, she was wearing the gold braceleted one her mum and dad had got her for her twenty first birthday, it read ten minutes after eight. Ideal, just what she wanted. She wanted him to see her walking in, and also be a bit worried that perhaps she wasn't coming at all. That would give her the upper hand right from the start.

DS Knight entered the restaurant and told the young woman behind the lectern that she was meeting a Mr Murphy, who had a table booked for eight o clock. The woman looked at a screen in front of her, before nodding and smiling at Knight.

'Ah, yes, you're in the private section of the dining room,' she said. 'Follow me please, Mr Murphy is already here.'

The woman led Knight through the restaurant to an area at the rear, which was curtained off, although the curtains were currently tied back so that the inside was only partly obscured. As Knight passed through, behind the other woman, she could see DI Murphy sitting at the table, with a half-drunk glass of red wine in front of him. He stood up as the two women approached and the waitress peeled away, leaving Knight on her own.

'Ah, Detective Sergeant Knight. I'm glad you could make it,' he said, smiling, his teeth stained from the red wine, and he reached out to shake Knight's hand.

DI Murphy had wondered if Knight would turn up, and he'd had his eye on one of the hotel bar staff in case Knight didn't show. But she had, and that sent out a clear message to Murphy that she was happy to meet him again. Murphy noticed that she was wearing a short black dress which showed off her smooth, slim legs. He knew there was a process to go through, a game to play, but they both knew what the ending was this time.

DS Knight shook his hand and then took her place at the table. As she made herself comfortable, she noticed that none of the four or five other tables in this area had been set for dinner which meant they would be eating on their own. It was a small round table, covered by a white tablecloth and laid out with various cutlery and glasses. She could sense that their knees were close to touching, hidden underneath the table.

Knight noticed that a glass of wine had already been poured for her and she took a sip from it, feeling the warm liquid trickle down her throat, through her chest and into her abdomen. It felt good.

'I'm glad our little misunderstanding in Birmingham hasn't put you off me,' DI Murphy said smiling at her and reaching across to touch her lightly on the back of her hand.

Before she was able to answer, the waiter appeared and recounted the day's specials. When he finished, he left and promised to return with some bread. As they looked at the menu, Knight's mind began to wander back to the police conference in Birmingham, the last time she had seen DI Murphy. "Our little misunderstanding" he'd called it. So that was how he saw it. Knight saw it somewhat differently.

Somehow, he'd followed her into her room and suggested they both have another drink from the mini bar. Knight wasn't sure how he'd got there. Maybe she'd made a mistake letting him in, but she could hardly have shut the door in his face. He was the senior officer. She knew she'd had enough to drink already and really just wanted to go to bed, but Murphy seemed friendly enough so she thought if they had a quick drink then he would get the message that it was time to leave. She took a couple of miniatures and cans from the fridge. She thought she could remember them as being vodka and cokes, but her memory was a bit hazy on that part of the night. She poured the drinks into two glasses which were sitting on the dressing table. She turned to hand one of the glasses to DI Murphy and found him sitting on the end of her bed. She remembered being surprised by that, the fact that there was a man sitting on her bed and he was old enough to be her dad. He shifted along the bed a bit and told her to come and sit beside him. Knight had looked around but there was nowhere else to sit. There was a chair in the corner of the room but it was covered with the clothes she'd been wearing during the day. She felt awkward standing up when he was sitting down, towering over him, so she sat down on the end of the bed, beside him.

She remembered he drank his drink really quickly and then teased her to try and make her do the same. At the same time, he moved along the bed until he was close to her. There was nowhere for Knight to go without going around the side of the bed which would have looked very strange. She felt his leg touch against hers and she looked down, suddenly surprised by how short her dress looked.

After that a number of things seemed to happen at once, all very quickly. He reached over and took her glass from her, she couldn't remember if she'd finished her drink or not. Then she was lying back on the bed, not quite sure how that had happened, but feeling dizzy as she stared at the light above. Then she felt his hand on her leg, moving upwards, until it was under her dress and at the top of her thigh. Right at the top. She could see him leaning over her, DI Murphy, who she had only met a few hours earlier. He had a serious look on his face as if he was really concentrating on something. She could feel him touching her, but somehow for a moment it didn't really seem like it was her, it couldn't be. It was somebody else and she just happened to be there watching what was going on. But that "somebody else" looked just like her, and then it was as if a switch flicked in her brain, and she realised what was happening.

She pushed him off and managed to stand up, smoothing her dress down as far she could. She told him as firmly as she could muster that he should leave now. Go back to his own room. She remembered he just sat there on the bed and smiled at her. He asked her if she was sure, and then again, after she said she was, he asked if she was definite. Knight remembered starting to feel a bit embarrassed, thinking maybe she'd over reacted. She *had* let him into her bedroom...but his hand. He stood up then and came towards Knight. Suddenly he lunged at her and tried to kiss her, but she managed to move her head just in time so that his lips only brushed across her cheek. At the same time, she felt him grabbing her breasts and she managed to get her hands on his shoulders and push him back. Before he had time to move, she drew her hand back and slapped him as hard as she could. The noise was loud, like a balloon bursting. That stopped him. Knight shouted at him to leave, even though he was only a few metres away from her. After a few seconds he started to laugh, then he turned and picked up his coat and started walking towards the door. Just before he left, he turned around and smiled at Knight,

'I'll see you again soon,' he said.

At that time, immediately after he left, Knight might have been persuaded that it was some sort of misunderstanding. She was confused, her emotions were all over the place. But, the next day, and thereafter, she knew it was much more than that. And what she'd discovered since, further confirmed that growing belief.

DS Knight suddenly realised someone had said something and it brought her back to the current day, and dinner with DI Murphy. He'd asked her if she wanted more wine and had begun topping her glass up before she could reply. DI Murphy replaced the bottle on the table and smiled at DS Knight. At the same time, subconsciously, he felt the two items in his jacket pocket. A packet of his magic blue tablets and a small vial of his magic potion. He'd left the box of condoms in his room upstairs, ready for use later that evening.

His mind drifted back to the last time he had been with DS Knight, in her hotel room, where she'd made him waste one of his precious tablets. They weren't cheap!

That night, everything had been going as normal, as he'd hoped it would. Detective Sergeant Knight had joined him at his table during the evening. They'd had a few drinks and then went back to her room. She was getting drinks from the mini bar, and he'd taken the opportunity to slip into her bathroom and pop one of his magic tablets. He knew it would begin to take effect pretty quickly, which would be just in good time. They'd sat on the bed and chatted. She was young, but pretty and quite funny.

She reminded him of Jane Walton, another detective who had worked for him when he was in the Manchester region. They'd be about the same age, Murphy guessed, but Walton had been quieter, with not so much personality as Knight, which could be a good or bad thing. He'd got six months out of Walton though. She had a good body, curves in the right places, but she wasn't keen on trying different things, which after a while, Murphy began to find a bit boring. Then the rumours about them, which had been going around for a while, had reached the ears of the Manchester Chief Constable. He didn't like it and made that clear to DI Murphy. However, equally he didn't want any scandal in his region, so Murphy had got a transfer to the Merseyside area, dressed up as a promotion, although most of the team in Manchester knew the real reason for him going, it didn't matter. Luckily no-one knew that the same thing had happened with Murphy twice before as he'd made his way up through the ranks in other areas of the police force. The trouble with Murphy was that he couldn't resist an attractive woman. Or any woman for that matter, given the right opportunity. The right time.

Take Sam Kelly for example. He wouldn't necessarily describe her as attractive, but she did the business okay. She was a young, rather plain looking, woman who worked in the administration team in the Merseyside region. Murphy had bumped into her while they were both working late one night. He was feeling frustrated, it had been a long day, and nothing had gone right. He asked her to come back to his office and that was the first time he had her. She hadn't seemed that keen, but she didn't say anything. She didn't stop him. Since then, any time he'd felt the urge, he'd call her in and lock his office door for ten minutes till he was done. Murphy liked how she never said anything, she just did whatever he told her to do.

Murphy's thoughts drifted back to that night at the police conference in Birmingham, him and Knight, moving closer together on the bed and then, just as things were beginning to happen, she'd suddenly stood up and started getting funny, asking him to leave. He'd gone to see if she was okay, she had drunk a lot that night, and she'd got even worse, slapping him in the face and shouting at him to get out. He couldn't seem to calm her down and so he decided the best thing was probably just to go back to his own room and let her sleep it off. Murphy had seen her at breakfast the following morning and she looked okay, but he hadn't had time to speak to her. He knew from his time in the police that alcohol could have all sorts of weird effects on people and obviously that was what had happened with Knight. She was attractive though, and he wondered if he should have used the magic potion on her. He'd, decided not to though. He thought it might have been too risky, especially at a police conference. Too many police around!

Besides, he hadn't perfected his usage of the drug yet. He'd only used it once before, on a woman he'd met in a hotel bar in Chester, and he'd given her a bit too much. He'd poured the whole vial of liquid into her drink when she'd gone to the Ladies. The woman had been pretty much out of it when the two of them had gone upstairs to her room. It meant she just lay there, a bit floppy, with Murphy having to do all the work. She was still a bit sleepy the next morning which allowed him to have a repeat performance. After that she had started to come to, but she couldn't really remember what had happened. That was good. The woman had been really embarrassed, she kept repeating that she was a happily married woman and she'd never done anything like this before. Murphy said he was the same, and they agreed they'd both made a stupid mistake, and no-one could ever know.

'So, I'm glad we could meet up again and get to know each other a bit better,' Murphy said, smiling across the table to DS Knight.

'Well, I think I know you quite well already,' Knight replied, smiling back at Murphy. 'I'm interested to hear about the job though. Is there actually a DI position going?' she asked.

'There's always a position for the right candidate,' Murphy replied, smiling. 'You'd come in at your current DS level but after a while, assuming you'd done everything asked of you, then you'd be in a great spot for a DI promotion.'

'And what would be asked of me exactly?' Knight replied. 'Would it be the same that was asked of Jane Walton? Or maybe Lizzie Hamilton. Or Sam Kelly? And all the other women?' Knight looked directly at Di Murphy.

Murphy lifted his wine glass and took a long slow drink. Knight sat back in her chair, waiting for him to speak, but maintaining eye contact with the detective. He put his wine glass down on the table and smiled at DS Knight.

'I'm not sure who you've been talking to, or what you are inferring DS Knight, but I have a clean record in the police force. On top of that, I have always looked to support women in the force, helping them to further their careers, where possible. I'd like to help you too, if you would like to progress, but if you have doubts about that then perhaps the police force isn't the right place for you….' Murphy stopped talking and shrugged his shoulders.

'Oh yes it's the right place for me,' Knight smiled back at Murphy. 'But not for you. Your time is up. Let's face it, Detective Inspector Murphy, you've had a good run, but it's come to an end now. You're a dinosaur. You're what the police used to be, but there's no place for the likes of you now. In a couple of years, you'll just be a miserable old man sitting at home on your own and everything that you did wrong, every woman that you used your position of power on, they'll all be on your mind, taunting you. Reminding you, who you really are. A sexist bully with no friends.'

'You think so,' DI Murphy laughed at Knight. 'Let me tell you something DS Knight, you're the one that's finished. You had a chance to make it, if you'd just behaved yourself, but now you've blown it. You won't be able to hide behind Mo Strong for ever you know.'

'I don't need DI Strong,' Knight replied, confidently. 'You see, since Birmingham, since our *little misunderstanding*, I've been doing my homework. I've spoken with some of your current and ex-colleagues. Jane Walton, Lizzie Hamilton, Sam Kelly and a few more. We now have a pretty damning dossier about you and how you've treated women throughout your police career. It'll finish your career, no doubt, and it should finish your marriage too, when your wife hears about it.'

'You wouldn't dare,' Murphy replied, hesitantly, and Knight could sense that a corner had been turned and she was starting to gain the upper hand. She could see that she'd knocked him off balance.

'Believe me I would, and I'm very tempted to hand the file over to your Chief Constable,' Knight replied. 'But I'm not a vindictive person and so I'm going to give you a way out.'

'What do you mean?' Murphy asked, and Knight noticed that all the colour had gone from his face. He suddenly looked smaller, like he'd somehow shrunk during the last few minutes he'd been sitting there.

In reality, as Knight had been gathering evidence on DI Murphy, her preferred course of action had been to present the final dossier to his Chief Constable. Get him thrown out in disgrace. It was all that he deserved. However, it had become clear to her that most of the women Murphy had wronged over the years didn't want it all brought to the fore again. Although they were prepared to tell their individual stories to DS Knight, some of them hadn't even told their partners or family. They didn't want what they'd gone through becoming public and have to go over it all in a court or a tribunal, where they could be grilled by Murphy's legal team. Knight understood that and so she'd had to come up with a plan B, which she hoped would at least finish Murphy's police career. Get him out.

'I'm going to give you two months,' she said, looking across the table at DI Murphy. 'Before that time ends, I want you to resign, take early retirement, whatever, but get out of the force. If you don't do that, then the Chief will get the file and you'll be finished in disgrace. Either way you're out. Believe me, with what I've got, there's no doubt. And if you're half a policeman, you'll know that, and if you're half a man, you'll do the right thing.'

DS Knight looked at Murphy and could tell that he was broken. If she hadn't known what an evil, misogynistic man he was, then she might have felt a bit sorry for him. But she didn't. She stood up, placed her napkin down on the table and picked up her glass of wine. She saw Murphy flinch as if he was expecting her to throw it over him and she smiled. Instead, she finished her drink, turned around and started to walk away.

'Wait,' DI Murphy called out, touching the capsule of liquid in his jacket pocket…if only…

But DS Knight kept walking, until she was out of the hotel and back at her car.

The next morning Knight bumped into DI Strong in the corridor as he was on his way to another meeting.

'Sorry I'm in a bit of a rush, running late. How did it go with Murphy last night?' Strong asked her.

'Emm…Yeh, it was interesting,' Knight replied, 'but not the one for me,' she added, smiling at her boss.

Chapter 32

The Serious Crime team were gathered together in the large, second floor conference room. Room 2.12. Most of them were sitting in the same seats they always sat in when there was a big team meeting on. Force of habit. Everyone had been called there for an update review on the Stephen Jones case.

Detective Sergeant Knight was leading the meeting, and, on this occasion, DI Strong was not in attendance. He'd been called away to another event, somewhere off-site, but he had met with Knight earlier that day to go over everything and give her his thoughts on the case. Despite DS Knight leading the investigation, Strong had stayed very much involved.

DI Strong still felt that Bradley Smith was the main suspect, even though they didn't have any clear evidence to pin it on him. They'd interviewed him twice now and Knight had also probed him informally over drinks. Dr Collins, the police psychologist, had also reviewed Bradley Smith's profile and although Smith had certain interesting characteristics, she found it all circumstantial. They had no direct evidence that Bradley Smith had attacked Stephen Jones and DS Knight didn't think he had. She also didn't think that Dr Collins believed Smith was guilty either, but neither of the two women had wanted to admit that in front of DI Strong, who clearly felt that Bradley Smith was the man they were after. Time, and evidence, would tell.

At their earlier meeting, Knight had asked Strong about why he had suggested Smith might have a scrapbook on the Stephen Jones killing and a copy of the same class photo, but he hadn't given her a straight answer. He'd just said that he wanted to get Dr Collins's perception of Bradley Smith and so he added in a couple of extra possibilities to see what she might think of him then. To Knight, it all seemed a bit tenuous, but he'd asked her to trust him, and she'd learned that, overall, that wasn't a bad approach to take. It had certainly done her no harm in her police career to date. On the contrary, Strong had been a great mentor to her and had definitely helped her reach her current level of Detective Sergeant, at what was still a relatively young age.

DS Knight had worked with her boss on a number of cases over the last few years and had begun to develop a better understanding of how he operated. Strong had a fantastic arrest record, there was hardly a major crime investigation that he had led, or played a significant role in, which hadn't been resolved in some way. Not always by way of a conviction, but usually resulting in the case being closed. That also came about when the known suspect had died. That had happened a few times, but it all counted the same with regard to the police statistics, which meant that his clean up rate was as good as, or better than, any other Detective Inspector in the whole country.

DS Knight knew how well DI Strong was regarded in the police force and she'd learned a lot from him. But this time, with regard to Bradley Smith, she felt he might be wrong. Maybe it was because she had been a pupil at Danesborough High School and she knew some of the characters involved, but Knight felt she had some sort of advantage over her boss in this case. She couldn't put her finger on it, but with it being so close to home she just believed she would come up with the answer.

Knight wanted to do that quickly, before DI Strong went too far with his belief that Bradley Smith was the assailant. She wasn't quite sure why, but she was worried about what DI Strong might do next, and she was convinced in her own mind that Bradley Smith was innocent. He was a slightly odd, maybe lonely individual, but not the type of man who would attack his ex-schoolmates for no obvious reason. Although Dr Collins had agreed that Bradley Smith should be considered a suspect, Knight felt that the Doctor wasn't fully convinced and had, to some extent, just felt that she should agree with DI Strong.

DS Knight opened the team meeting by summarising the latest position with Bradley Smith. With Strong not being in the room, she played his involvement down, without writing him off as a suspect completely. She wanted to get him out of the way first so that they could then move on to discuss other aspects of the case. Maybe things that they'd overlooked previously.

Knight went on to talk about her meeting in the hospital with Nigel Harrison and how she felt he was hiding something. She believed there had been someone with him when he had broken his ankle, but whether that person was to blame for his injury or not, she didn't know. Only Nigel Harrison could tell them that, but for whatever reason, he was staying silent.

'I've gone through all of the statements we took from the interviews with the ex-pupils,' Knight went on to tell the room. 'There's definitely some connection between Nigel Harrison and Stephen Jones. A number of the statements mention them as being close friends at school, and the fact that Jones is now dead, and Harrison is in hospital within a few days of each other seems like too much of a coincidence. Dr Collins, our police psychologist, thinks it relates back to something that happened when they were at school. Some sort of incident. Maybe something that went wrong and impacted one of the other pupils. I agree. We need to find out what that was and that will lead us to the person we're looking for. It might be Bradley Smith, but it could also be somebody else. We're not there yet.'

DS Knight paused and took a sip of her coffee. She looked around the room to see if anyone wanted to add anything, but everyone remained silent. At least they all seemed to be listening to her.

'Okay, so what we need to do now is to re-interview all of the class pupils again, but this time more formally,' she said. 'I'll allocate them out amongst you all with a brief on what we need to ask them. Basically, we are looking for something out of the ordinary that happened at the school, involving Stephen Jones, Nigel Harrison and at least one other person, where that third person may have come off badly. Maybe it was a prank that went wrong. Maybe it was a fight or perhaps just some bullying. We need to find out.'

DS Knight looked around the room and saw some of the team nodding, while others were making notes in their notebooks. They were a good team.

'Myself, I am going to go and see the class teacher, Miss Hardy,' Knight continued. 'We didn't manage to talk with her previously because she was said to be ill. I am hoping she might have a different view on the class, coming at it from another perspective.'

Just then Knight noticed a hand being raised in the far corner of the room. It was a young Police Constable who had been allocated to work on the case, alongside the Serious Crime team.

'Guv, PC Morton,' he said introducing himself. 'I, emm…took a call yesterday from a neighbour of Irene Hardy, the teacher,' Morton said looking at his notebook.

'It was a Mrs Joan Branson,' he continued. 'She said that she was concerned for her neighbour, Miss Hardy. She said Miss Hardy had not been answering her calls and that she'd seen a young man coming and going from her house, who she didn't recognise. She sounded a bit upset about it all.'

'Okay, I think I read that her nephew was staying with her,' Knight replied. 'I guess it was him.'

'Yes, that's correct Guv,' DC Harris spoke up. 'When I went to see her, it was the nephew that answered the door, and he said Miss Hardy was ill. James Hardy he said his name was. I asked her to get Miss Hardy to call us when she could, but I don't believe she has yet.'

'I did say that to Mrs Branson, that it could be her nephew, just to try and calm her down,' PC Morton said. 'But she said Miss Hardy had never mentioned having a nephew before and she was worried who the man was. She seemed quite definite about it, so I said we'd send someone round to check it out, just to put her mind at rest.'

'Okay, well I have it on my list to go and see Miss Hardy,' Knight said. 'So, I guess I can clear up this "who is the nephew" question while I'm there. I'll get straight onto it when we are finished here.'

Chapter 33

DS Knight walked up the steps to Irene Hardy's front door. It will be funny seeing her again after all these years, Knight thought, as she knocked on the door. She could feel a sense of anticipation, a tingling in her tummy, as if she was fifteen again and had been sent to see the headmistress.

Inside the house, James Gray had seen Knight approaching through the front window and he'd immediately guessed that she was a police officer. She was ordinarily dressed, wearing a dark blue jacket and skirt, but there was something about her demeanour, the way she walked, that just identified her as a police officer.

'It looks like the police are determined to talk to you. I think we'll have to do it this time, or they're just going to keep coming back,' James said to Miss Hardy, who was sitting in her normal chair in the conservatory. 'We might be able to find out where they are with things too.'

'Yes okay. So you've told them that you're my nephew. Assuming they don't know who you really are, why don't we have a bit of fun, shall we? Let's pretend I'm going a bit doolally. I'll get things mixed up and that, confuse them a bit. Just for a laugh,' Miss Hardy replied, with a mischievous smile on her face.

'Oh, God, really?' James replied, but he knew he wouldn't be able to stop Miss Hardy. She was a force of nature, and besides, he knew it might be fun to watch her.

James went to answer the door and Detective Sergeant Knight introduced herself and showed him her warrant card. It had been at least fifteen years since they had last been in the same place and neither of them recognised each other, as they stood on Miss Hardy's doorstep. James explained he was the ex-schoolteacher's nephew and that he was staying with her for a few days.

'She hasn't been very well unfortunately,' James told DS Knight as they stood in the hallway. 'She's emm…she's getting a bit old now and sometimes gets a bit confused. I don't think the medicine she's taking helps. She might be asleep, she sleeps a lot during the day.'

James led DS Knight through to the conservatory where Miss Hardy was sitting. Thankfully she was awake, and James explained who their visitor was. DS Knight stepped forward and shook Miss Hardy's hand. Although she was older looking, DS Knight definitely recognised her as being her old Geography teacher from Danesborough High school and despite what her nephew had just told DS Knight, the detective thought Miss Hardy looked well.

'I don't know if you remember me, Miss Hardy,' she said. 'I'm Laura Knight. I used to go to Danesborough, and I was in your Geography class for a while. I'm afraid I wasn't much good at it though,' Knight laughed as she let go of Miss Hardy's hand.

That surprised James, he looked at the police officer again, but he didn't recognise her. The name rang a faint bell somewhere in his mind, but he'd only been at Danesborough for two years and he didn't remember many of the other pupils who had gone there.

'Laura Knight,' Miss Hardy repeated back. 'Laura Knight. Yes, I think I do remember you. Didn't you get pregnant and have a baby? A little girl, wasn't it? How is she now? She must be all grown up,' Miss Hardy said, with a smile.

'No, no that wasn't me. It must have been someone else,' Knight replied laughing and glancing across at James, who was standing to her left and also seemed to be supressing a laugh.

Knight took a seat across the room from Miss Hardy and leant forward, looking directly at her ex-schoolteacher. James had remained standing in the corner of the room, and Knight was just aware of him out of the corner of her eye.

'I'm in the police now, Miss Hardy, I'm a detective, and I just wanted to ask you a few questions about one of your former pupils, Stephen Jones. Do you remember him?' she asked, hoping that she didn't think he'd got pregnant too. 'That's him in the photograph there,' she said handing Miss Hardy the class photo and pointing out Stephen Jones to her.

'Stephen Jones,' Miss Hardy repeated the name. 'Stephen Jones, oh yes, I remember him, lovely boy wasn't he, but a bit cheeky I seem to remember. Oh, look at me. I looked so young then,' she said with a smile on her face as she saw herself in the school photo.

'Yes, I think Stephen had a bit of a reputation for getting up to mischief,' Knight replied. 'Can you remember anything specific that he might have done at school? Anything that was a bit over the mark?'

James Gray could feel himself tensing up in the corner of the room. He could remember a few things that Stephen Jones had done. All of them had been way over the mark. It was apparent from her line of questioning that the police suspected what had happened to Stephen Jones was to do with something that happened when he was at school. That was correct. But it also seemed they didn't know what that was. They didn't know that he had been an out and out bully. And furthermore, the police didn't know who the victim of Stephen Jones's "mischief" had been. They didn't know about James Gray, probably because he wasn't in the class photo. James was waiting to hear what Miss Hardy's reply was going to be. He couldn't guess.

'Oh, I'm sorry,' she said. 'Would you like a cup of tea. How rude of me not to have offered. Let me make you one… emm...Lucy.'

Miss Hardy made to get up from her seat, but DS Knight replied quickly.

'No, that's okay, honestly, I'm fine,' she said, and Miss Hardy sank back down into her seat again. 'Is there anything you can remember about

Stephen Jones, or perhaps Nigel Harrison? I believe they were best friends at school,' Knight asked her.

James noted that she'd also brought up Nigel Harrison. That probably meant that the police had linked the two incidents, but if that was the case, he couldn't fathom how they didn't seem to know about him. Surely Nigel Harrison would have told them?

'That's Nigel Harrison there,' DS Knight said, pointing him out in the school photo.

'Ah yes, Nigel Harrison, He was a bright boy. I'm sure he got an A star in Geography,' Miss Hardy said, seemingly staring into space. 'Or was that Bradley Smith?'

'Do you remember Bradley Smith then?' Knight asked, beginning to wonder if she was wasting her time here. Miss Hardy's memory was obviously not as good as it used to be. Knight could remember when, as a teacher, she could reel off all of the capital cities of the world and lots of other interesting facts for her pupils. They would often try and catch her out with an obscure geography question, but she always seemed to know the answer. It was sad now to see her losing that sharpness.

'Yes, I remember Bradley Smith. Him and that shy girl, Alison Kirkbride, used to sit together at the back of the class and hardly say a word all lesson,' Miss Hardy replied, getting animated for the first time since Knight had started talking to her. 'It used to wind me up something terrible. I tried to include the whole class in my lesson but those two would just sit there with their heads down, doing all they could to avoid eye contact with me.'

Standing in the corner of the room, James Gray could also remember Bradley Smith. Although they hadn't been particularly close friends at school, they looked a bit similar, and people often used to get the two of them mixed up. During his period at Danesborough High school, James had spent a lot of time telling the other pupils that his name wasn't Bradley Smith.

'Mmm…just going back to Nigel Harrison and Stephen Jones,' DS Knight interjected. 'Can you remember anything about them? We've been told they got up to a few pranks while they were at school. Can you remember anything they did that got them into trouble with the school?'

Miss Hardy sat for a few moments, staring into space, seemingly lost in her own thoughts. Suddenly she focused back on DS Knight.

'Sorry, what did you say? Would you like a cup of tea?' she asked.

'No thanks, I'm fine,' Knight replied, smiling. 'I was just asking you about Stephen Jones and Nigel Harrison. Did they do anything wrong at school? Can you remember? Is there anyone they might have picked on?' DS Knight asked. Out of the corner of her eye she saw James Gray put his hand over his mouth and cough.

Miss Hardy sat still for a few seconds again, before answering softly.

'No. I'm sorry, my memory isn't as good as it used to be,' she replied. 'I used to be able to remember all of my pupils but not any more,' she said with a sad look on her face. 'Are you sure you didn't have a baby, a little girl?' she asked, hopefully.

DS Knight decided there was not much to be gained by continuing to question her old teacher. Clearly her memory wasn't good, and even if she did come up with something, it might not actually be real. They'd certainly not be able to use her as a witness in court, should it come to that.

'Okay, don't worry,' Knight replied. 'I know it was a long time ago, but if you do happen to remember anything please give me a call. I'll give your nephew my contact details.'

DS Knight stood up and shook the school-teacher's hand again.

'Goodbye Miss Hardy,' she said. 'Thank you for your time.'

'Goodbye Emma, it was nice to see you again and thanks for doing my shopping. Give my love to your mother please,' Miss Hardy replied smiling.

James coughed again, then followed DS Knight out of the room and along the hallway to the front door where they both stopped and turned to face each other.

'I'm sorry about that. Her memory is getting worse now. Some days she hardly knows who I am, or even that she has a nephew,' James said. 'It's very sad. She used to be so with it.'

'Yes, I know,' Knight replied. 'I remember her from school days, she was so sharp then, we could never catch her out.'

'I guess you didn't get anything from that, today' James said. 'But from what you were asking, I'm guessing something has happened to the two men you mentioned. Stephen and Nigel. And it has something to do with their time at school, when my aunt was teaching them. Is that right.'

'Yes, we think so, but we don't really know enough yet,' Knight replied. 'If your aunt remembers anything at all can you give me a call please?'

'Of course,' James replied. 'But you've no idea yet who did it or why?'

'No, not really,' Knight replied with a frown and a shake of her head. 'Where do you live by the way? In case we need to get in touch with you?'

'Oh, it's okay. I'm staying here with my aunt for a bit, you'll be able to get me here,' James replied.

'Oh, okay, that's fine, but just for the record, because I've spoken to you, I need to take your name and home address,' Knight replied, smiling.

'Oh, okay I see. Well, I don't really have one at the moment. I'm kind of in-between houses and just staying with friends and that,' James replied, forcing an embarrassed giggle.

'Okay, sorry to go on,' Knight replied, 'but maybe just give me the address of the last place you were then. As I say it's just for the record. Have you got your driving licence handy? I can just copy that.'

'Emm…no. No, I don't sorry, but let me write it down for you,' James replied, deciding it would be safe enough to give her the address of the friend's flat he had been planning to stay in for the fortnight of his mission of revenge. Now that he was staying with Miss Hardy, he wasn't going to be there anyway.

James Gray watched DS Knight walk down the path and turn along the street, before closing the door and returning to the conservatory to where he found Miss Hardy sitting with a big grin on her face.

'Ooh, that was fun,' she said. 'How did I do? I think I make a very convincing old dear!' she added, before bursting into laughter.

James couldn't stop himself joining in and they both laughed until it began to hurt, and they had to stop.

'You are a wicked woman!' James said, still smiling at what had just happened.

'Well, when you get to my age, you have to take any opportunity you can to have a bit of fun,' Miss Hardy replied. 'We didn't do anything wrong really. Just a bit of mischief. They'll find out the truth soon enough, when we're ready to tell them.'

'Yes, they don't seem to have got very far in identifying me,' James replied. 'They seem to know it's school related in some way, but they haven't nailed it down to what exactly. They don't know about the bullying and Nigel Harrison obviously hasn't said anything. I think we're pretty safe for now.'

As Detective Sergeant Knight walked back to her car, she felt a touch sad. Sad for Miss Hardy who had been a very intelligent woman and who, now, was beginning to succumb to the ravages of old age. It was slowly eating away at her once sharp memory, changing her irreversibly for however long she had left to live. As she opened her car door, she heard a voice calling out.

'Excuse me.'

Knight turned around and saw an elderly woman walking towards her.

'Are you from the police?' the woman asked and continued without waiting for a reply. 'I'm Mrs Branson. I spoke to one of your colleagues. About Miss Hardy. And that young man who seems to be there with her now.'

Joan Branson had now reached DS Knight and stopped directly in front of her, breathing heavily, her face flushed. She leaned against DS Knight's car.

'Yes, I'm with the police.' DS Knight replied. 'How can I help you Mrs Branson?'

'I saw you coming out of Miss Hardy's house just then. Is she okay?' Joan asked the detective.

'Yes, she's fine,' Knight replied. 'I used to have her as a teacher so it's sad to see how she is now, but she seems happy enough.'

'What do you mean, sad?' Joan replied.

'Well, just with her, you know. Her memory not being so good. I assume it's some sort of dementia or something,' Knight replied.

'Dementia?' Joan exclaimed, a confused look on her face. 'Irene doesn't have dementia.

She's as bright as a button. She still does the crossword in the paper every day.'

'Oh, right,' Knight replied, slightly taken aback by this turn of events. She'd just been with Miss Hardy and her ex-teacher had definitely been in a confused state. Maybe this Joan Branson had it wrong. Maybe she was confused too?

'And did you find out who that man is that's in her house now? She's never mentioned having a nephew before and he's not letting me talk to her. I'm worried for her safety,' Joan replied.

'Don't worry Mrs Branson,' DS Knight replied. 'Miss Hardy's fine. She's just been a bit sick lately. I'm sure you'll see her again soon.'

With that DS Knight got into her car and the old woman turned and walked back to her own house. She had made Knight think though, and the detective sat in her car for a few minutes, going over everything that had just happened. She picked up her mobile and dialled a number.

'Hello DC Morgan?' she said as the phone was answered. 'Can you do me a favour. Can you check out a James Hardy for me please? He's the nephew of Miss Irene Hardy, the teacher in the class photo. See what you can find out about him please.'

'Yes, Guv, will do,' Morgan replied, and DS Knight ended the call and started up her car. She looked at her watch and smiled. She was going out for dinner tonight and she was really looking forward to it.

Chapter 34

Detective Sergeant Knight had never been in the French Room restaurant before. She'd heard about it. She'd been told that it was good. But she'd also heard it was expensive and so she'd been waiting for a special occasion as an excuse to go there. That hadn't happened yet.

When Dr Collins had called her and asked if she wanted to meet at the French Room for dinner and a catch up on the case, she thought, why not? It would kill two birds with one stone, so to speak. She would see what the restaurant was really like, as well as finding out a little bit more about Dr Collins.

Knight had been impressed by the psychologist when they had met at the police station. Surprisingly so. Ordinarily she didn't have much time for that sort of thing in her policework. She thought psychology was all a bit too airy fairy, not real, factual stuff, but Strong had told her that Collins was different. She was very practical and had been a great help to him in a previous case.

'Give her a shot, you'll see,' he'd said.

And, of course, he had been right. Knight had found Dr Collins to be thorough and clever, and she had provided some good input to their investigation. And apart from that she was really likeable. Knight was also pleased that a young, attractive woman like Collins was making a good name for herself, a good career, and it was wholly due to her expertise and confidence, not her looks. Knight knew what it had been like for her trying to make a career for herself in the police force, and she imagined Dr Collins would have had a similar struggle in her field of work. Maybe she would find out more over dinner and a couple of glasses of wine tonight.

DS Knight arrived at the restaurant a few minutes ahead of their agreed time and, rather than sit on her own at the table, she decided to have a drink at the bar.

'What can I get you, madam?' the barman asked her in a sexy sounding, French accent. Knight wondered if it was real or just put on for the setting.

'Oh, can I have a gin and tonic please,' she replied, smiling at the waiter. Regardless of whether his accent was real or not, he was still very good looking.

Knight sat on a barstool and waited. The barman placed her drink in front of her and smiled at the detective.

'There you are madam,' he said in that French accent again. 'Are you dining with us tonight, perhaps you are waiting for someone?' he asked DS Knight.

'Yes, I'm waiting for a friend, a colleague,' Knight replied, 'Miss Collins,' she added as the barman watched her. He was very handsome, and that accent…

'Ah, Miss Collins, of course. I know her well. A beautiful lady, if I may say so,' the barman replied, a wide smile on his face as he thought about DS Knight's dining partner. 'Miss Collins comes here often,' the barman explained. 'She is one of our best customers and a very kind lady.'

Wow, DS Knight thought. Maybe she should have gone down the psychology route rather than becoming a detective. If Dr Collins could eat here regularly then she must be doing well. Better than Knight anyhow. With her mortgage payments, coming to this restaurant was only ever going to be a once a year type event, if she was lucky. Perhaps she could find a reason to meet Dr Collins more regularly!

As she mulled that thought over in her mind, Dr Collins walked through the restaurant door and was warmly greeted by two of the restaurant staff at the entrance. There were lots of smiles, hugs and kisses on the cheeks, before they let her go.

One of the restaurant staff said something to Dr Collins and they both looked across to DS Knight sitting at the bar. Dr Collins gave her a friendly wave and smile and DS Knight did the same back, although slightly awkwardly, conscious she couldn't match the psychologist's natural beauty.

Dr Collins was wearing a yellow and white summery dress which stopped just above the knee. It was perfectly tailored to show off her slim waist and long legs. DS Knight watched her as she approached and saw a few of the men sitting at their dining tables, turning their heads as she walked across to the bar. A number of the women did the same.

'Detective Sergeant Knight,' Collins said. 'I'm so glad you could make it,' and she leaned forward to give Knight a friendly hug and a peck on the cheek.

'Have you been here before?' Collins asked. 'It's my favourite place, I have to admit,' and she smiled at the barman as he placed a drink in front of her. 'Merci, Jacques,' she said, before turning back to face DS Knight.

'Well thank you for inviting me,' Knight replied. 'No, this is my first time here and please call me Laura. We're off duty tonight,' she added, smiling.

Dr Collins raised herself up onto the bar stool next to DS Knight, her knee brushing lightly against Knight's leg and her dress riding up a little as she made herself comfortable on the stool.

'Well cheers Laura,' Dr Collins replied. 'I'm Sam,' and she clinked her glass against DS Knight's.

The two women chatted for a while, ordering a second drink while they waited for their table to be made ready. Knight learned that Dr Collins had gone to University in Manchester before moving back down south to London and joining a Psychology practice. Her specific interest in criminal psychology had led her to being asked to do some work for the police a few years ago and more recently she'd worked with Detective Inspector Strong on one of his major cases, tracking down the man the press had dubbed as The

Anniversary Killer. Strong had asked her advice on a couple of occasions since that case, but this latest one, the Stephen Jones death, had been the first major investigation since that original case.

The waiter led them to their table, which was set in the far corner of the restaurant, almost hidden away in a little alcove of its own. Dr Collins explained that she'd asked for this table specifically so they could have a private conversation without the worry of being overheard. The two women studied the menus and a few minutes later the waiter returned and took their order. DS Knight hadn't understood most of the menu, so she had just picked the items which had some words in there that she recognised and hoped that the rest of the, unknown, ingredients were something that she also liked. For her starter she had chosen a ravioli fish dish, on the basis that she recognised the word ravioli along with some of the types of fish listed alongside it on the menu. Luckily it turned out to be delicious, although she was surprised that there were only three pieces of ravioli on the plate. She'd expected more than that. Still, it was only a starter, she thought.

'So, what do you think then Sam?' Knight asked as they sat at their table, starters finished and a half drunk bottle of wine sitting in front of them.

'About the case I mean,' Knight added. 'Do you think Bradley Smith is our man?' she asked, taking a sip of her wine and watching the police psychologist over the rim of her glass.

Dr Collins smiled at DS Knight and took a sip of her own wine before answering her.

'Well Laura, I sense that's a bit of a loaded question, isn't it?' she responded. 'I'd say the person asking that question doesn't believe that Bradley Smith is a guilty man. Am I correct?' Dr Collins smiled at Knight and took another sip of her wine as she waited for the detective to reply.

'Ah, you're playing the psychologist, are you?' Knight laughed. 'But I'm interested in what you think Dr Collins. What's your professional opinion?' Knight asked, more formally, but still smiling back at Dr Collins before taking another drink of her wine.

Dr Collins laughed. 'Okay I'll go first then, shall I? I don't think at this point there is enough evidence to say that Bradley Smith is the man you are after. Don't get me wrong, it could be him, but equally it could be someone else. I get it that DI Strong would like to make a quick conviction and close the case but, from my viewpoint, I couldn't honestly say that Bradley Smith is the guilty man.'

'Mmm…and getting down off the fence Sam. In your opinion, did Bradley Smith do it? Yes or No?' Knight responding, now with an even bigger smile on her face. She was enjoying this little game.

'Wow, you're a tough detective Laura,' Dr Collins replied, laughing. 'Okay, I give in. No, I don't think he did it. There you've got me. Banged to rights! But I do understand the pressure on DI Strong, and of course yourself too, to close the case.'

'Yes, we certainly do get that. But that's part of the job,' Knight replied. 'I have to admit though, just between you and me, DI Strong does sometimes, emm…you know, push things a bit. He sometimes cuts a corner or two to speed things up and get the right result. It's just his way.'

DS Knight stopped talking and took another drink of her wine, suddenly conscious that she was talking, maybe a bit too freely, about her boss to Dr Collins. Now that she had established, what she had already thought, that Dr Collins didn't think Bradley Smith was the man they wanted, maybe now it was time to move the conversation on to something else. Something away from DI Strong and police work. But before she could change the subject, it appeared Dr Collins wasn't yet ready to do that.

'Do you like working for DI Strong?' she asked DS Knight. 'The two of you seem to make a good partnership.'

'Yes, I do,' Knight replied, nodding her head. 'He's helped me a lot in my career. Mentored me, I guess. The police force is still a bit of a big boys club really, and so it's not so easy for a woman to make it. We have to work bloody hard. Men like DI Strong are few and far between in the police, so I've been lucky to have got him as a boss.'

'Yes, I can see that,' Dr Collins replied. 'He seems a genuinely nice guy and I appreciate what he's done for me too. There's a lot of police officers who still think that what I do is a pile of crap,' Collins laughed. 'You and DI Strong are different though Laura, you both see what I can bring to the game, and I love working with the two of you.'

'Well, I have to admit Sam, I was probably one of those other officers before DI Strong persuaded me to bring you in!' DS Knight replied laughing across the table. 'But I'm a convert now. You've definitely helped us on this case and it's a pleasure working with you too.'

'Well thank you Laura,' Dr Collins said, reaching across the table and squeezing the detective's hand, before suddenly pulling it away as she realised a waiter had appeared at the table.

'I'm sorry,' the waiter said. 'I didn't mean to intrude. I was just checking to see if you two ladies wanted another bottle of wine. I see that this one is almost finished,' he said, lifting up the bottle and pouring the remaining wine into the two glasses.

'Yes, why not?' DS Knight replied, smiling at Dr Collins and then at the waiter.

'Okay. A beautiful wine for a beautiful couple, it is,' he said, before turning and walking away. The two women looked across the table at each other and laughed.

'So, going back to DI Strong,' Dr Collins said, smiling at DS Knight. 'Have you ever…, you know…he's a good-looking man,' the Doctor laughed.

'What! No, of course not,' DS Knight replied with an exaggerated look of open-mouthed shock on her face. 'He's my boss and he's old enough to be my dad! No way!' Knight laughed. 'Oh no, that just wouldn't be right!' she added before taking another drink of her wine.

'Well, I had to ask. Some women like older, handsome men with a bit of power and DI Strong certainly has all of that,' Dr Collins replied.

'Yeh that's true. We did hug awkwardly once at the end of a case, after a few drinks. Probably a few too many. But that's not my type, maybe it should be though. I haven't exactly got a great track record on relationships,' Knight replied, laughing.

'So do you have a boyfriend, Laura?' Collins asked, having noted that Knight didn't wear an engagement or wedding ring. ' A young attractive woman like you, I bet a lot of your fellow police officers have tried to chat you up, haven't they?'

DS Knight's thoughts immediately jumped to DI Murphy. It was still raw in her mind and although he had been the worst, he hadn't been the only one to try it on with Laura during her time with the police. Most of it was innuendo and she'd grown used to that, but in the early days especially, there had also been a lot of touching. Thankfully that seemed to have stopped now, maybe because she was older and at a more senior level, or maybe things really were changing with regard to how the men treated their female colleagues. It had certainly seemed that way to Knight until she'd encountered DI Murphy at the police conference.

Dr Collins realised that Knight had hesitated at her question.

'Sorry, I'm being a bit presumptuous and personal, forgive me. Of course, I should have thought. Men may not be your preference,' Collins said, smiling at Knight. 'I'm sorry I didn't think.'

'No, no it's okay. It's fine,' Knight replied, shaking her head and smiling back at the doctor. 'I do like men, but there's no-one special at the moment. I'm just a sad lonely girl. It's actually quite difficult with the job, the odd hours, that sort of thing. It's hard to find anyone who can understand that and put up with it. I can see why many police officers end up getting together, but I'm not sure I'd want to live with another police officer. I think it would be too much. That's my excuse anyway.'

'I know, I get it, and also most men don't understand a career girl do they? Someone that wants to be successful and doesn't just want to get married and have babies,' Dr Collins replied, shaking her head.

'Exactly, you're completely right,' Knight replied. 'Maybe us women should all stick together and just forget about men. Maybe there's something in that,' Knight replied, laughing and Dr Collins laughed along with her.

'Have you got anyone Sam?' Knight asked the psychologist, suddenly realising that she didn't know much about her personal life.

'Yes. I've got Chris at home,' Dr Collins replied. 'We've been together for about four years now,' she said, smiling at the thought.

'Oh right,' Knight replied, forcing a smile. She wasn't sure why, but she suddenly felt a little deflated and was worried Dr Collins would notice.

'Ooh, I love this music,' Knight said as a song played across the restaurant, and she felt the need to change the subject.

'Yes, me too. Its Adele, isn't it?' Dr Collins replied. 'I love her songs. I often listen to her albums when I'm at home alone, curled up on the sofa with a glass of wine.'

'That's exactly what I do!' Knight exclaimed, clamping her hand over her mouth as she realised it had come out louder than she had intended. 'Excuse me a second, I'm just going to nip to the loo,' Knight said as she got up from her chair and made her way across the restaurant floor, towards the ladies toilet.

The female toilet was just as she had expected it to be in such a classy restaurant. It was spotlessly clean and smelled of fresh summer flowers. Knight stood at the washbasin, washing her hands and looking at herself in the mirror. She couldn't stop smiling. Maybe it was partly due to the wine, but it was also because she was having such a good night. She hadn't laughed so much in ages. She was getting on so well with Dr Collins, Sam, she almost couldn't believe it. It was like they were old friends who had known each other for years. Prior to this evening, she'd admired the psychologist professionally, but she hadn't really known anything about her as a person. Now that they'd spent a bit of time together, outside of work, it also seemed that they had a lot in common. Knight moved her hair back behind her ears, brushed her skirt down and returned to the table.

'All okay?' Dr Collins asked her with a smile as Knight sat down at the table again.

'Yes, good,' Knight replied. 'The toilets are immaculate,' she said giggling.

'I know,' Dr Collins replied. 'I hate a dirty toilet,' and the two women broke into another spell of laughter.

The waiter arrived with their main courses and the conversation quietened somewhat as the two women became engrossed in their food. Once again, DS Knight had chosen one of the meals where she recognised at least some of the ingredients on the menu. The waiter gave it the big announcement as he put the dish down in front of her.

'One roast duck magret with choux farci of confit leg, heritage carrot cooked in liquorice butter, creamed savoy, and a red wine sauce.'

Duck and carrot and a red wine sauce. Knight had latched on to those, the rest was a bit of a blur.

'Oh my God, try this Laura,' Dr Collins suddenly said, holding out her fork with a piece of fish attached to it.

DS Knight leaned forward and ate the piece of fish from Dr Collins's fork, savouring the flavour as it hit the back of her mouth.

'Oh, wow. That is so delicious Sam. I wish I'd ordered that now,' Knight said. 'Here, try a piece of my duck.'

She stabbed a piece of meat with her own fork and held it out for Dr Collins to eat.

'Mmm, that is delicious too,' Collins replied. 'I honestly don't think I've ever had a bad meal in here though. Everything is so yummy,' she said, 'and they always seem to have different things on the menu every time I come here.'

'Is it just me or has it got darker in here?' Knight asked Dr Collins with a puzzled frown on her face.

'Yes, I think they've put the lights down. They're on the romantic setting now,' Collins replied laughing. 'This is obviously the place to come to impress your date.'

The two women finished off their dinners and spent the rest of the evening sharing stories about their lives, and giggling. Lots of giggling. At the end of the meal, Dr Collins insisted on paying the bill.

'Don't worry, I've got an account here. They'll just stick it on that,' she said. 'It's easier that way.'

DS Knight had tried to argue, but on her current salary as a Detective Sergeant, she was partly relieved that she wasn't having to pay for the dinner, and so she didn't push it too much. She told Dr Collins that the next time she would get it. She didn't say it might have to be a Nandos though, on her salary.

DS Knight felt the cool night air hit her face as she stepped outside the restaurant, and she shivered just as Dr Collins joined her on the pavement.

'Well thanks for a lovely evening, Laura, I really enjoyed spending time with you,' Dr Collins said, and she stepped forward and hugged the detective warmly. 'Ooh, are you cold?' she said closely into DS Knights ear as she could feel the detective shivering in her arms.

‘A bit,’ DS Knight replied softly, while enjoying the warmth of the police psychologist’s embrace.

‘We must do this again sometime. Soon.’ Dr Collins said, and she slowly undid her arms and kissed DS Knight on the cheek, before giving her another quick, final hug.

‘Yes, I’d like that,’ DS Knight said smiling at Dr Collins, still shivering, but at the same time feeling much warmer. It had been a great night.

In the taxi on her way home, DS Knight messaged Dr Collins to thank her again for dinner and telling her next time she would get the bill. After a few moments thought, she added a smiley face and a kiss to the end of her text and then hit send. A few minutes later she got a reply from the Doctor, saying how much she had enjoyed it too and that she was looking forward to the next time. Knight was pleased to see that the psychologist’s message also ended with a kiss.

Dr Collins opened the front door and entered her house. She hung her coat up on the bottom stair banister and walked into the living room. Her partner, Chris, smiled at her as she entered the room. Chris was sitting on the sofa, wrapped overall in a large white bath robe.

‘Hello darling, did you have a good evening at the French Room? Who were you with?’ Chris asked.

‘Oh, just a detective from the police. We were catching up on a case we’re both working on,’ Dr Collins replied.

‘Oh right, was he nice?’ Chris asked her.

‘Well, it was a “she” actually,’ Dr Collins replied, smiling at her partner. ‘A detective sergeant Knight, from the Serious Crime team.’

‘Oh. I hope you didn’t tease her too much. I know what you’re like,’ Chris replied grinning at Dr Collins.

‘Ha-ha, well maybe just a little bit,’ Dr Collins replied laughing. ‘She was nice though, I liked her, it was a fun evening.’

‘Was she as nice as me though?’ Chris replied, smiling, before standing up and letting the bath robe fall to the floor.

Dr Collins smiled and stepped forward, cupping Chris’s naked breasts in her hands, before leaning down and kissing her passionately on the lips.

Chapter 35

Flicking through the file again, DS Knight stopped at a document which had obviously come from the school. She hadn't seen it before. Someone in the team must have just filed it recently without saying anything. Or maybe she'd just missed it. It was on Danesborough High School headed paper, and Knight realised it was a list the school had provided of all of the pupils in Miss Hardy's class that year. The year the class photo had been taken. She glanced through the names, recognising some of them personally and others from the statements she'd read. Most of them had been interviewed in person, although two had moved away, and so they'd been contacted over the phone to give their statements. But none of them had provided much of interest. So far.

DS Knight knew that there was no magic solution in crime investigation. More often than not it involved going over and over the same documentation or photos or videos, time and time again, until something stood out. Something that didn't look quite right. It could be a simple thing like two slightly contradictory statements, or a person appearing in a CCTV film for a few seconds that they hadn't spotted before. Hard, basic police work. That was often the thing that cracked a case and that was why she was looking through the case file once again. To find the one thing that they'd missed.

DS Knight picked out a copy of the class photo and laid it on her desk, alongside the school class list. She then took all the individual statements and put them in a pile beside the other two documents. Slowly, she checked through the statements, ticking off each one against both the school photo and the class list as she finished reading them. Twenty minutes later, Knight reached the final statement and cross referenced it against the other two documents, sitting back in her chair as she finished. She looked carefully at the photo and confirmed that there was a small tick against the head of every pupil. They'd contacted, and spoken with, each and every one of the pupils and staff in the class photo. She then picked up the Danesborough High School class list and looked down the list of names, checking that there was a tick against each one of them. That was when she noticed there was one without a tick. There was nothing against a boy called James Gray.

She picked up the statements again and flicked through them, one by one, looking for the one which referenced James Gray, but she couldn't find it. She checked once again, but it still wasn't there.

Suddenly she had a thought, and she counted the names on the school list. There were thirty. She then picked up the class photo again and counted the heads of all the pupils. There were twenty nine. James Gray was missing. He had been in Miss Hardy's class, but for whatever reason, he wasn't in the class photo. The one they'd all been working from. Knight slammed her hand down on the desk. Why had no-one thought of that, why hadn't she thought of that? Of course there could have been someone missing from the class photo. Kids were off school all the time.

Oh shit, Knight thought. Maybe it didn't mean anything, but she knew that they had to find this James Gray. Her mind was racing, and she pulled out the statement they had from Jenny Broughton and typed her ex-schoolmates' number into her phone. After a few rings, Jenny answered.

'Jenny, Hi, it's Laura Knight here. Have you got a minute?' DS Knight asked her old schoolfriend.

'Oh, hi Laura, yes sure, I'm just doing some baking, but how can I help you?' Jenny replied.

'Well, you know when we last spoke, you were trying to remember the name of a boy at the school, but you couldn't?' DS Knight asked her. 'You thought Stephen Jones might have done something to him,' Knight added.

'Yes, but I'm sorry. I've been racking my brains and I still can't remember his name,' Jenny replied. 'I don't think he was at our school for long, but it's very annoying!' Jenny said, laughing at her own frustration as she spoke.

'Okay. Well, I'm going to say a name now and I want you to tell me if you remember him. He was in the same class, but he's not in the class photo, which is why we missed him. Maybe he was off sick or something,' Knight replied.

'Okay, what was his name?' Jenny asked, suddenly feeling excited but nervous at the same time.

'James Gray,' Knight said slowly, making sure she pronounced it properly, not leaving any room for error.

'That's it!' Jenny immediately exclaimed. 'James Gray, that was his name. Oh, Laura, I'm glad we finally got it! I've been so frustrated trying to think of it. I think he left the school at some point, maybe his family moved away or something, I can't remember. Oh, I do hope that helps you.'

DS Knight ended the call and then immediately made another call to Detective Constable Morgan. She explained what had happened, how they had missed one of the pupils.

'I need you to find out everything you can about James Gray. Where he lives, where he works, everything you can get. And a recent photo, if possible, too,' Knight said to her colleague. 'Ring me back as soon as you have anything.'

A few minutes later, DS Knight's phone rang and, seeing it was DC Morgan, she answered it immediately.

'Yes,' she said, 'that was quick.'

'Yes, sorry Guv,' Morgan replied. 'I meant to say when we were on before, but I forgot. I've been looking for Miss Hardy's nephew, James Hardy, like you asked me to, but strangely I haven't been able to find him. He doesn't appear on any of the usual PNC systems. To be honest I can't find any trace of him at all.'

'Okay, don't worry about him for now,' DS Knight replied. 'Just focus on finding out about James Gray. I need to find out where he is. He's the priority now.'

'Okay, will do,' Morgan replied and ended the call.

It didn't take Detective Constable Morgan long to find out the relevant details for James Gray, he was on all of the usual Government systems the police had access to, but after that everything became frustratingly slow. Morgan explained to Knight that they had his home address but that he didn't appear to be there. They'd asked his immediate neighbours and none of them had seen him for a week or so. Morgan had also established that James Gray worked as an anaesthetist at the Royal College Hospital, but when they contacted the hospital, he was told that James Gray was on two weeks annual holiday. DC Morgan had also got a mobile phone number for Gray, but he wasn't answering it and it appeared to be switched off. They were monitoring it in case he switched it back on again so that they could then trace its location, but they had had no luck so far.

'I spoke with one of his colleagues at the hospital and he told me that Gray is a nice guy, but he's a bit of a loner and has been known to go off before on his own. You know camping in the wilds somewhere with no communication. Off grid. That sort of thing,' Morgan explained. 'It's not for me, that,' he added. 'Too uncomfortable, sleeping in a tent in a field somewhere. Rain pouring down. Cow dung everywhere. Give me the sun, a swimming pool, and a nice cold beer any day.'

'Okay, keep trying,' Knight replied. 'He's certainly a person of interest, hopefully he'll turn up soon. When he does, let me know. I want to speak to him.'

Chapter 36

'Sophie, are you up yet?' Catherine called upstairs to her daughter. 'There's a package arrived here for you. I'll leave it at the bottom of the stairs,' she added before heading back into the kitchen.

Upstairs, Sophie stretched her arms and legs out across the bed, still underneath the duvet. It was a Saturday morning, she didn't need to get up yet. In fact, she didn't have much planned for today and didn't really have to get up at all, apart from when she needed to eat. She could have a PJ day. She'd done that a few times in Leeds with her flatmate Emily. Oh, they had been good times. Granted they didn't have much money, but it was amazing how much fun they could have just sitting chatting and eating directly from a box of Rice Krispies. She missed those days.

Sometimes she wished she was back there, being a student again. But now, somehow, she was back living at home with her mum and dad again. How had that happened? On top of that, she had also become one of the millions of office workers who trudged back and forwards to their workplaces, just so they could get some money into their bank accounts at the end of each month. She was in the rat race.

Sophie stretched again and yawned. What had her mum said? Something about a package. It must be something she had bought on-line, she did a lot…no, she did *all* of her shopping on-line, and there was a constant stream of packages being delivered for her. She usually knew what they were, and when they were coming, due to the regular notifications she got on her phone, but this time she couldn't think what this one could be. She wasn't expecting anything today. She looked at her phone, but no, there was nothing due.

It was bugging her now and she knew she was going to have to get up and see what it was. She briefly considered calling her mum and asking her to bring the package upstairs, but although she knew her mum would do that for her, she also knew that was pushing it a bit too far. Her mum did a lot for her already and Sophie had to be careful she didn't just take advantage of her.

Reluctantly, Sophie kicked off the duvet and swung her legs over the side of the bed. She stood up, stretched her arms above her head and sat back down on the edge of the bed again. That was her exercise for this morning. She didn't want to overdo it! Sophie had never been into exercise. Like most of her friends, she'd joined a couple of gyms over the years, but like most of her friends, she'd stopped going after a few weeks. She just didn't enjoy it and she couldn't understand people that did. Sure it would be great to have a toned, muscular body, but the effort and pain it took to get there –

well it just wasn't worth it. Luckily for Sophie, she seemed to have the kind of metabolism that meant, despite her lack of exercise, she didn't put on any weight. She'd always been slim, and even through her university years, when she'd probably drunk much more alcohol than was medically advised, she had managed to maintain the same physique.

Sophie stood up again and made her way downstairs. It was too early to get washed or dressed yet, she could do that after breakfast. She walked into the kitchen, where her mum was doing something in one of the higher cupboards. She was always doing something, Sophie's mum. She never sat still for long. There was always something to do in the house, and outside of that, she seemed to be on every local committee, or a member of every local club that existed. Sophie sat down on one of the kitchen bar stools and yawned.

'Morning darling,' her mum said, looking over her shoulder as she reached up to the kitchen cupboard. 'I'm just doing a spot of cleaning. It's amazing what you can find in some of these cupboards. Can I get you something for breakfast? Cornflakes, Weetabix, some toast?'

'Cornflakes please,' Sophie replied, not really interested in what was in the cupboards. Just kitchen stuff she assumed. They were in the kitchen after all.

Her mum placed a bowl of cornflakes and a spoon in front of her, on the kitchen island, and Sophie, suddenly feeling very hungry, started to greedily devour it.

'Cup of coffee?' her mum asked her.

'Mmm…' Sophie replied, through a mouth full of cornflakes.

'There you go,' her mum said, placing a red mug of coffee in front of her, the alluring aroma hitting Sophie's airways.

'Did you get that package?' her mum asked her.

'No,' Sophie replied, shaking her head, as she scooped up another spoonful of cornflakes. She swallowed most of them before adding,

'Where is it?'

'I left it at the bottom of the stairs for you. You must have walked straight past it! Hang on, I'll get it for you,' Sophie's mum replied, and she walked past her daughter and out of the kitchen.

She returned a minute later and put a large brown envelope on the kitchen island to the right of Sophie's, now empty, breakfast bowl. Sophie glanced at it, before taking a drink of her coffee, inhaling the aroma as she drank, feeling the warm, comforting liquid descend through her body. She put her cup down and picked up the envelope. It had a typed address label on it and Sophie guessed it was probably from someone trying to sell her something. Probably a new gym opening up or something. There seemed to be another one almost every week. She turned the envelope towards her and slipped her index finger under the flap, moving it along the top, tearing the envelope open as she did so. She reached inside the envelope and could feel some paper, which she gently pulled out. As it emerged, she began to see that the top sheet was a photograph, and by the time she had pulled it out completely she realised it was a photo of her boyfriend Keegan. Or to be more accurate, a photo of her boyfriend Keegan sitting very close to an extremely attractive woman in a short red dress. Sophie stared at the photo for a while, but she didn't recognise the woman.

She put the photo down on the worktop and looked at the next sheet. It was a photo too. Another photo of Keegan and this same, beautiful woman. But this time they seemed even closer and Sophie glanced back at the first photo to confirm that. This time the beautiful woman's hand was on Keegan's leg and her face was turned towards him and smiling. A beautiful, irresistible smile.

'What was in the envelope?' Sophie's mum asked her and she walked across to where Sophie was sitting.

'Ooh is that a photo?' she asked, looking at the photo Sophie had put down on the counter top. 'Oh, it's Keegan. Who's that he's with? That's not his sister, is it?'

'No mum, it's not his sister,' Sophie replied as she sat staring at the next photo. This one showed Keegan with his hand on the beautiful woman's leg. Why was he doing that? Just why?

She put it down on the work surface and her mum saw it, and immediately understood.

'Oh,' she said, and she moved closer to Sophie and saw the photo she was now looking at.

In this one, the final one, Keegan and the beautiful woman, the beautiful woman in the stunning red dress…they were kissing. Sophie was staring at it and her hands started shaking. Her mum put her arm around Sophie's shoulders and pulled her close to her, her cheek brushing against Sophie's hair and ear. Sophie started to cry.

'Oh, my love,' Sophie's mum said, as she pressed her mouth closer into Sophie's ear.

Chapter 37

Miss Hardy was sitting in her conservatory, staring at the class photograph, looking at all of the pupils faces, one by one. She could remember all of their names and also a little bit about most of them. What they had been like in her classroom. Some shy, some cheeky, some loud and a few, no matter what she did, just not interested in what she was saying. There was nothing wrong with Miss Hardy's mind.

Miss Hardy had always tried to make her lessons as interesting as possible and engage as many of the class as she could. She had some really good pupils, very clever, but there were always one or two who were impossibly resistant to anything she tried, and just did not want to be there.

While she was looking at the photo, James Gray came into the room holding two cups of tea. He put one down beside Miss Hardy and then sat down across the room from her, sipping his own drink. Although he'd only been there a short time, he'd settled into a nice, comfortable routine with Miss Hardy.

Miss Hardy was still going through the photo. She was feeling disappointed that they were nearing the end of their little bit of fun. That was how she saw it, a bit of fun. It had been an exciting, refreshing break from her normal daily life. She hadn't quite realised how much of a routine she'd fallen into since she had retired, until James had appeared on her doorstep, and she'd loved the excitement of it all. But now it was coming to an end and her life would soon have to go back to how it was before. Miss Hardy worried that she would find that too boring now, after all the fun of having James staying with her.

James had told her that there was only one other person that he wanted to get his revenge on for bullying him at school. He was called Danny Blake and Miss Hardy could remember him well from his schooldays. He was always getting into trouble then, getting into fights, breaking things in the classroom, all sorts of things. He had been a handful at school and from what Miss Hardy had heard, he hadn't calmed down much since he'd left. Various people she'd bumped into locally had told her that he'd been in trouble with the police a few times and that he wasn't a very nice young man. She hoped James would be able to get his revenge on him, without it going wrong. So far, he didn't have a great track record in that respect. But Danny Blake definitely deserved punishment for what he'd done. Miss Hardy looked up from the photograph.

'What about some of the girls, didn't they have a go at you, call you names and stuff like that?' Miss Hardy asked. She knew that some of the girls she had taught could be very vicious. Not with their fists, but definitely with their tongues.

'Well, some of them did,' James replied. 'But it wasn't that bad. I got used to it really and, to be honest, a lot of people had nicknames at school. No, I think after I've seen Danny Blake that will be enough. Him, Nigel and Stephen were the worst, and I can't go round the whole class - that would be too much!' James said, laughing. 'I think from the outset, when I decided I was going to do this, it was going to be those three and so I'm going to stick to that. After that, whatever happens, happens.'

'What about Debbie Craig though? She was a right bitch as I remember?' Miss Hardy said with a mischievous smile.

'Oh, Miss Hardy, stop it will you please,' James replied, laughing at his old teacher.

Miss Hardy took the hint and put the photo down on the table by her chair. She looked at the young man sitting across the room from her with a feeling of genuine affection. She'd loved having him stay with her, but she knew it was inevitably coming to an end.

'Are you ready for Danny Blake?' she asked him, with a serious look on her face. She knew this was going to be his toughest challenge yet.

'Yes, I think so,' James replied, a touch nervously.

James went on to explain to Miss Hardy what he planned to do. He'd found out that Danny Blake worked as a doorman at a nightclub in town. It was called Club Extream and Danny started his shift at eight pm. The club was generally quiet at that time of the evening, with most of the young people not arriving until a couple of hours later. As well as there being less people around, it also meant that Danny Blake would be on the door on his own at that time of the evening. James had decided that would be the best time to carry out his act of revenge.

'When are you going to do it?' Miss Hardy asked.

'Tonight,' James replied. 'It's time to get this finished,' he added in a determined voice.

Miss Hardy nodded in agreement, it would soon all be over for James, but she'd already started thinking about what she had to do now to make sure that he got the outcome he deserved. As she'd said to him already, she'd let him down once before and she wasn't going to let him down this time.

James walked past the black painted doors to Club Extream. He looked at his watch, it was seven forty and the club wasn't open yet. He'd decided to come early so he could have a look around and get his bearings, as well as planning his escape route. There was an alleyway which ran down the side of the club building, and the other end of it led out onto a busy main road where he would be able to flag down a taxi if he needed to. James was confident that he would be able to outrun Danny Blake if it came to that. Although Danny was built to fight, he didn't look like he would be able to run that quickly. He looked too solid.

James went into a café across the street and ordered a black Americano before sitting down at a window table, with a clear view over to the club doors.

Ten minutes later, one of the doors slowly opened and a man dressed in a black suit, and a long dark grey overcoat, stepped out onto the pavement. He stood with his back to the door and looked up and down the street. As his head turned in the direction of the Cafe, James recognised that it was Danny Blake. James took one last drink of his coffee and made for the door. It was now or never. Let's get it done.

He walked quickly along the street, crossing the road just before he came level with the club, and marching the final few steps to end up standing in front of Danny Blake.

'We're not open yet mate. Come back later,' Danny said eyeing him up and down before a look of realisation crossed his face.

'Pigface. Its fucking Pigface innit? It's you. Fuck me that takes me back,' Danny said, and he began to laugh loudly. 'It must be, what....'

'What the fuck is that?' James suddenly shouted loudly at Danny, and he briefly noticed that the doorman had stopped laughing and a frown was spreading across his face.

It was only brief though, because a second later James's fist slammed into Danny's face.

'Shit!' James shouted out as the pain hit his hand.

He felt like he'd broken it, but he came to his senses quickly and turned and ran down the alley. He thought he could hear someone shout out behind him, but he didn't dare turn around. The adrenalin was pumping through his veins, and he quickly reached the far end of the alley. As he emerged out onto the street, he saw a bus just starting to pull away from the bus stop a few metres away. He sprinted towards it and banged on the door with his open hand, causing him to wince again in pain. The bus stopped and the doors sprang open. James jumped on and took the first empty seat he could find, breathing heavily, his hand aching, but also feeling a sense of exhilaration. All the other passengers were looking at him, but no-one spoke. James didn't care. He'd done it. He'd finally done it. It was over.

Danny Blake was furious. He could still feel his nose blocked up with dried blood and it was throbbing. It was probably broken, but that didn't bother Danny so much. It had been broken a few times before and it always set again pretty quickly. It was the fact that Pigface had hit him and run away, that was what angered him most. That, and the fact that the policeman behind the counter was laughing at him.

'C'mon Danny,' the policeman said. 'You don't expect me to take you seriously, do you? How many fights have you been in? Must be hundreds.'

'Yeh, I know,' growled Danny. 'And every time you guys have been quick enough to arrest me and throw me into a cell. So how about you do the same now, when the boot's on the other foot?'

The policeman laughed again which made Danny even more angry. Surely he had the right to be treated like anyone else. Someone had attacked him, for no reason, he hadn't even seemed drunk. He'd just hit him and run away. The police should be out there trying to find him. Danny felt a rush of cold air and he turned around to see DI Strong walking into the police station.

'Mr Strong,' Danny said. 'Thank God you've turned up. This clown here isn't taking me seriously,' he nodded towards the policeman on reception who was still laughing. 'I've been assaulted. Some bloke, Pigface, came up and just punched me and ran away. For no reason. He should be arrested. I would have been if it had been me, Mr Strong, you know that.'

'Pigface?' DI Strong replied, with a puzzled look on his face.

'Yeh, he's somebody I went to school with. I hadn't seen him for a long time, and he just turns up at the club and lamps me. For no bloody reason. I think he broke my nose. I want him charged with GBH,' Danny insisted to the detective.

'Okay, calm down Danny,' DI Strong replied. 'Come on, come through here with me and you can tell me all about it,' he said as he opened the door to the right of the police reception desk and led Danny Blake along the corridor to the interview rooms.

DI Strong knew Danny Blake very well. He had encountered him numerous times over the years, and he'd even arrested him two or three times. Always for fighting or breach of the peace. Danny, it seemed, was one of those people who was never going to learn. He was destined to go through life, continually getting into trouble until one day he got seriously injured himself, or he encountered a tough judge who ran out of patience and gave him a long jail sentence. On the whole though, Strong knew that Danny Blake was relatively harmless. He wouldn't attack anyone for no reason, and he would never use a weapon. Danny was strictly a fists only fighter. Well, fists and feet. And maybe an elbow or a headbutt. But definitely no weapons. Just body parts.

Strong listened to Danny's story of what had happened, appearing to take some notes, but not really. He was going through the motions, letting Danny get it off his chest. If someone had punched Danny Blake, he probably deserved it. Danny told the detective that if he ever came across the guy again, he'd make him pay for what he'd done. Strong advised him it was probably best he didn't do that, or he'd just end up inside again. After a while, Danny finally ran out of things to say, and seemed to calm down again.

'Okay, well thanks for coming in Danny. I'm sorry to hear about what happened and we'll let you know if there's any news,' Strong said as he led him back down the corridor.

'Funnily enough I was just speaking with another of your old schoolmates, Bradley Smith,' Strong continued. 'He's the manager at the Co-op supermarket in town now. Do you remember him?'

'Nah, not really,' Danny replied as he walked through the door back into reception, leaving DI Strong standing in the corridor.

As he left the police station, Danny's mind was working furiously, and his rage was rising again. Bradley Smith. That was Pigface's name, wasn't it? Well, if the police weren't going to do anything about him that was fine, but he certainly would. No-one was going to hit Danny Blake and get away with it.

That was a definite.

Chapter 38

'Hi, is that Laura…Knight, sorry I mean Detective Knight?' the voice on the phone tentatively enquired.

'Yes, this is Detective Sergeant Knight,' came the reply. 'Who is this?'

'Oh, it's emm…it's Jenny Broughton,' the caller replied.

'Oh, hi Jenny. Sorry I didn't recognise your voice then. I suppose with me being in work mode, it was kind of out of context,' DS Knight laughed.

'Yes, that's okay, I understand,' Jenny replied. 'How's it going with the Stephen Jones…emm…case? Have you…emm…managed to solve it or anything yet?'

'We're working on it,' Knight replied. 'We're making some good progress.'

'Oh, that's good. That's good,' Jenny replied. The line went quiet.

'So, what can I do for you Jenny?' DS Knight asked.

'Oh yes, sorry, well, you know you asked me to give you a call if I remembered anything else after we remembered that boy's name, James Gray?' Jenny replied.

'Yes, that was good, thanks for that,' Knight replied.

'Well, I've remembered what they did to him. Or at least what the rumour was,' Jenny said. 'What everyone said happened, but you know what it was like at school, people making up all sorts of things. But this one seemed to be…you know…people said it definitely happened, so it could be right.'

'What was it, Jenny? What happened?' DS Knight asked her old school friend, hoping to bring her more quickly to the point. But she knew from experience with witnesses that sometimes you just had to sit and listen until they got there in their own time.

'Well, the rumour was, what people said, was that someone flushed his head down the toilet,' Jenny replied.

DS Knight immediately sat forward in her seat, holding the phone more tightly to her ear.

'And can you remember who did it, Jenny,' she asked, but she felt she already knew the answer.

'Well, nothing was ever proven as far as I know,' Jenny replied. 'But everyone seemed to believe that it was Stephen Jones and his mates who were responsible for it.'

Chapter 39

'Can you tell me where I can get some fresh ginger, please?' Miss Hardy asked the young shop assistant who was crouched down, filling up the bottom shelf with small jars of assorted spices. 'I'm making a Caribbean casserole and I thought I had some ginger at home, but I couldn't find it anywhere.'

The shop assistant stood up, smoothed down her blue uniform, and led Miss Hardy to the top of the aisle, pointing out where the fresh ginger was to be found.

'Ah thank you,' Miss Hardy said, smiling, and the shop assistant returned to her previous duties.

Irene Hardy stood for a minute, pretending she was looking at the different pieces of ginger on display, but in truth she wasn't planning to buy any. She did have a two-pint bottle of semi-skimmed milk, and a small box of tea-bags in her trolley, but she wasn't really here to shop. She was hoping to "bump into" someone. Someone who she hoped would give her the little bit of information she was keen to get.

As she picked up another piece of ginger, seemingly weighing it in her hand, feeling how soft or firm it was, she finally saw the person she was waiting for, walking down the aisle towards her. It was Doctor Cathy Elton, who, Miss Hardy knew, was a police forensic pathologist.

'Cathy, how are you? How's Eloise?' Miss Hardy asked, as the woman drew level with her.

'Oh, hello Irene. I'm good,' Cathy replied. 'Eloise is doing well too. She's at University in Bristol, doing a law degree. She seems to be enjoying it. We went down to see her last weekend and took her out to lunch. It gave her a break from eating student meals!'

'Oh, that's good,' Miss Hardy replied. 'She was always a good pupil when I taught her. Always well behaved and keen to learn. How about you? Is the job still keeping you busy.'

'Yes, it is. I still enjoy it though. I know it can sound a bit gruesome to an outsider, but I get some satisfaction out of it, finding out what happened, why someone died, you know?' Cathy replied, hoping Irene Hardy understood, at least a little bit.

'Yes, I get that. Actually, I heard that another of my ex-pupils, Stephen Jones, had been found dead in unexplained circumstances. Did he pass through your laboratory?' Miss Hardy asked Dr Elton.

'Yes, he did. That was sad. He was still quite young. Early thirties I think,' Dr Elton replied. 'But he had a heart problem. He was on various medications for it, but it seems it just packed up. Sadly, he had a fatal heart attack. Sometimes these things just happen.'

'Oh, I see,' Miss Hardy replied. 'That's sad. You never expect it to happen at that age. So young,' Miss Hardy frowned. 'Do you still see Mo Strong at all? I think he's pretty high up in the police now.'

'Yes, he heads up the Serious Crime team now,' Dr Elton replied. 'Funnily enough I did see him regarding Stephen Jones, with it being an unexplained death. I think he was looking at it with one of his team, a young detective, Detective Sergeant Knight.'

Miss Hardy carried on the conversation with Dr Elton for a few minutes longer, but she'd already got everything she needed in this supermarket. She looked at her watch and made an excuse that she had to go, saying she was meeting a friend for coffee.

'It was lovely to see you again Cathy. Give my love to Eloise when you next see her,' Miss Hardy said, and she turned away and walked towards the checkout tills.

Chapter 40

Detective Sergeant Knight had updated DI Strong on what she had found out about James Gray. Strong agreed that they needed to find him, and that should now be their number one priority.

'It was definitely worth investigating Bradley Smith though,' Strong said. 'There was something not quite right about him, and although Dr Collins said that he fitted the profile of the man we were after, I have to say, I still wasn't wholly convinced. I think he was just an oddball, like you said at the start, but sometimes you need to just make sure. I'm pissed off with Smith, that he wasted so much of our time like that, but I'm sure he'll get his comeuppance at some point. I'm afraid Dr Collins maybe didn't quite get it right this time, but I guess we can't always expect her to be correct.'

DS Knight felt that was a bit of a harsh assessment of Dr Collins. From what she had witnessed, DI Strong had been the one that had pushed the idea that Bradley Smith was the main suspect, but she didn't want to contradict her boss.

She asked DI Strong if they should get Dr Collins back in to assess what they now had on

James Gray, to get her opinion on him. But Strong didn't think they needed to.

'Now that we have identified James Gray as the main suspect, we don't really need any psychological profiling. We've gone beyond that point now,' Strong concluded.

Knight agreed with his logic, but she couldn't help but feel disappointed that they wouldn't be meeting with Dr Collins again. She hadn't seen the psychologist since their dinner meeting at the French Room, although they had swapped a few brief text messages since that evening. Knight was keen to meet her again and return the favour of dinner, but so far they hadn't been able to nail down a date. It seemed that Dr Collins had a very busy diary and DS Knight was still waiting to hear back from her.

After meeting with Strong, DS Knight had quickly called the rest of the team together in the large conference room on the second floor of the police station, so that she could bring them all up to speed on the latest development. DI Strong had gone off somewhere to another meeting, but Knight carried on without him, telling the team that their number one suspect was now James Gray. But frustratingly, they still hadn't been able to find him.

'If he does what he said he was going to do, then he should be back to work at the hospital on Monday,' DC Harris told the team. 'He's supposed to be working at the hospital all next week.'

'Okay, well that'll be interesting to see if he does that,' DS Knight replied, 'but it would be nice to get him before that. He might be planning to attack some more of his ex-schoolmates. At this stage we just don't know, but we have to assume he may do that. Did we manage to get a photo of him yet?' she asked the room generally.

There were a few murmurs before DC Morgan held up his hand.

'Yes Guv, we managed to get a blown-up version of his identity card from the hospital,' he said. 'It's not great, but it's the best we can get at this point. We couldn't find anything on the usual social media sites. Do you want me to get it circulated around the team, or even wider?' he asked.

'Yes, just send it around the team for now. Do you have a copy here? I'd like to see it, see what he looks like now,' Knight replied.

DS Knight couldn't remember James Gray from their time together at Danesborough High school. They had been in the same year, but different classes and it seemed James had only been there for a short time. Knight waited while DC Morgan shuffled some papers around in his file before finally finding what he was looking for. He handed it across the table to DS Knight and she looked at it, her eyes widening and her mouth falling open. The reason for her shocked look was that she had immediately recognised the face staring out at her from the photograph.

'Wait. This isn't....this is James Gray? Are you sure?' she said, still looking confused and staring at DC Morgan.

'Yes, that's correct Guv,' he replied. 'As I said we got the photo from his hospital Id card.'

'But…this is James Hardy,' DS Knight exclaimed. 'Okay, okay, let me think. I know where we can find this man,' she said excitedly. 'I need to go and see DI Strong first. Can everyone go back to work for now but be on standby please. We may need to move quickly on this.'

Chapter 41

It had been a long time since Irene Hardy had been in this pub. Or any pub when it came to that. Since she'd retired, she'd led a much quieter, parochial life. More sedate, spending a lot of time in her garden or just having tea and cake with her neighbour Joan, listening to all Joan's gossip.

But here she was, sitting at a small wooden table in the corner of the pub, facing out towards the pub entrance, an empty wooden chair waiting on the other side of the table.

Although it had been a while, and she quite fancied a half pint of beer, she had resisted the temptation and ordered a small glass of fresh orange juice instead, deciding she needed to keep her wits about her, and so avoiding any alcohol at this point. Maybe afterwards she could have a small one.

Irene had deliberately arrived at the pub early so she could choose where to sit and watch for the arrival of Detective Inspector Strong. She was keen to see his reaction when he finally saw who she was, "The Social Worker," although she didn't expect he would recognise her. They'd only ever met once, and that had only been very briefly, a long time ago. However, Irene had seen photos of Strong in the newspapers and she'd also come to understand some of Mo Strong's personality over the years, when she had been regularly feeding him pieces of information over the phone. From those calls she'd learned that he liked to be in control. He wanted to know everything, so that he was prepared for any eventuality. Irene knew, especially in the early days of their relationship, that Strong was frustrated about not knowing her real identity. She knew that he'd tried to find out at various times. He'd even attempted to trick her on a few occasions to make her reveal herself, but Irene had taken a lot of care to remain anonymous, and up till now she'd been successful in doing that.

Irene knew, right from the start, that she was putting herself in some danger by passing on information about individuals and suspected criminal activities. But she still felt strongly that it was the right thing to do. Her position in the local community enabled her to find out things that others didn't know. Especially the police. It was amazing what some people would freely tell a respected schoolteacher. Sometimes she felt like a priest taking confession, but of course she didn't have the same privacy restrictions as the clergy.

To help keep herself safe, she decided that the less people who knew about what she was doing, the better. That was how "The Social Worker" had come to be. It was a spur of the moment response, the first time she had called the police, and a younger Mo Strong had answered.

'Who am I talking to?' he'd asked.

'Just call me The Social Worker,' Irene had replied.

It had simply been the first thing that had come into her head, and she was forever glad that she hadn't said "The Schoolteacher", that could have been a give-away. And as far as she was aware not one single person knew who she was, or what she had been doing, all those years. Not until today.

But now the situation was different. It wasn't just about her this time, and although she had spoken with him again recently, she knew she had to meet the detective, even if it meant breaking her most important rule and exposing herself. Him finally finding out who she was. But it was too important to try and cover it all in a phone call. She needed to see the whites of DI Strong's eyes when she spoke to him. She needed to see that he understood what she was saying, and what she wanted him to do. What she needed him to do. That was crucial if she was going to be able to help James Gray this time, and not let him down again, like she had once before.

Irene had phoned DI Strong's special mobile number once more and left a message, just like she had done recently and just like she had done many times in the past. But this time the message was different. This time it was to arrange a meeting, and she knew DI Strong would not be able to resist that. He'd want to see who "The Social Worker" was. After all these years he'd finally find out and maybe, in his mind, he would feel that, at last, he was in control of everything again.

Irene watched him walk confidently into the pub. He looked like a policeman. He was tall and slim. Not as young as he used to be, but still a good-looking man, nevertheless. She watched him for a few seconds as he looked around the room, his eyes adjusting to the darker interior of the pub. Irene let him wait. She was still the one in control. At least for a little bit longer. She kept watching him carefully as he scanned the room, until his eyes settled on her. He gave a small, almost imperceptible, nod of his head and Irene smiled and nodded back. He'd finally found her. DI Strong walked across to Irene's table and stood, towering over her. He held out his hand and spoke,

'So, The Social Worker. At last, we finally meet,' he said, grinning down at Irene.

Irene smiled back and shook his hand. The detective took his seat at the table and settled himself in.

'Am I allowed to know your real name now?' Strong asked. 'It seems a bit daft to keep calling you The Social Worker.'

Irene smiled. As ever, Strong was straight to the point. He wanted to know everything, he wanted to be the one in control. She decided to ignore his question for now, although she knew he'd ask again later.

'Why don't you get yourself a drink,' she said to him, 'and then we can have a chat.'

'Okay,' Strong replied smiling, and he went to the bar, returning a few minutes later with a glass of coke. 'So, what is it you want to talk to me about, after all these years?' Strong asked her as he took a sip of his drink.

'I need you to do something for me,' Irene replied. She'd thought long and hard about how she was going to approach this meeting until she was sure in her head that she had got it right.

'Later today, a young man will come into your police station to talk about Stephen Jones, Nigel Harrison and Danny Blake,' Irene started.

'How do you know this?' Strong jumped in.

'Please don't interrupt me, Mr Strong, let me finish, then we can discuss anything you want,' Irene replied and then, without waiting for a response from the detective, she carried on.

'The man is called James Gray and the three other men I mentioned, bullied him terribly when they were all at school together,' Irene said. 'He didn't get any help from the school or anyone else, and things got so bad for him he had to transfer to another school. They made his life a misery and he has never been able to forget it.'

Irene paused to take a sip of her drink. She looked at DI Strong as she drank it, but she couldn't read anything from his blank facial expression. She put her glass down and continued with her story.

'Recently, James happened to come across these three men again and it was apparent that they hadn't changed. They were still bullies. Just a few years older, but just the same. It was obvious that they had no regrets or remorse for what they had put James through when they had been at school. It was at that point that James knew he needed to do something to clear his mind and be able to start living his life again, without the memory of what they'd done to him being constantly in the back of his mind. Always niggling away at him, reminding him. So, he decided to act. You might call it revenge but it was really an act of retribution. Justice. Justice for James.'

Irene paused and had another drink but was disappointed to see Strong's expression was still the same. She didn't know what she was expecting of him, but at least something. What was he thinking? She just couldn't read him at all.

'So, in simple terms, James decided to do to them, what they had done to him, all those years ago,' Irene said. 'And basically, that's what he's done.'

Irene stopped again and took another drink. This time she saw a slight smile appear on DI Strong's face. At least that was some kind of reaction.

'And who are you? The lawyer for the defence,' Strong said smiling across the table at Irene. 'Of course, you've missed out some key facts from your story. Stephen Jones is dead, potentially unlawfully killed. Nigel Harrison ended up in hospital and Danny Blake has a broken nose. The man we are looking for in connection with these three incidents could face charges of murder and GBH, or at the very least common assault.'

It was DI Strong's turn to pause and have a drink, and Irene's turn to smile. So far it was going just as she had been expecting. It was like chess and she was in control of the game.

'Okay, you want to talk facts? Well, here's some *you* missed,' she replied. 'Stephen Jones died of a heart attack. Nigel Harrison fell over and broke his ankle and Danny Blake is in some sort of fight every week as far as I can tell. His nose has been broken more times than you or I have had hot dinners.'

'How do you know all of that?' Strong asked, unable to keep a surprised tone from his voice, as he looked at the lady sitting across the table from him. The Social Worker.

'That doesn't really matter. The fact is it's all true and it means there isn't really much of a case against James Gray,' Irene replied. 'What happened to him was much, much worse than what happened to those other three. And besides that, you head up the Serious Crime Team, don't you? I'd hardly call this a serious crime. Surely you should be focusing on more major crimes?'

DI Strong took a drink of his coke and looked at Irene, trying to work her out. By name, he still only knew her as The Social Worker, but, over the years, he had formed his impressions of her character. She had always been extremely diligent. The information she had provided him in the early days on local criminals and their various activities had always been spot on. A lot of the detail she had given him had enabled Strong to more easily secure convictions and keep a lid on the local crime scene when he had been a younger police officer. That had certainly helped him climb up the career ladder in the police force. She had also come across as a very determined character. If there was something she wanted Strong to know then she made sure he understood. Conversely if there was something she didn't want Strong to know then she was equally good at concealing that too, like her identity. Strong had tried a number of ways of finding out who she was, but without success. No-one seemed to know. Even now, although he was sitting with her, he still didn't know her real identity.

What was interesting now though, with her sitting across the table from him after all these years, was that she was now defending this man she had named as James Gray. Strong couldn't work out why she was doing that. What was he to her? He decided to see if she would tell him, although he suspected he knew the answer already. He put his drink down and smiled at her.

'Okay, so I get this guy was bullied at school and, years later, for whatever reason, maybe an understandable one, he decides to get his revenge,' Strong said. 'I get that. But what I don't understand is why you are here now. Why are you asking me to…I don't know what you're asking exactly, but what is this James Gray person to you?'

'He's someone who was let down. By me and lots of other people,' Irene replied. 'I should have been able to help him when he was younger, but I didn't. I let him down then. So now I want to try and make up for that, in some small part at least,' Irene paused for a quick drink before continuing.

'As to what I want from you Mr Strong, I want you to let him off without any charge,' she said. 'He's no danger to anyone now. He's done what he set out to do and that's it. I can guarantee that. There's nothing to be gained from arresting him. You should just let him go free.'

'I can't do that,' Strong replied, shaking his head slowly as he spoke. 'You've just told me this guy attacked three people. Two of them ended up injured and one died, arguably due to the assault. I can't just let him go when he's done all that.'

He looked across the table and saw that Irene Hardy was smiling at him. She had a nice smile, somehow comforting, perhaps like a good social worker should have. Maybe that's what her job was, although he had looked into that to see if he could identify her, but without any success.

Irene was enjoying the conversation with Detective Inspector Strong. The game of chess. Although this was the first time that she had really met him, she felt she already knew him well. In addition to feeding him pieces of information, she'd also followed his police career through the years, and she'd developed an understanding of how he worked. He liked to get results and he'd been very successful at doing that, helping him to quickly reach the level of Detective Inspector. But, watching how he worked, Irene had noted a number of cases where he appeared to have manipulated the information that she had given him to secure quick convictions. And even more than that, she was very suspicious that he might have also planted evidence, weapons or drugs, in several of his suspects' houses, again to help get an easier conviction. However, the worst case, which was one of the reasons she came to the decision to stop supplying him with information, was that of a man called Bobby Forest.

Bobby lived in the Campbeltown Estate with his mum and dad, two brothers and a sister. Six of them in total, living in a three-bedroom flat. Bobby was the eldest in the family and by the time he had reached his mid-teens, he was becoming uncontrollable at home, and he was already getting into trouble with the police. Initially it was minor stuff. Shoplifting, breaking into garages, handling stolen goods, that sort of thing. Then, as he got into his late teens, his crimes gradually became more serious, but he'd become cleverer too, learning from his earlier mistakes, making it harder for the police to pin anything on him. The police suspected that he had been involved in two armed robberies at local factories, where guns had been used and two of the security guards had been shot. Both of them had been taken to hospital with life threatening injuries. Thankfully they'd both survived, but the police had not made any arrests.

Bobby's younger brother, Jamie was a pupil at Danesborough High school, and his class teacher was Miss Hardy. Irene could see that Jamie didn't have the best of times at home, he'd often come to school looking tired, dishevelled and hungry. Irene took him under her wing and began to look out for him, like she did with several of the pupils at the school. She would sit with them during break times, or after school and chat, let them simply talk, it seemed to help them just getting things out of their systems. Stuff that was going on at home, things they didn't understand or were frightened of. They were only young. Jamie told Miss Hardy how he'd seen his brother hiding a gun in his bedroom and how he'd overheard him talking on the phone.

'The things he was saying weren't nice. Like he was happy he'd shot someone, and he wished they'd died so they couldn't name him. It just wasn't right, you know. I wish he wouldn't do these things. He used to be fun. We used to play together. Football and stuff, you know. It was fun. But now he just shouts at me. tells me to….he swears at me, you know.'

Irene had passed on the information about Bobby Forest to Strong, and the following week she heard that Bobby had been found dead. He had been shot, and the official police report said that he had committed suicide. Jamie hadn't come into school for a week and when he returned, he avoided Miss Hardy, somehow sensing that she had something to do with his brother's death.

Irene had spent the last twenty four hours going over all of this at home. Everything she had told Strong over the years. She had kept extensive notes, as well as typing up a summary document which she had previously deposited with her solicitor. She knew how potentially dangerous her situation was, apparently from both sides, criminals and the police. That was why she'd taken pains to conceal her identity, as well as keeping documentation of everything that had happened, in case she ever needed to use it.

'You said you can't just let him go, but of course you can,' Irene said, more forcefully to the detective. 'You're the head, the man in charge. You can make the call. He's no danger to anyone,' Irene said excitedly, she was getting into her stride now, everything she'd planned to say was coming out.

'You can slap his wrists, give him a caution, and let him go. Let him get on with his life. Let him do his job at the hospital. You can do all of that. It's your decision. But, Mr Strong, you can make the right decision,' Irene stopped talking and took a long drink, not taking her eyes off DI Strong. She hoped he would see sense without her having to push him further.

'I am in charge, yes. But these things aren't just down to me to decide. I have a team, a lead detective on the case and all of the evidence we collect is put together and presented to the CPS. It's they who decide if we should prosecute, not me,' Strong replied. 'You see it's out of my hands.'

'No, it's not really. The CPS only get involved if you want to charge someone,' Irene replied, glad that she'd learned about the internal workings of the police force over the years she'd been an informant for Strong. She knew that CPS stood for the Crown Prosecution Service and, crucially, she also knew what power they had.

'If you decide there's no case, no great evidence, no reliable witnesses, and let him off with a caution then that's it. Case closed. I've met your DS, Knight, isn't it? She seems a sensible girl. I'm sure she'll do what you suggest,' Irene finished, looking straight at the detective.

Strong was impressed by the woman's knowledge but not surprised. He realised she would know all of this. She had always been extremely thorough, and what she was saying was correct. Assuming they found James Gray, he could just let him off with a caution, but doing that would mean that he hadn't got a conviction for the three assaults. Although the case would be closed, it still wouldn't look quite as good on his record. Or DS Knight's, with her being the lead detective on it. And he'd have to convince her that letting James Gray off with a caution was the right thing to do. Weighing it all up, it would be much easier just to charge James Gray, close the case, take the plaudits, let justice take its course and move onto the next one.

'No, I'm sorry,' Strong replied. 'I don't think I can do that.' He glanced at his watch. 'Look it's been nice meeting you, seeing you in person for the first time and all that, but I must get back now,' he said, and he started to stand up from his seat.

'Wait,' Irene replied, a steely, determined look on her face which stopped DI Strong in his tracks, and he sat down again. 'Before you go, just think about all of the information I supplied to you. Remember how it often led to you getting arrests and convictions. How it helped you enhance your reputation in the police force. How you got promoted.'

'Yes, I appreciate that,' Strong replied. 'You were a great source of help, especially in the early days and I thank you for doing that. It definitely helped us clear some of the criminals off the streets.'

'Yes,' Irene nodded. 'And I watched you progress through the ranks. I kept a close watch. I kept detailed notes on what I had told you, and what happened subsequently. It wasn't difficult to put two and two together and see what you were doing. How you were getting so many successful prosecutions… and other outcomes,' Irene paused to take a drink and to let the detective think about what she had just said. Hopefully it would sink in.

'It wouldn't do you any good if I shared what I have with your bosses, the Chief Constable,' she went on, with a fixed, hard look on her face. She knew this was almost her last move, she had hoped it wouldn't come to this, but she needed to get Strong to believe that she was being deadly serious.

Strong remained silent and Irene softened her look, with a slight smile, as she caught his eye.

'All I'm asking is that you do this one thing for me,' she said. 'Maybe look at it as a thank you for all the help I gave you before, if you want to. But, either way, it's a one off. I'm only doing this for James because he deserves it. After this you won't hear from me again, and don't bother trying to find out who I am, it won't help you. As I said, I'm doing this for James Gray. He deserves justice.'

While Irene had been talking, Strong's mind had been working furiously, going through all his options. He knew this woman sitting opposite him, The Social Worker, was very clever. Whatever she had on him, it would be safely stored away somewhere, not just sitting at the bottom of her bedroom wardrobe. She was too clever and careful for that. Her information was probably deposited with a solicitor, only to be accessed if needed. He couldn't help but admire her tenacity. Whatever it was she felt she owed this James Gray, it was obviously something she thought to be very important, something that she was prepared to put her neck on the line for.

Strong realised that what she potentially had on him could be career ending. She was right, in the early days he had used her a lot and it wouldn't take a genius to work out what he had done, how he had manipulated evidence to get some results. It was also possible, maybe even probable, that she'd worked out that he didn't always get justice through the courts. Sometimes he had arranged punishments in other ways, when it looked like the police system was not going to be able to deliver a fair outcome. In that respect, Bobby Forest was a name that came to mind, although there had been others too.

Weighing it all up, it seemed to Strong that he didn't have too many options. He'd have to persuade DS Knight, but he was fairly confident he could do that. He'd think of something.

'Okay, I'll see what I can do about James Gray,' he said to Irene. 'But that's it. After that we're done, okay?'

Irene smiled, nodded, and finished her drink. She stood up from the table.

'Goodbye Mr Strong. It was good to meet you,' she said, and she turned and walked out of the pub, leaving DI Strong still sitting at the table.

Irene walked briskly along the road until she found a café. She went in and ordered a black Americano, taking a seat in an empty area of the room. Sitting at the table, she felt herself trembling a little with excitement. The meeting with DI Strong had been very interesting and also very tense at times, but she'd really enjoyed the challenge. It was the most thrilling thing she'd done for a long time, but she'd achieved what she set out to do. She took a sip of the hot liquid, feeling satisfied, as it flowed down her throat.

Irene took out her phone and looked around the room, making sure no-one was within earshot, before dialling a number.

'Hello, James. Okay, I've done what I wanted to do,' she said. 'I'm sorry I couldn't tell you what, but it's best that way. You'll just have to trust me, okay? Anyhow, you can now hand yourself in and tell them what you've done. Ask for DI Strong, he's a good man. Trust me, you'll be okay.'

Chapter 42

Detective Inspector strong returned from his meeting with The Social Worker to find DS Knight waiting outside his office, looking flushed.

'Ah DS Knight,' he said. 'I'm sorry I didn't make your team meeting. Something important came up that I had to attend to. Did everything go okay? Are you alright? You look a bit hot and flustered.'

The two detectives went into Strong's office and sat down on either side of his desk.

'You know James Gray is our main suspect, but we haven't been able to find him so far,' DS Knight blurted out excitedly.

'Yes,' Strong replied, sensing that there was more to come from the detective.

'Well, I know where he is. Where he's been hiding,' DS Knight replied. 'He's been at Miss Hardy's house, claiming to be her nephew. Calling himself James Hardy.'

'Miss Hardy's house? The teacher?' Strong asked. 'But didn't you go there to see her?'

'Yes, and he was there then, but he said he was her nephew and to be honest she wasn't quite with it,' Knight replied. 'I never knew him at school, and it was only when DC Morgan showed me a photo of him at the meeting today that I realised who he was.'

'I see, that's great. And what about Miss Hardy? Do you think she knows who he is and what he's been doing?' Strong asked.

'I don't know. She was a bit doo lally to be honest, so it was hard to say what she knew or didn't know,' Knight replied. 'What I'd like to do now though is get James Gray in so we can question him. I don't think there should be too much of a problem getting him, but with Miss Hardy being there too, we need to be careful nothing goes wrong.'

'Yes, agreed,' Strong replied. 'We don't want anything happening to her.'

'Thanks Guv, so, to be on the safe side, I'd like your permission to get a SWAT team organised. I think it would be wise to have them on standby, just in case we need to use them.'

'Okay, if you think so, I'll get that sorted. It may take a couple of hours, but I'll let you know,' Strong replied.

Chapter 43

Keegan Summers was walking aimlessly when he suddenly saw the sign on the wall. Police Headquarters it proudly announced in silver letters, set against a dark blue background. It was a spur of the moment thing. But he thought, why not? He'd tried everything else. Why not this? It couldn't make things any worse. Could it?

The truth was, Sophie had been ignoring him. She'd been refusing to speak to him or even return any of his messages. Nothing since that first night when he'd called her, and she'd said she didn't want to see him again. It was over. She didn't explain why, and he didn't get it. He hadn't done anything wrong. Or nothing that he could think of. He knew he'd let her down a bit a couple of times when they'd been supposed to be seeing each other and something else had come up. But that wasn't that major surely? Not something you'd dump someone for. He was sure she'd done the same to him once or twice, although he couldn't be precise on that. But either way, he still felt that was a fairly minor thing. It wasn't like he'd got off with anybody. He hadn't been unfaithful to her. Absolutely not. He wouldn't be. He was loyal to her, he had been. He'd surprised himself sometimes, when the opportunity had been there, but his feelings for Sophie had been too strong that he found he just couldn't do it.

He walked up the steps, through the double doors and into the reception area. There were two people sitting there on grey plastic chairs. A man and a woman. Keegan wasn't sure if they were together. They weren't talking, they were both just sitting there looking down at the floor. Keegan guessed that maybe they were waiting for their son to be released after a night in the cells. But that was just a guess.

Keegan approached the counter, which had a glass shield with a little round, grey speaker on the ledge at the bottom. Behind the partition, there stood a middle-aged policeman with a shock of unruly white hair. He was a big man, with a stuck out chest, and he looked up as Keegan reached the counter. Keegan bent down slightly to talk into the speaker.

'Hi, I was…emm…wondering if I could speak to Detective Strong,' Keegan said into the device while trying to simultaneously look at the policeman in front of him.

'Is he expecting you? Does he know you're here?' the policeman replied.

'Emm…no, not exactly. No, he doesn't know I'm here. I'm…I'm just a friend of the family,' Keegan replied, wondering if he'd done the right thing, coming into the police station. Maybe he should have just walked on by.

The policeman looked Keegan up and down as if he was making some sort of assessment before he made any decision.

'What's your name?' he asked.

'Keegan, …it's Keegan Summers,' Keegan replied.

The policeman turned off the intercom and picked up a phone from the desk. He turned away slightly as he made a call. Keegan could see him talking into the receiver, but he had no idea what the policeman was saying. After a minute he put the phone down and switched the intercom back on. He turned to face Keegan.

'Detective Inspector Strong will be down in a few minutes,' the policeman said. 'Please take a seat and wait,' and he nodded towards the row of seats behind Keegan.

The seats were now empty, although Keegan hadn't noticed the man and woman leave. Did they get up and leave, or did they go further into the police station? Keegan would never know. He took the seat nearest to the door, half-wondering if he should just go. The seat was cold, and he sat on his hands as he waited.

A few minutes later there was a buzzing sound and a heavy steel door, adjacent to the reception counter, opened outwards. DI Strong stepped through it and into the reception area. Keegan saw him appear and he was tempted to just make a run for it, but Strong had spotted him. The detective walked towards him with a smile on his face.

'Keegan, nice to see you,' he said, extending his hand out to shake Keegan's.

The detective's friendly demeanour had taken Keegan by surprise, and he automatically returned Strong's handshake.

'Come on, let's get out of here. I'll buy you a coffee. I could do with a break from this place,' Strong said and he guided Keegan towards the door.

Strong had set the process in motion to get the SWAT team organised for DS Knight in case it was needed for the arrest of James Gray, but he knew that would take an hour or two to organise and get the required approvals. When the call had come to say that Keegan Summers was asking for him in reception, Strong thought he might as well see him. He had some time to spare, and he was intrigued to see what Keegan wanted. Also, as always, his mind had already started working on how he might be able to use this meeting to his advantage in some way. Strong led the way, guiding Keegan towards a café just around the corner from the police station. It was one that Strong used when he wanted to have an informal, off the record, chat with someone. It was never too busy and the way the tables were laid out meant it was always easy to find a spot where he could have a private conversation without the risk of someone listening in. He bought two coffees and the two men sat down at a table towards the rear of the café. They exchanged a few minutes of conversation about nothing in particular and then they both went quiet, escaping into the safety of their drinks.

Keegan took another slurp of his coffee, before putting his cup back on the table, banging it down more loudly than he had intended. He looked around but no-one else seemed to have noticed. He glanced at the detective, Sophie's father, sitting across from him, and finally worked up the courage to start talking about what he really wanted to.

'How's Sophie? Is she okay?' he asked, immediately lifting his cup with both hands, and taking another drink of his coffee. He held it by his mouth, waiting anxiously for the detective's reply, watching him over the top of his cup.

'She's good,' Strong nodded. 'All well, I think.'

'Oh good,' Keegan replied. 'Has she…has she…emm…said anything about me at all? It's just emm…she doesn't seem to be talking to me, or returning my messages, but…but…I don't know why. I don't know what I've done.'

'Yes, I heard she'd emm…she'd had some sort of change of plan I think,' Strong replied.

'Change of plan…what's…emm…that? What…emm…does that mean?' Keegan replied, still holding his cup in front of his face.

'Well, she's a young girl still,' Strong replied. 'I know she's been away at university and done that, but I think there's lots of other stuff she still wants to do. I don't think she'll be at home for much longer, I think she'll probably be off somewhere again at some point.'

'Oh right,' Keegan replied. 'I know she'd spoken about maybe going travelling or something. We'd both chatted about doing that, maybe in the summer, but…do you know why she's not talking to me now? She's not returning any of my calls or messages. It's like I've done something wrong, but I haven't. I don't get it.'

'Mmm…I know. I'd heard. I guess it's just one of those things that happens,' Strong said, looking sympathetically at the young man across the table from him. 'Sometimes there's no rational explanation, Keegan. Things just come to an end. People move on.'

Strong stopped talking and looked around the café, but he didn't recognise anyone and there was no-one within earshot. He leaned forward over the table.

'I've never told anyone this before, so this is just between me and you, okay?' Strong said, looking directly at Keegan. Keegan nodded and Strong continued.

'A while ago, before I met Sophie's mother, I was seeing a girl called Amanda. She was beautiful, long blonde hair, great personality, always laughing. I couldn't believe she was my girlfriend. At the time, I was totally besotted with her. I thought she was the one, I couldn't envisage us ever not being together. But then, after a couple of months, she left me and went off with a biker. At the time I was devastated, I couldn't believe she'd gone. But afterwards, looking back, I could see that it had all happened really quickly, and I came to realise that she wasn't right for me, and I wasn't right for her. She was a free spirit, and I was really seeking stability. It was never going to work long term. Sometimes these things happen. It's inevitable. A few weeks after she left, I met

Catherine, Sophie's mum, and, well, the rest is history.'

Keegan had been listening intently to the detective's story and, as Strong paused, he took the opportunity to ask a question.

'And this Amanda, did you ever hear from her again?' he asked DI Strong.

'No. I heard she'd gone off with her biker friend, somewhere in Europe, travelling around I think,' Strong replied. 'So, you see, what I'm saying is things happen for a reason. There's no telling why, but sometimes one door closes and another opens. I guess you and Sophie…maybe it's just run its course and you'll both move on to something else, something better for you both. You're both young. I'm sure she'll talk to you again at some point.'

'Mmm…I guess,' Keegan replied. 'It's just so hard when she won't tell me why.'

'Yeh, well, I think you maybe just have to leave it. You've tried, and if she wants to talk to you, she knows where you are. Sometimes there's no satisfactory explanation, you know?' Strong replied, smiling at the young man.

'Yeh, I guess you're right,' Keegan replied, putting his now empty cup back down on the table.

He wasn't sure exactly why, but somehow the chat with Sophie's dad had helped him feel better. Maybe it was just the act of getting it all off his chest, but what Sophie's dad had said was right. He had tried to contact Sophie and she knew how to get back to him, if she wanted to. Maybe he needed to just "man-up" a bit and move on with his life.

'Thanks for the coffee and chat Mr Strong,' Keegan said. 'I think I just needed to talk to someone, but I think you're right. If Sophie wants to talk to me, she knows where I am. Meantime, I need to get on with my life.'

'Yes, I think you're right,' Strong replied. 'And remember my story about Amanda, that's just between us, okay? In fact, its probably better if no-one knows we met, let's keep it to ourselves, okay mate?' Strong said and he winked across the table at Keegan.

'Yes, of course,' Keegan replied, nodding back at the detective.

'Well, I'm glad our little chat helped, Keegan,' Strong said. He glanced at his watch. 'I need to get back now, duty calls,' he said, smiling across the table at the young man, his daughter's ex.

The two men rose from the table and left the café, going their separate ways. Strong walked back to the police station, smiling to himself as he went. He was giving himself a virtual pat on the back for coming up with the "Amanda" story. Of course, it was completely made up, but Strong had to congratulate himself for inventing such a creative and convincing story. It seemed to have done the trick. It looked like, finally, Keegan wouldn't be bothering his daughter Sophie again any time soon.

Chapter 44

Detective Inspector Strong had got the approval through for a SWAT team to be on standby, if needed, to extricate James Gray from Miss Hardy's house. DS Knight was in the midst of getting that organised which, frustratingly, meant filling in several more forms, duplicating the same detail over and over, before she had all the necessary police approvals to act. Just as she was completing an on-line risk assessment form, her phone rang, and she picked it up while continuing to type in the details on screen.

'Hello,' she said into the phone, wedged under her chin.

'We've got a James Gray in reception,' the voice at the other end announced. 'He says he wants to talk to someone about the Stephen Jones case. He asked for DI Strong, but I thought it best to call you.'

DS Knight almost dropped the phone but managed to recover it. She stopped typing and looked at her phone screen to see who the caller was.

'Sorry Stan, ...can you just repeat that please? I was in the middle of something,' she said to the Desk Sergeant, not sure she could believe what she thought she had just heard.

'Sure. I said we have a James Gray here at the front desk. He just walked in a couple of minutes ago. He wants to see DI Strong about the Stephen Jones case,' the Desk Sergeant replied.

There was no response and after a few seconds the Desk Sergeant spoke again.

'Hello, are you still there?' he asked, more loudly.

DS Knight shook her head, trying to bring herself back into the current moment. Her brain had been working overtime with all sorts of thoughts. What was James Gray doing here? What did he want? It had taken her completely by surprise.

'Yes, sorry, …yes I'm here,' she replied. 'Listen, Stan, I need a few minutes. Can you put him in one of the interview rooms for now and I'll be down shortly.'

Knight hung up and rose from her chair in one movement, instantly forgetting about the incomplete data on her computer. She walked quickly to DI Strong's office and knocked twice, firmly, on his door before opening it and entering the room. Strong was sitting behind his desk, looking at the screen in front of him. He turned to look at DS Knight as she approached his desk.

'Ah, everything okay? Are we ready to roll?' Strong asked her.

'He's here Guv,' she replied excitedly. 'He's downstairs. I just got the call. Apparently, he just walked in. Says he wants to talk about Stephen Jones. Stan said he asked for you.'

Strong sat forward in his seat.

'Hold on, slow down,' he said. 'Who's here? I'm not quite with you.'

'James Gray,' Knight said, unable to stop a smile appearing across her face. 'He's downstairs, just walked in. I've told Stan to put him in an interview room. I'm going down now. Do you want to join me Guv?'

'Sure,' DI Strong nodded and he rose from his seat, picking up his glasses from his desk as he joined his colleague.

Ten minutes later DI Strong, DS Knight and James Gray were sitting in Interview Room Number One on the ground floor of the police station. It was a fairly sparse room, just a table and a few chairs surrounded by plain grey walls, but it also held a lot of technology. There were multiple cameras and recording devices, all connected to even more technology in an adjacent room, where other police officers could also sit and observe the proceedings.

Gray had declined the option of having a legal representative with him, saying that he didn't need one. DS Knight pressed the record button on the table mounted device and introduced the three people present. She then asked James if he could tell them why he had come into the police station today. James took a deep breath before starting to talk.

He spoke for about ten minutes and neither of the police officers interrupted him throughout that time. Knight scribbled a few notes at various points and Strong sat completely still, his hands interlocked, resting on his lap.

James Gray told his story. How he had been bullied at school. How it had affected his life - not just then, but ever since. How he had seen the bullies again on the night of the school reunion. And how he had decided it was time for him to get his revenge. How he had got his justice, by doing to them, what they had done to him. He said it was the only way that he could put an end to it.

Firstly, he had pushed Stephen Jones's head down the toilet and flushed it over him. He made a point of stressing that was all he did, and that he had left Jones's house straight after doing that. Apart from putting the school photograph in Jones's lounge. He said he didn't know why he had done that. It had just been a daft idea he'd had. Some sort of reminder for Jones when he got up again from the bathroom floor. But of course Jones had never got up again. Gray was at pains to make it clear that he hadn't killed him. All he had done was repeat what Jones had done to him many years before in the school toilet. If he had known that Jones was suffering in any way then he would definitely have stayed and helped him.

After that he went on to tell Strong and Knight how he had visited Nigel Harrison, intending to burn his arm with a cigarette, just as he had done to him when they were both at school. But Nigel had run out of the room and fallen, breaking his ankle. James had called an ambulance and left the scene after making sure it had arrived to attend to the injured man.

Then, finally he had attacked Danny Blake. Danny had continually bullied him physically at school. Pushing, nipping, kicking, pulling his hair, spitting and punching. All of that, and at every opportunity he could. James knew that he worked as a bouncer at Club Extream and so he went to confront him there.

'He remembered me. Called me Pigface again, so nothing had changed really, it was like we were still at school,' James explained to the two detectives. 'So, I punched him as hard as I could. Hopefully I broke the bastard's nose. I certainly hurt my own hand,' he said raising his right hand slightly in a fist shape and rubbing it gently with his other hand. 'After that I ran, and that was it really, I'd done what I set out to do, it's finished, and now I'm here.'

James stopped talking, satisfied that he'd told his story how he'd wanted to. He looked across the table at Strong and Knight.

'And why did you come here? Now, I mean,' DS Knight asked him.

James smiled at the detective.

'Because I'm finished. That's it. I've done to them what they did to me,' James replied. 'They were the three worst. There were others of course, at different times, but Stephen Jones, Nigel Harrison and Danny Blake were constant bullies. They couldn't resist it. But I've finally got my own back now, and I'm ready to move on. I'll accept any punishment you think is appropriate, but I'll say again I did not kill Stephen Jones and I'm sorry it ended that way. If there was anything I could have done...'

'And you were living at Irene Hardy's house while you were doing all of this?' Knight asked him.

'Well, no, not to begin with,' James replied. 'I went to see her after I'd visited Nigel Harrison and of course, well you've seen her, she's not well. So, I stayed with her for a few days to help her out. It seemed to suit both of us. It gave me a place to hide out until I was finished. I knew you'd be looking for me and so I couldn't stay at my own house.'

'Did Miss Hardy know what you were doing? Did you discuss it with her?' Knight asked.

'No, she didn't know a thing,' James replied. 'Sometimes I think she knew who I was, from schooldays, and other times I'm not sure. You saw her,' he said to DS Knight. 'She gets very confused. But what I did, I did on my own. It was my mission to complete, no-one else's.'

DI Strong turned sideways to face his colleague, DS Knight.

'Okay, let's take a break for a bit,' he said, nodding towards the recording machine and Knight reached across and turned it off.

The two detectives left the room and made their way silently back upstairs to Strong's office, after a short stop in the kitchen to arm themselves with some fresh coffee.

'So, what do you think?' Strong asked as they took a couple of seats at the long table in his office.

'Well, he's confessed to at least attacking them all, hasn't he? So, I guess we could at least charge him for that, although I do feel sorry for him after everything he went through at school. I didn't know,' she added, shaking her head slowly. 'That sort of thing can definitely affect you for a long time. I've read about it. Maybe he's right what he said though, …I mean that he's got some sort of redemption now and that's him finished.' Knight replied. She took a sip of her coffee before continuing.

'I don't know what to think to be honest,' she sighed. 'What do you think Guv?'

'Well, I think, let's look at the facts,' DI Strong began. 'Stephen Jones died of a heart attack, a natural cause, and he isn't with us now to be able to say anything different. Sure, Gray has confessed to flushing his head down the toilet, but that's not really a serious crime, is it? Nigel Harrison, for whatever reason, probably shame, isn't talking either. So, we have no witnesses from those first two, incidents, let's call them for now. The third guy, Danny Blake has a criminal record as long as your arm. He is probably the most unreliable witness we could ever imagine using. The defence would rip him to bits. I wouldn't be surprised if he ended up jumping out of the witness box and lamping the defence lawyer,' Strong laughed.

'Mmm…yeh, I wouldn't put it past him,' DS Knight laughed along with her boss. 'So, what are you saying? What should we do with James Gray?'

'I think what I'm saying is that it's not straightforward,' Strong replied. 'Let's sleep on it and reconvene in the morning. We'll hold him overnight for now and decide what to do with him tomorrow.'

'Okay, sounds like a good idea,' Knight agreed with her boss. 'And what about Miss Hardy? She did seem very confused when I saw her. I'm thinking there's nothing to be gained from investigating her any further…what do you think?'

'I agree,' Strong replied.

Back downstairs, James Gray had been taken to a police cell. It was a small, narrow room and James was sitting on the bench against the wall. He'd wedged himself into the corner trying to get as comfortable as possible. He was satisfied that he'd been able to tell his story. Right from the beginning, when he'd started planning his scheme, he'd known that this time would come at some point. The time when he'd be telling the police exactly what he'd done, and so he'd rehearsed it in his head, over and over. He wanted them to understand not just what he'd done, but more importantly, why he'd done it. He was content that he'd now been able to do that.

However, he had been surprised at the police's lack of follow up questions, and then the detective suggesting they have a break. They'd only been in there for about thirty minutes. And now it seemed they weren't going to talk to him again until the morning. He'd never been interviewed by the police before though, maybe that was how they did it. Get the accused talking and then take a break. Leave him overnight, make him sweat. But James wasn't sweating. He felt relaxed, relieved that it was almost over. He'd done everything that he had wanted to do. It almost didn't matter to him what their questions were, or what happened next, or when. To him, it was finally all over.

He took a deep breath and wriggled his bottom further back into the corner of the police cell, ready to wait for what was yet to come.

Chapter 45

'Morning Guv, I got your message. You wanted to see me?' DS Knight asked as she entered her boss's office. 'I guess you want to talk about what we should do with James Gray?'

'Yes, take a seat,' Strong replied, nodding towards a chair.

Strong took his glasses off and put them on the desk in front of him. He picked up a pencil and started to twiddle that around in his hands whilst, at the same time, leaning back in his chair and stretching his legs out under the desk.

'I've been thinking more about James Gray,' he began, 'and I had a quick word with John Moore in the CPS about him too.'

'Really?' Knight replied frowning. She was surprised that Strong would have discussed the case with the CPS office without her being involved too. It was *her* case after all.

'You went to the CPS with it?' she asked him.

'Well, no, not exactly,' Strong replied. 'Obviously I wouldn't do that without you being there, but I had to talk to John about some other things and it just came up in the conversation. He asked how we were getting on with it and it just came from that.'

'Oh, okay…and what did he say then?' Knight asked, still feeling slightly miffed at what her boss had done, behind her back.

'Well, I gave him a quick outline of where we were with James Gray,' Strong replied, 'and his opinion was that, well, in essence we should just let him go with a warning not to do anything like that again. Just give him a caution.'

'Really?' Knight repeated, unable to keep the surprised tone from her voice. 'And what did you say?'

'Well, I discussed it with him of course. I had to, now that it had come up. His main concern was that we would get crucified because of the whole bullying background to the case,' Strong replied. 'And I think he's probably right. It's very topical, politically, at the moment. You may have seen some of the stuff on the TV News lately, and John's advice was that we should steer clear of it. It's a minefield, he said. I think that, along with our lack of any reliable witnesses, means he may be right.'

'So, we're just going to let him go? James Gray?' Knight asked.

'Yep, that's the sensible thing to do.' Strong replied, nodding his head. 'We'll give him a simple caution, but I think he's done everything he intended to do now. He's got his own justice for the terrible bullying he had to endure. Just like he said. I don't think he'll concern us again.'

DI Strong paused to take a drink from the cup on the desk in front of him.

'Don't worry about it though,' he continued. 'I'll clear it upstairs with the Chief. I'll make sure he knows what a great job you did in tracking Gray down and why we let him go with a caution,' Strong said, and he walked around his desk, reaching out to give DS Knight a squeeze on her shoulder.

Before Knight could respond, her phone started to ring, and she saw the call was from Dr Collins. She really wanted to speak to the police psychologist and so she stood up, turned away from her boss and spoke quickly and quietly into her phone,

'Give me two secs,' she said.

Knight turned back to face her boss again.

'I've just got to take this, but I agree with you about James Gray. Leave it with me. I'll get it all sorted,' she said before quickly walking out of Strong's office.

'Sorry about that,' she spoke into her phone as she walked down the corridor in the direction of her desk.

'Oh no worries, it's Sam, Sam Collins. How are you?' Dr Collins replied.

'Oh, hi, I'm fine,' Knight replied. 'How are you?'

'Yeh, good. Listen, I'm sorry I haven't returned your calls. I've just been so busy. Too much going on. I know that's a crap excuse, but…you know,' Dr Collins replied.

'No, that's okay, I understand,' Knight said, warming to the sound of Collins's voice.

'Ah good, well listen. It would be lovely to catch up again. I'm intrigued to find out what's going on with the Stephen Jones case. But I wondered, rather than just having another meal, if you fancied doing something else, something a bit different?'

'Well, yeh, I guess we could. What were you thinking exactly?' Knight replied, just as she arrived back at her desk.

'Well, I wondered if you fancied a bit of R and R, and maybe doing a day at a Spa?' Collins asked.

'Ooh, well that does sound nice,' Knight replied, smiling. In her mind, she was already looking forward to it.

'Great, I hoped you'd say just that,' Collins replied. 'My friend is the manager of a new Hotel and Spa that's just recently opened up, and she's given me a couple of free passes, including dinner and an overnight stay. It's not really my partner Chris's thing, a Spa Day, so I thought I'd ask you. I was thinking it would be a great way for us to catch up.'

'Yeh, that sounds great, I'd love that,' Knight replied with a big smile. A Spa Day was just what she needed at this time.

'We'd have to share a room, but I'm okay with that, if you are,' Collins added. 'I'm sure it would be fun.'

'Yeh, sure that's fine,' Knight replied. That should be no problem, she thought, she'd done that before when she'd been on school trips and the like.

She ended the call, still with a smile on her face, and somehow feeling a lot happier than when she had left DI Strong's office just a few minutes beforehand.

A few hours later, James Gray walked out of the police station, apparently a free man. He'd been given a caution, which meant that he was on the police database, the PNC they called it, but that seemed to be it. Nothing else. He took a deep breath of the fresh outdoor air and smiled. He wasn't quite sure what had just happened, but the fact was that he was a free man. They'd just given him some sort of warning, like a slap on the wrists, told him not to do it again and then let him go. Just like that! He'd been expecting to be charged with assault at least, with the prospect of a term in jail, but it hadn't happened, and he wasn't going to complain about that!

James stood on the pavement outside the police station. He threw his arms open wide, arched his back and, smiling broadly, he took the deepest breath in he could manage. For the first time in his life he felt different, and as he exhaled, he called out as loudly as he could,

'I'M FREE!'

Chapter 46

'It's funny we've never done this before,' Strong said to his daughter, Sophie. 'I thought about it a few times, and always meant to do it, but somehow never got around to it. There was always something else going on.'

'Ha-ha, yes, I remember asking you when they had those "take your daughter to work" days at school,' Sophie replied, 'but I think you were a bit worried it might be a bit scary for me, and you'd end up giving me nightmares. It wasn't everyone's dad whose job was the Head of the Serious Crime unit in the police.'

'No that's true, but I think you're old enough now, and I'm glad you've been able to come in and see where I work, and meet a few of the team, the people I work with,' Strong replied. 'And it's not all gruesome stuff, most of it is pretty ordinary really.'

The Strongs, father and daughter, were sitting in the Detective Inspector's office. It was a quiet day in the police station, and Strong had already shown his daughter around his place of work, proudly introducing her to everyone that happened to be in that day.

There was a knock at Strong's office door, before it opened, and Carter the Mailman stepped inside.

'Last post Guv,' Carter said cheerily. 'Anything…' he stopped as he realised DI Strong wasn't alone. 'Oh, sorry…I…I didn't realise you had someone…there… emm was someone else here.'

'Oh, don't worry,' Strong replied, smiling and stepping out from behind his desk. 'This is my daughter Sophie. Sophie this is Carter the Mailman. He's been here, …how long Carter?'

'Fifteen years Guv,' Carter replied.

'Wow that's a good gig,' Sophie replied smiling and holding out her hand to Carter.

Carter shook her hand, hoping his own hand wasn't too sweaty. DI Strong's daughter was a good- looking girl, but not what he'd expected. She looked different from the photos he'd seen. Her hair was a different colour, and style, but he guessed she'd just gone for a new look.

'Oh, hi, you've changed…I …emm like your new hairstyle,' Carter blurted out nervously, unable to stop himself voicing his inner thoughts.

'Oh, …thanks,' Sophie replied, slightly puzzled. 'Have we met before then?' she asked Carter.

'Oh, no it's emm…,' Carter stumbled. He realised he couldn't admit to having seen her photos, without it being obvious he'd taken them out of the envelope. 'I, …emm, I think I saw a photo of you once, in a night club, with your boyfriend, I think,'

Shit! Why did I say that? Carter thought. His mind was racing. He had the images of the photos in his head and that was the first thing that had come to mind. But he didn't need to say anything about a night club, or a boyfriend. It had just come out.

'Right,' DI Strong said, stepping forward to come between Sophie and Carter, handing him a few envelopes. 'Good to see you Carter, you better get moving. You don't want to miss the final post, do you?' he said, and he gently took Carter's elbow and guided him towards the office door.

'Oh, yes, okay, Guv. I better get on, more mail to pick up,' Carter said as Strong opened the office door for him.

Strong turned back to look at his daughter who was still standing in the middle of his office.

'Fancy a coffee and then we best get you on your way?' Strong asked smiling. 'A latte okay?' he asked, and Sophie nodded her head and smiled.

Strong left his office to get the drinks and Sophie sat down on the chair by her dad's desk, thinking. That had been a strange encounter. Carter the Mailman. She hadn't expected that. Why would he have seen a photo of her in a night club with a man? Maybe something posted on social media, but she couldn't recall anything like that. Usually the photos were just ones of her with her girlfriends. She couldn't remember any being taken of her with a man, and she certainly hadn't posted any like that herself.

Her dad reappeared with two cups of coffee, and they sat there drinking them, while discussing

Sophie's job. Although she seemed to be getting on well in her new company, she'd settled in nicely since returning back down South, Strong sensed that there was still something missing for her. It wasn't everything she wanted, and he knew that wouldn't be good enough for Sophie. At some point the itch would become too irritating, and she would go on to do something else, something more fulfilling. Strong and his wife both knew that their daughter had a sense of adventure and she'd spoken about going off travelling a few times, but it hadn't happened. Not yet anyway, but Strong thought she would do it sometime.

'We ought to be heading home now,' Strong said, looking at his watch. 'Your mum will be waiting for us.'

'Yes, okay,' Sophie replied, finishing her coffee and sliding the empty cup across the table towards her dad.

DI Strong put the two empty paper cups into the bin and turned off his desktop computer. He put his laptop into his briefcase, picked it up and walked to his office door. He held it open to allow Sophie to pass through, before pulling it closed behind him.

'I'm just going to nip to the Ladies before we go,' Sophie said, and she walked across the office towards the corridor where the toilets were located.

A few minutes later, as she was coming back out of the Ladies toilet, she almost bumped into a man who was hurrying down the corridor behind her.

'Oops, sorry,' he said, and Sophie turned around to see that it was Carter the Mailman.

'Oh, no worries,' Sophie laughed. 'Actually, I'm glad I bumped into you again,' she said, moving in front of Carter, effectively blocking his way. 'You know you said about seeing me in a photo in a night club with my boyfriend…I was trying to remember where that was,' Sophie said.

Carter could feel the blood rushing to his cheeks. He wanted to get out of this situation as quickly as possible, but he couldn't get along the corridor without pushing Sophie out of the way. He was looking down at his feet, trying to think how he could escape.

'I know you said my hair was different…Was it one where I was wearing a red dress, can you remember?' Sophie asked with a quizzical look on her face.

Carter remembered the red dress, the tight red dress, showing off all of Sophie's womanly curves. She'd definitely looked good in it.

'I…emm...I think so…it might have been…I can't remember. I…emm, I think maybe I got you mixed up with someone else. Sorry.' He said, raising his head to look at her on his last word. 'I…I need to get…you know, going, work stuff,' he said, and he made to ease past Sophie, forcing her to step aside to let him through.

Sophie remained there for a few seconds, thinking about Carter and what he had said, or hadn't said. He was definitely hiding something, but Sophie couldn't quite work out what it was or what it meant. Had he seen the photos of Keegan with the other woman? If so, how could he have, and what did that mean? She'd never really thought much about who had sent her the photos before, it hadn't really mattered. The photos on their own had been enough. Could it have been Carter that sent them? She saw her dad walking across the office and went to join him.

'Come on then, we better be going,' Strong said and the two of them walked out of the police station, into the car park. Strong opened the passenger side door of his car to let Sophie in, before getting in himself, on the driver's side.

'That Carter is a strange little guy,' Sophie said as her dad drove along the road.

'Yes, a bit I guess,' Strong replied. 'Change the radio station if you want,' he added nodding at the car audio system.

'It was funny how he thought he knew me, or that he'd at least seen a photo of me in a night club,' Sophie said, a puzzled frown on her face as she thought about it.

'Yes, he probably just got you mixed up with someone else,' Strong replied. 'As you said, he's a bit strange. Who's this singing now? I think I recognise it,' Strong asked.

"Got me mixed up with someone else"…funny, that's exactly what Sophie had been thinking. Carter had got her mixed up with the girl in the photos she'd been sent. The ones where the girl was with Keegan, kissing him. But then how would Carter have seen those? Unless he had taken them? But how…and why? It didn't make sense. Carter was just the mailman at her dad's work.

Sophie sat back in her seat and closed her eyes. Whatever it meant, maybe none of it really mattered any more. Keegan had let her down. The photos were proof of that, regardless of where they came from. Keegan obviously couldn't be trusted. She thought he'd grown up and changed, but she wasn't going to make that mistake again.

At first, Keegan had tried to contact her, leaving messages for her almost every day, but she'd just ignored them. As far as Sophie was concerned, it had been Keegan's last chance and he'd blown it.

Lately though, his attempts to contact her seemed to have stopped, and she hadn't had anything from Keegan for a while. So maybe he'd finally realised that she didn't want to see him again and given up. Sophie certainly hoped so.

Chapter 47

Detective Sergeant Knight was feeling bored. There wasn't much happening, work-wise. No serious crimes had been committed lately and so she'd spent the last week catching up on her admin. At least she'd got her expenses submitted. Finally. Doing that was a tedious task.

First you had to fill in a spreadsheet, every line detailing an individual item of expense – date, description, purpose, location, amount, VAT, another amount. Who really needed all that information? What was it ever used for? And then after that you had to write a number on each of the paper expense receipts, the number corresponding to the relevant spreadsheet line number, before stapling the receipts to the back of a printed-out version of the expenses spreadsheet. Then that whole bundle had to be put in an internal envelope and sent to the police accounts department. Knight had even seen some of her colleagues photocopying everything, and keeping a copy, just in case it got lost. Personally, she couldn't be bothered doing that, and instead she put her trust in Carter the Mailman to deliver it safely.

Knight had come to believe that you couldn't make the whole process more annoying if you tried. She did wonder if it had deliberately been designed that way, in the hope that it discouraged police officers from submitting expense claims, and so saving the police force some money! Whatever the case, at least she'd got it done and she wouldn't have to do it again for another month.

Although work wasn't currently the most exciting thing for DS Knight, on the plus side, her social life had picked up a bit lately. She'd not heard any more from Sam Collins about the Spa day, but she'd been out a few times with someone she'd met through a dating app. His name was Harry, and he seemed a nice bloke, a good laugh. When she was with him, he was able to make her forget all about her police work, and any other worries she had at the time. And he wasn't bad looking too!

DS Knight was now on her way to a local hotel. The New Alexandra Hotel to be precise. She was going there to attend a presentation which had been set up to highlight some recent changes that had been made in the process of arresting a suspect. It was a location they often used when they didn't have a big enough room in the police station.

'It's not like the old days,' DI Strong had told her. 'When I first started in the police, as a young police constable, you could get away with almost anything. I saw a few of the older Sergeants getting stuck in. They weren't averse to handing out their own punishment, but they wouldn't get away with that now. Too many rules and procedures.

Victims' rights. And cameras. Everything gets recorded now, you have to be very careful.'

DS Knight had heard her boss talk like that before, banging on about there being too many rules and so on, and she knew, having worked with him for a while now, that he had his own ways of getting around some of these. All he wanted to do was clear the criminals off the street, and get justice for their victims, and he had been very successful at doing just that. Knight couldn't argue with that.

All of the senior officers in the Serious Crime Team, from Detective Constable upwards, took it in turn to attend these types of events. There were usually around five or six per year, and this time it was DS Knight's turn to go along. She would have to sit through it, take some notes, or, if she was lucky and there were handouts, get a copy of those. Then afterwards she would have to summarise what she'd learned and feed it back to the rest of the team, either via an email if it was brief and simple, or, more often, through a presentation at their next team meeting.

This one was quite important, and to emphasise that point, DI Strong, as a senior officer, had come along to show his face, and to say a few words at the start of the event. After that, having said his piece, he would be able to disappear, but Knight would have to sit through it all and deliver a presentation back to the team the following week. Luckily there were a few pages of handout material that would help her put it together. The gist of it was that you could only arrest a suspect if you explained to them exactly why you were doing that.

No worries that they might just run away while you were in the middle of your explanation. You couldn't use any physical force unless you could demonstrate that you were in physical danger yourself. It didn't matter if the suspect was verbally abusing you, which was often the case, you couldn't respond back in any way in case you made the situation worse. All of the arrest process had to be recorded on the police officer's bodycam.

To be fair it was mostly common sense, protecting both the suspect and the police officer, but in Knight's experience it was rarely required. The only people it seemed to benefit were the suspects who could afford expensive lawyers. They would pick the whole scenario apart, and if the correct arrest process wasn't followed, exactly to the letter, then they would claim that it wasn't legal, and their client should be set free.

There must have been around a hundred people in the room, all from the police and other public sector related organisations. Knight recognised a few of them and nodded, smiled and mouthed a hello across the room as they saw each other. She sat through the presentation, making a few notes and bagging a copy of the handout documentation, satisfying herself that she had all she needed. She was keen to get back to the police station to do some "proper" police work. However, there was a final, networking coffee event, she had to attend first, before she could escape. She decided she'd do that as quickly as she could.

As she got up from her seat and headed towards the door along with the other attendees, she repeated her nodding, smiling and mouthing "hello" routine to the people she knew. Just as she was leaving the room, funnelling through the door, she felt a touch on her shoulder and turned to see a man smiling at her. Knight recognised him as being from the Crown Prosecution Service, or CPS as they were more commonly known, but she couldn't quite remember his name. She quickly ran through the alphabet in her head…was it Ken…or Keith, something like that?

'Hi, DS Knight, isn't it?' the man said. 'We've met a couple of times, I'm Kevin Bond from the CPS office.'

Kevin, of course that was it, Knight smiled back at the man. He was a handsome man. A bit like her new friend Harry, but older than him. Knight had just come back from a weekend away with Harry and it had gone well, although she'd had to cancel her planned Spa day with Sam Collins. She felt a bit awkward phoning Dr Collins to tell her she couldn't make it, but the psychologist seemed okay about it, just saying they'd have to do something else, another time. Knight knew she still owed her one, with Dr Collins having paid for their meal at the French Room.

Kevin Bond was tall and slim, probably in his mid-forties, grey hairs beginning to poke through at the sides. Kevin Bond was wearing the conventional dark business suit and white shirt, offset with a red tie.

'Hi, how are you doing?' Knight replied as they moved forward, side by side, into the corridor, gradually arriving in the adjacent room where the networking coffees were being served.

'Good, yeh, thanks,' he replied. 'A bit quiet in the office at the moment, hence me being here,' he laughed.

'Yeh, same with me,' Knight replied, returning his laugh.

'Do you want a coffee?' he asked DS Knight and when she replied she did, he went off, returning a few minutes later with two coffees in white cups and saucers.

'So, what are you working on now?' Bond asked her. 'I must admit I was surprised with what happened with the Stephen Jones case. I heard you were working on that. We were expecting someone to be charged with it.' Bond added, taking a sip from his cup of coffee.

'Well…no…it's dead and buried now,' DS Knight replied. 'We knew what happened and who did it, but apparently, there wasn't enough there for us to get a conviction,' Knight said.

'Oh, really. I hadn't heard that. I thought maybe you hadn't got anyone, or maybe it was still an open case,' Bond replied. 'But then I heard someone say it had been closed.'

'Yes, as I said, we knew who did it, but there wasn't enough evidence for you guys in CPS to take it forward,' Knight replied, smiling, before taking a drink from her cup.

'Oh really? Who actually said that then?' Bond asked, a confused frown on his face.

'Well, as I understand it, DI Strong spoke with your boss, John Moore, I believe….and that was the message we got back,' Knight replied. 'I think it was done as part of a phone call when they'd been covering other things, but sometimes that's how these things work I guess, and then we have to just get on with it.'

'Oh, I see,' Bond replied. 'Strange he didn't say anything, he….'

The CPS man was suddenly interrupted as DI Strong appeared and wedged himself in between the two of them. Strong recognised Kevin Bond and said a quick hello to him before turning back towards DS Knight. His face was slightly flushed. He edged her a step backwards.

'I don't think we're going to be losing you to the Merseyside region anytime soon,' he said quietly, smiling at DS Knight as he spoke.

'Oh, why's that?' Knight asked and, over Strong's shoulder, she noticed Kevin Bond turning away to speak with another two similarly suited men, neither of whom she recognised.

'Well, I just heard, so keep it to yourself for now, but apparently DI Murphy has decided to take early retirement. I think that means there will be a bit of a shake up in Merseyside. It was a bit of a shock, him going, no-one knew he was going to do that. I certainly didn't, he'd never said anything to me. I'm not sure why he wanted to meet with you if he was planning on leaving. Strange that. In fact, I thought he was going to be there till they kicked him out for being too old. Anyway, it's come sooner than everyone expected.'

Well, maybe not everyone, DS Knight thought, as she took another sip from her cup of coffee.

Chapter 48

'Where are we going today, exactly?' Sophie asked with a hint of irritation in her voice. 'I can't remember you saying anything about there being a barbeque.'

'Yes, I told you last week, after you'd come home from work,' Catherine replied patiently. 'Thursday, I think it was.'

'And who's is it again?' Sophie replied, still feeling irritated.

'It's Roger and Sally's, they live in the next street, you remember them. Sally used to run the Brownies for a while, when you were there. I told her we were all coming,' Catherine replied, still patiently. She knew her daughter well enough to know patience was the best approach when she was like this.

'What's it in aid of? Is it someone's birthday or something?' Sophie asked, now with less irritation and more resignation in her voice. She knew when she was beaten.

'I'm not sure,' Catherine replied. 'I think Sally might have said it was something to do with her son, Freddie. Do you remember him? I think he was a year or two older than you.'

Sophie thought for a minute or two, but she couldn't remember him. He had never been part of her crowd.

A couple of hours later, the three of them, the Strongs, Mo, Catherine and Sophie, were on their way to Roger and Sally's house. Mo was carrying a blue cool bag which contained two bottles of wine. As they turned into the street where Roger and Sally lived, they saw a young man approaching from the opposite direction.

'Isn't that the guy that works with you at the police station, the mail guy?' Sophie turned to ask her dad.

'Yes, I think it might be,' her dad replied, thinking it definitely looked like Carter the Mailman, but he was surprised to see him here.

The Strong family soon reached their destination, Roger and Sally's house, where they saw a side gate with a written sign announcing, "Enter this Way". The gate led down a pathway into Roger and Sally Field's back garden. As they stood there, about to go in, Mo saw that Carter the Mailman had almost reached them, and he held out the cool bag to his wife.

'You two go on ahead and I'll join you in a minute. I'll just say a quick hello to Carter,' he said, and he guided his wife and daughter towards the gate.

Carter had been walking with his head down and earphones on. He was listening to a sports podcast and hadn't noticed the Strong family up ahead, until he almost bumped into DI Strong.

'Oh, sorry, oh, it's you…Guv,' he said with a shocked look on his face, and he quickly took his headphones off and straightened himself up.

'Afternoon Carter,' Strong replied, smiling. 'I don't often see you around this neck of the woods.'

'Oh,…emm…no,' Carter replied, still not quite over the surprise of meeting his big boss, outside of the police station, in the street. What was he doing here?

'So, what brings you here?' Strong asked, echoing Carter's thoughts.

'Oh…emm…well. I'm actually going to a barbeque at my uncle and aunts' house. In fact, they live just here,' Carter replied, nodding towards the house the two men were standing outside.

'Roger and Sally? They're your uncle and auntie?' Strong asked, with a surprised tone to his voice.

'Yes, that's right,' Carter replied. 'Why, do you know them?'

'Yes, they're friends of ours. We just live around the corner. Well, well, it's a small world,' Strong replied. 'I never knew.'

'Listen,' Strong continued, a thought coming to him. 'My daughter Sophie's here too, she's just gone in with my wife. Remember you met her a few weeks ago at the police station, when I had her in with me one day?'

'Oh…emm, yes I think so,' Carter replied hesitantly.

'Well, you might recall there was a bit of a mix up,' Strong continued. 'You thought you'd seen a photo of Sophie in a night club, but it was someone else. A case of mistaken identity, as we say in the police,' Strong laughed.

The detective looked at Carter the Mailman, expecting some kind of response, but the young man didn't say anything.

'The thing is Carter,' Strong carried on, 'if you bump into Sophie today, it would be best if you don't mention anything about any photos. If she brings it up, just say you were confused and got it wrong. Then make an excuse that you need to go to the toilet or something and walk away. Got it?' Strong asked looking directly at Carter.

'Oh…emm…right,' Carter replied, feeling his cheeks going red.

'Good, probably best try and avoid her altogether, then there'll be nothing to worry about,' Strong said, putting his arm around Carter's shoulder. 'Shall we go in?'

'Emm…you go in Guv, I'll just be a minute,' Carter replied, easing himself away from Strong's arm.

Carter stood watching as DI Strong marched with his long stride towards the side gate. It had been a shock meeting Strong here, outside his uncle and aunt's house. And then to find out that Strong's daughter was here too…

Carter had really been looking forward to the barbeque. He didn't do social occasions often. He didn't get invited to many. But he hadn't seen his uncle and aunt for a while, and he was keen to catch up with them. They had always been very kind to him. And he'd been eagerly anticipating seeing his cousin Freddie again. Freddie was a great laugh, and very talented too. He played guitar and was a very good singer, although he hadn't really pursued it as a career. It was just more of a fun thing for him. Carter had always enjoyed spending time with his cousin, but he hadn't seen him for a while.

But now, standing outside the house, and having had the warning from DI Strong, and he was clear it had been a warning, he wasn't sure what to do. The thing was, Carter wasn't a good liar. He never had been. He always tried to tell the truth and anytime he didn't, which wasn't often, people seemed to know right away. He just couldn't get away with it. He knew it would be the same with Sophie. And he also knew she'd question him about the photos he'd seen, and it would all come out, what he'd done. Looking at them in his post-room. She'd picked up on it when they'd bumped into each other outside the toilets at the police station. She knew there was something there, and Carter could see she wasn't the type to let it lie. She might have made a good police officer. Like father, like daughter.

Carter couldn't face it. The whole idea about having to try and avoid the Guv's daughter, it would make him a nervous wreck and spoil his day. He turned around and started walking back in the direction he'd just come from.

Strong walked into Roger and Sally's garden and found Catherine and Sophie standing by a patio table, talking to each other. His wife handed him a drink, and he took a sip of it before looking around. There were already twenty or thirty people in the garden, all standing around in small groups chatting, with drinks in their hands. Luckily the weather had stayed fine, and it was pleasantly warm.

Sophie spotted the barbeque standing on the patio, up against a wooden fence, near the sliding patio doors leading into the house. It didn't appear to be lit yet which was disappointing as Sophie was feeling hungry. From her limited knowledge of barbeques, as a student, she knew that they were supposed to be lit for an hour or so before they were ready to cook. She'd be starving by then.

She looked around and saw a table with some nibbles. Crisps, nuts, and other stuff. Thank God for that, she thought, she'd be able to stock up on those until the burnt chicken and sausages were ready to eat. She walked over to the table and was immediately joined by a young man dressed in a casual shirt, jeans, and beach shoes. He had a short-trimmed beard, was that a hint of ginger in it, and brown hair. He was around six feet tall and quite fit. Not bad looking at all, thought Sophie. The man smiled at Sophie and offered her a bowl, laden with crisps. Sophie took a handful.

'Hi, I'm Freddie,' he said. 'You're Sophie Strong, aren't you?'

'Ah, so you're Freddie, I wasn't sure,' Sophie said smiling. 'So, you must be some sort of local celebrity then, having everyone coming to a barbeque for your birthday.' Sophie said, still smiling at Freddie as she crunched down on a crisp.

'Ah, well I don't know about that,' Freddie replied, laughing. 'It was my mum's idea. She wanted to do something, and I couldn't stop her.

You know what they're like, mums, always wanting to do things for you. It's not my birthday though, it's more of a farewell thing. I'm going off travelling in a few weeks time.'

'Oh, are you?' Sophie replied, feeling interested, but also surprisingly disappointed.

She could only imagine the feeling of disappointment was because she'd always wanted to go travelling herself. It was her dream to see a bit of the world, and here was someone standing in front of her who was going to do just that.

'Where are you going?' Sophie asked, before popping another crisp in her mouth.

'Well, I'm flying to India first and planning to spend some time there before working my way down through Thailand, Malaysia and Indonesia and ending up in Australia. That's the plan anyway,' Freddie laughed, 'but I'm sure things will change on the way. I'll just see what happens.'

'Wow, that sounds great. I've always wanted to do that,' Sophie said, smiling.

'You should,' Freddie replied. 'What's stopping you? Just go for it,' Freddie smiled back at Sophie.

Just then, someone called out Freddie's name and the two of them looked around and saw a middle-aged woman waving at him from the patio door.

'It's my mum,' Freddie said. 'I better see what she wants. I'll see you later,' he said, and he reached over and squeezed Sophie's arm before walking off in the direction of the house.

Sophie grabbed another handful of crisps and walked back to re-join her parents, offering them both a crisp from her hand.

The rest of the afternoon passed pleasantly enough. The weather stayed fine and the three Strongs spent the day mixing with the other guests, who were also largely neighbours of Roger and Sally. To Sophie's great surprise, the food turned out to be delicious. It was a feast of both barbequed and non-barbequed food and Sophie filled her plate before going back for seconds. Although she enjoyed the food, she couldn't get the earlier conversation with Freddie out of her head. It was the travelling bit. All those countries he'd mentioned, she wanted to see them, to experience them too. She'd always said she was going to do that, go travelling, but what was she doing now? She had done her degree and now she was working in an office job, just like everyone else. "What's stopping you, just go for it," Freddie had said, and he was right. There was nothing stopping her really. She could go anytime.

Sophie's thoughts were interrupted by the sound of music, and she looked up to see Freddie sitting on a stool, playing guitar, and singing. She had to admit, he was actually pretty good! She caught his eye and smiled, and he smiled back at her as he sang.

After playing a couple of songs, Freddie stood up and took a bow as the assembled guests applauded his performance. He turned and disappeared into the house, guitar in hand.

'I'm just going to the loo,' Sophie said to her mum, and she walked across the patio towards the door that Freddie had just passed through.

Sophie found herself in a large, open-plan kitchen and seeing a door on the far side of the room, she headed towards that. She went through the door, which opened out into the hallway. Sophie stood for a second, at the bottom of a staircase, looking around, wondering where to go next. Wondering what she was doing. She heard a noise from up above, a door closing, and she decided to go upstairs. She reached the top landing and saw four identical white, wooden doors. All closed. She walked along the corridor and could hear a noise coming from behind the second door on the right. Sophie stepped forward and gripped the handle, gently easing it open. Inside the room, she could see a man leaning over a bed, putting a guitar back into a black case. It was Freddie.

Sophie stepped inside the room and shut the door. At the sound of the door closing, Freddie stopped what he was doing and looked around.

'Oh, it's you,' he said with a smile.

Sophie walked forward and put her arms around Freddie, pulling him into her. He didn't resist. She felt his arms go around her waist and she angled her head upwards as he bent his down. Their lips locked and, to Sophie, it felt just perfect.

'It's funny,' Freddie said, unconsciously playing with a long strand of Sophie's hair as the two of them lay naked on his bed. 'I remember I was at my mate William's house one day and we could see into your garden from his bedroom window. We stood there, watching you on your swing and I felt really jealous. I wanted to have a go on it.'

'What? You were spying on me, a little girl. You're not some sort of weird pervert, are you?' Sophie exclaimed and she poked her finger into Freddie's chest.

'Ouch, no,' Freddie said, 'I was only a kid at the time.'

Sophie shifted her position on the bed and eased herself up, leaning on one elbow so she could see Freddie's face. Her hair fell across his chest.

'I've decided I'm coming with you,' Sophie said, staring straight at Freddie who was still lying flat out on his back.

'What do you mean?' Freddie replied, his eyes wide open.

'I'm coming with you,' she replied, running her hand across his chest. Some hair, but not too much. Sophie didn't like hairy men. 'It's obvious,' she added.

'What's obvious?' Freddie replied, his face only a few inches from Sophie's as she looked down at him from above.

'You need a backing singer,' Sophie replied, and she kissed him on the lips before swinging her legs around and getting off the bed.

'We better get back downstairs, back to the barbeque, people will be wondering where we are. I know my mum and dad will,' she said as she began to get dressed.

'But I don't even know you, really,' Freddie said, still lying on the bed, not moving.

‘Yes, you do, I’m the girl every boy wants,’ she said. ‘I’m the girl from next door,’ Sophie replied smiling.

Chapter 49

DI Strong watched from the side of the courtyard as the Chairman of the local council cut the ribbon to officially open the new hospital. Although it looked open, it wasn't fully there yet, with a few of the wards having to remain empty due to a combination of budget cuts and problems with suppliers. Still the reception area looked bright sparkling new and that was what the local media were now photographing.

Strong wasn't intending to hang around, it was one of those events where he just needed to show his face to represent the police force. After that he could just disappear and get back to his job of arresting criminals and keeping ordinary people safe. He was just about to make his way back to the car park when he felt someone touch his arm. He turned around and saw that it was Councillor John Aitken. The two men greeted each other and shook hands firmly.

'I meant to ask you, did you get that email, the stuff I sent you on that teacher I was trying to get back from Switzerland?' Aitken asked Strong. 'Remember we spoke about it at the Community Awards dinner a few months back?'

'Oh yes, I did. I had a chat with a few people I know in Germany, but I'm not sure if they could do anything,' Strong replied. 'Sorry I should have got back to you about it.'

'That's okay. Well, actually, you don't need to do anything now,' Aitken replied. 'Sandown was found dead in his swimming pool last month. Apparently it was an accident. They say he'd been drinking, and he slipped and fell into the pool and, well he just drowned. They found him the next day.'

'Oh, right,' Strong replied. 'Well, I suppose that's good news in some ways then. You don't have to worry about him any more. He's gone. Out of your lives.'

'Yes, to an extent you're right,' Aitken replied, 'but most of us would have liked to have got him in court. Made him go through it all. Make him admit it and let people hear what he'd done to us. We won't get that opportunity now.'

DI Strong smiled ruefully. It was hard to please everyone. Strong had learned that sometimes you had to get justice in whatever way you could. Aitken and his friends would have wasted years of their lives trying to get Sandown into the British courts, with no guarantee of a successful conviction. One call from Strong and Sandown had been brought to justice. He'd paid for what he'd done to those schoolboys. He'd paid with his life.

Chapter 50

It was the day of Sophie's departure. Her big trip. It had come around quickly. Much quicker than any of them had imagined, especially Catherine, Sophie's mum. She was going to miss her only daughter terribly, but she knew she had to put a brave face on it and let her go.

Both Catherine, and Sophie's dad, DI Strong, had been shocked when Sophie had suddenly announced that she was going to go off around the world with Freddie Field. After they'd got home from the barbeque, Sophie suddenly announced she had something to tell them, and then she just came out with it. She said Freddie and her had discussed it that day, and they'd just decided to do it. Catherine had noticed that Sophie had gone missing for some time while they were in the garden and she assumed that must have been when Sophie and Freddie had talked.

He seemed a nice enough young man, but they didn't really know him, and as far as they knew, Sophie had only really met him at the barbeque, just a few weeks before. However, they knew she needed a change, and they couldn't help but admire her spirit of adventure.

'She's only young once,' Catherine had said. 'But she's old enough to know what she's doing. She's been to university, and she always spoke about going travelling. I think it'll do her good. I sometimes wish I'd done a bit more travelling when I was her age. Seen a bit more of the world.'

Strong agreed with his wife. His only concern had been how quickly she seemed to have hooked up with Freddie Field, but he'd got Marsha to do a few checks, and Freddie seemed to be a good, clean-living guy. No criminal record, and a much better choice than Keegan Summers, of that he was sure.

Sophie and her dad, DI Strong, were standing in the kitchen, killing time before Sophie's lift arrived. Freddie's dad was taking the two of them to the airport. Sophie's dad had offered too, but Sophie said she preferred to say her goodbyes to them here, at the house. If her mum came to the airport, it might just get too much. Too emotional. Best just to do quick goodbyes at the house, then go. Although Catherine had been a bit reluctant with that idea at first, she had eventually come around to it. Strong glanced at his watch.

'They should be here soon. Where's your mum?' Strong asked his daughter.

'Probably looking round my room again, for the millionth time, making sure I haven't forgot anything,' Sophie replied, smiling.

'That's what mums do,' Strong replied. 'I don't think she can quite believe you're going yet. It all seems to have happened so quickly.'

'Yes, I know,' Sophie replied. She'd thought that herself, and worried that maybe it had all happened too fast, but she knew that the longer she had to think about it, the more chance something else would come up that would give her a reason to change her mind again. It was better just to get on and do it. She was happy with Freddie too. After that initial day of instant passion, she'd found him to be very laid back and easy to get on with. She was sure he would be a great travel companion, but if things didn't work out between them, then she'd carry on regardless. She'd always wanted to see a bit more of the world and she knew this was the time in her life to do it.

'I think that's a car outside now,' Strong said and he left the kitchen to have a look out of the front window.

'They're here,' he called back, then, 'Catherine, the car's here,' he called upstairs to his wife.

Catherine came down the stairs and the three of them met in the hallway. Sophie's dad picked up his daughter's case and walked to the front door.

Sophie turned to face her mum. This was going to be her one biggest worry, how much she'd miss her mum. But she had got through three years at university in Leeds okay, although that wasn't quite as far away as Australia. There was always WhatsApp though, and other technology. She could see, and talk to her mum, as if they were in the same country, not ten thousand miles away on the other side of the world. It would be okay.

Her mum hugged her tightly and Sophie almost started crying, but she managed to hold it in. Her mum was doing exactly the same, she wanted to stay strong. There would be plenty of time for tears after she'd gone. They stood together in the hall for a few precious moments longer until their husband and father called from outside the front door.

'Come on, or you'll miss your flight.'

Chapter 51

'The thing is mate. If he gets beat up, they're immediately going to suspect it was me, especially since I've not long since been in complaining about him assaulting me. I need to have a good alibi. Like being on shift here, so loads of people will have seen me on the door which means there's no way I could have done it, do you see?' Danny said.

'Aye pal. No need tae worry,' Scotty replied. 'It sounds like the wee guy needs a guid kickin' an am yer man for that,' he laughed.

Danny had known all along that his fellow doorman, Scotty, would be up for doing it. He knew Scotty liked a scrap, even more so than he did. It was like a perk of the job for the Scotsman. Danny just hoped he wouldn't go too far. He'd had to pull Scotty off people a few times when he had got a bit carried away. Sometimes Scotty didn't seem to know when to stop. Or maybe he just didn't want to.

'So, remember Scotty, just a couple of punches, nothing more than that. I don't want you seriously injuring the guy or nothing like that,' Danny said.

'Aye nae bother,' Scotty replied smiling. 'He'll get what he deserves, dinnae ye worry.'

Danny had told Scotty that Bradley Smith worked in the local Co-op supermarket and on a Thursday night, he would leave the building through the back door at nine pm.

'He parks his car, it's a red Honda, in the yard at the back,' Danny had told him. 'It's pretty dark and quiet round there so you shouldn't have anyone disturbing you.'

Scotty was standing, leaning against the corner of a rusty, yellow skip. He was dressed in dark clothes, a black woolly hat, sweatshirt, and jeans and if you didn't know he was there, it's unlikely you'd spot him. He had a perfect view of the rear exit to the shop which was about twenty metres away. Scotty looked at his watch, any minute now he thought, and he could feel the adrenalin start to pump. He was excited. He always enjoyed this bit. A minute or so before it happened when he was in control, and he knew exactly what he was going to do.

He heard the lock turning and saw the crack of light from inside grow brighter as the door opened. A man stepped outside and closed the door behind him. He fitted the description Danny had given him, but Scotty wasn't too bothered about that anyway, he was just ready to do his thing. Nothing could stop him now.

He waited until the man had walked a few paces. He was now diagonally across the yard from Scotty and only ten metres away. Scotty started to move. Nine metres, eight, seven, six. He was now close enough to see the man's face, but the man still wasn't aware of Scotty's presence.

'Oi Pigface,' Scotty growled, and the man turned around with a startled look on his face.

But he didn't stay startled for long as Scotty's right fist collided with his nose. Scotty recognised the familiar feeling of bone crunching and breaking against his solid knuckles. The man fell to the ground, immediately unconscious. Scotty looked down at him and drew his right foot back, giving him two kicks to the head and face for good measure. Satisfied with his work, Scotty brushed himself down and looked around to check all was well. There was no-one around. It had all taken less than thirty seconds and Scotty walked away to find the nearest pub so that he could quench his raging thirst.

Chapter 52

Detective Sergeant Knight was in the police station kitchen, making herself a cup of coffee, her second of the day, when DI Strong walked in.

'Oh, hi Guv. I was about to come and see you. We got a flag on the PNC system this morning,' DS Knight said. 'You remember Bradley Smith? Well, apparently, he's been attacked. We got a red flag notification because it linked it to the record of us interviewing him recently.'

'Oh, okay,' Strong replied. 'Any details on what happened?' he asked.

'Yes, from the notes on the PNC system, it seems he was attacked as he left his work at the supermarket, around nine pm,' DS Knight replied. 'He was taken to hospital and the police interviewed him there. He has no idea who did it, or why. He says it was all very sudden. Someone shouted something, he turned around and that was when he got hit. It was dark, and all so quick, that he didn't manage to see his assailant.'

'Is he badly hurt?' Strong enquired.

'I think he's got a broken nose, a couple of teeth missing and a few other bumps and bruises, but they let him out in the morning,' DS Knight replied.

'Do you think it could have been our man, James Gray?' Strong asked his colleague.

'The thought did cross my mind Guv, but I did a quick check and found out he was working at the hospital all day yesterday,' Knight replied. 'So, it couldn't have been him.'

'Ah well, probably just a disgruntled customer upset at the price of his mange tout,' Strong laughed. 'Let's leave it to the locals to sort it out, I'm sure they'll find out who did it.'

DI Strong picked up his freshly brewed cup of coffee and walked back to his office ready to start another day. Of course, he had a good idea who had attacked Bradley Smith and he knew the local police probably wouldn't find him, but then Bradley had brought this on himself. He'd got what he deserved for lying in the first place and wasting police time. Wasting DI Strong's time and almost making him look like a fool. Nobody did that without getting punished.

Justice had to be served after all.

Acknowledgements

There are a few people I'd like to thank for helping and encouraging me to write this latest book. As always, these things are a team effort, and their support has been invaluable. Firstly, my family and friends, especially my wife and daughter, Gill and Megan, for just letting me get on with it - and supplying teas and coffees…along with the occasional biscuit as I sat writing. It's a lonely task!

I'd also like to thank my regular team of first readers who have helped with the final draft – (Wee) Jean Farrell in California and Jim Anderson in Scotland. Thanks to both of you for your extremely helpful input, suggestions, and just picking up on the bits I'd missed.

Now that it's all done, it's time to start writing the next book….

Due for release in Summer 2023, the next book in the DI Strong series. Following on from School Reunion, find out what happens next in the lives of DI Strong and DS Knight.

Other books by Ian Anderson:

Jack's Lottery Plan

This is the funny and moving story of Jack Burns. One day he finds out that a friend has secretly won the lottery and he embarks on a clandestine plan to get a share. But his plan goes hopelessly wrong impacting Jack and his friends in ways he would never have imagined.

Jack's Big Surprise

Jack Burns is planning a surprise proposal for his girlfriend Hannah. But as is usually the way with Jack, his plan doesn't quite go the way he was hoping it would. Instead he finds himself hopelessly involved in a series of hilariously funny, and sometimes, unfortunate incidents. This is the sequel to Jack's Lottery Plan and finds Jack just as chaotic as he always is.

The Anniversary

In the first book of the DI Strong crime thriller series, Andy Austin's family are killed in a road accident. With a sense of injustice, he becomes obsessed on seeking revenge. He befriends DI Strong and uses him to help carry out his plan. As the police get closer to catching him it becomes clear that not everyone is without a guilty secret.

The Deal

Detective Inspector Strong hatches a plan to use Andy Austin, a wanted murderer, to help him deliver justice to serious criminals the police aren't able to convict by conventional means. This is the second great book in the DI Strong crime thriller series, following on from The Anniversary.

Loose Ends

The third book in the DI Strong Crime Thriller series, following The Anniversary and The Deal. Strong has been bending the law, but is he taking too many chances and arousing suspicion? Too many people are becoming involved, too many loose ends, which Strong knows he will have to do something about.

Two Wrongs

Two Wrongs is the fourth book in the DI Strong Crime Thriller series. Detective Constable Knight is keen to progress her career but is struggling to shut down a criminal turf war. Strong looks to help, unaware that DI Campbell and DC Harris have their suspicions on his methods of working.

For more information, please visit my website at:
www.ianandersonhome.wixsite.com/ianandersonauthor

Or find me on Facebook at:
www.facebook.com/IanAndersonAuthor

Printed in Great Britain
by Amazon